VIRAGO
MODERN CLASSICS
517

Elaine Dundy

Actress, journalist, novelist and biographer, Elaine Dundy was born and raised in New York. She has been there, done that – and loved it all. She jitterbugged with Piet Mondrian in Madison Square Garden; shared a symbiotic relationship with her sister, Oscar-winning film-maker Shirley Clarke; drank *Papa Dobles* with Hemingway in Havana; shared a psychiatrist with Tennessee Williams; turned a dalliance with Cyril Connolly into a leading character in her second novel; watched Gore Vidal win by losing a congressional campaign; married the *enfant terrible* of British theatre critics, Kenneth Tynan; and was a bestseller on both sides of the Atlantic with *The Dud Avocado*.

D0238239

By Elaine Dundy

Novels
The Dud Avocado
The Old Man and Me
The Injured Party

Plays
My Place
Death in the Country

Biographies
Finch, Bloody Finch
Elvis and Gladys
Ferriday, Louisiana

Autobiography
Life Itself!

THE OLD MAN AND ME

Elaine Dundy

With an Introduction by the author

Virago

VIRAGO

Published by Virago Press in August 2005
Reprinted 2007

First published in the UK by Victor Gollancz Ltd 1964

Copyright © 1963, 1964 Elaine Dundy

Introduction copyright © Elaine Dundy 2005

A CIP catalogue record for this book
is available from the British Library

ISBN 978-1-84408-124-0

Papers used by Virago are natural, recyclable products made from
wood grown in sustainable forests and certified in accordance with
the rules of the Forest Stewardship Council.

Typeset in Goudy by M Rules
Printed and bound in Great Britain by
Clays Ltd, St Ives plc
Paper supplied by Hellefoss AS, Norway

Virago Press
An imprint of
Little, Brown Book Group
Brettenham House
Lancaster Place
London WC2E 7EN

A Member of the Hachette Livre Group of Companies

www.virago.co.uk

INTRODUCTION

The Moving Finger writes; and having writ,
Moves on: nor all your Piety nor Wit
Shall lure it back to cancel half a Line,
Nor all your Tears wash out a Word of it.

At sixteen, *The Rubaiyat* ruled my life. Now at eighty-two I see it makes good poetry but bad sense. Re-reading *The Old Man and Me* forty years after its first publication, my Moving Finger has re-writ, or rather, edited my novel with I hope, all my Piety and Wit. From today's prospect, I was able to cancel a word or half a line throughout, understanding what I didn't then that in this novel, speech read is preferable to speech spoken. The latter is full of 'um', 'oh' and 'ah' – dead foliage that smother the text. I eliminated most but not all of them. Some were too stubbornly embedded in the text. Words such as the all-purpose 'just' that runs around this book as in 'you just want to', 'just a moment', 'just in time', 'just the wrong way'. I cut some of the beginnings of sentences that use such weakening qualifications as 'well' and 'I'm afraid' followed by I, you, he, she, it. I cut 'perfectly' and 'definitely'. These, being eliminated, I felt released the core of the text to glow. I wanted the two protagonists to express them-selves through exchanges that are brisk, crisp, direct and unadorned, sometimes to the point, often around it, even at times, soul to soul.

My first-person narrator, a young American girl, speaks a jumble of jargon *du jour*, college-speak, popular Madison Avenue advertising idioms and basic black musician talk. Jazz great, Miles Davis, whom I had loosely based a character on, after he read the book, had only one comment: 'Watch out for slang,' he said. 'It dates fast.' I had occasion to recall that in the '70s when a friend said the narrator's slang was dated. Again in the '80s, when another reader thought it was 'period' (i.e. quaint). Now, in the new millennium, it is historic. The way we talked way back when we dug things, made the scene, went to Happenings and all that jazz. When the cigarette was not a prop but had a life of its own, an indicator of mood, a gesture denoting anything from seduction to boredom. Smoking round the clock was universally acceptable. In the novel, one Bright Young Thing with a long cigarette-holder smokes during the meal and nobody leaves the dining room.

Cigarettes and slang stay, I decided; dead weight vegetation goes.

Incidentally, the other protagonist, Englishman C.D. McKee, the narrator's worthy opponent, described as 'too distinguished to do anything', speaks a brand of standard educated English which never went through the dated or period cycle but was and is historic.

My specific aim in writing this novel was to present an anti-heroine in response to all the anti-heroes so popular of the day, beginning with Kingsley Amis's Jim Dixon in *Lucky Jim*, John Osborne's Jimmy Porter in *Look Back in Anger* and all the anti-heroes who followed in their wake. Loosely bound together as Angry Young Men, they hit out at everything phony, pompous, priggish, prudish and pretentious. Their anger was exhilarating. To their delight (and to his later embarrassment), Somerset

Maugham called them 'scum'. Creating the female counterpart I knew would be tricky, as in those days when relationships between men and women were at an all-time low, females were depicted as passive and put upon. (Then came the '70s – Gloria Steinem and her Ms magazine, Germaine Greer and her *Female Eunuch*, Carmen Callil and her all-female publishing house Virago. And nothing was ever the same again.) Back in the '60s I was aware that my anti-heroine might scare people off. But I did it anyway. And it was fun. After all, Cyril Connelly had advised me about my private life: 'Make up your mind, you can either be a monster or a doormat.' I opted for the former.

My Angry Young Woman hates everything English – Soho, Mayfair, the West End and country houses. She is a girl with a plan, with lots of opinions, operating on a short fuse. Almost everything about English people annoys her, her irritation at times boiling up to fury even as her adversary's irony slides down into sarcasm.

But what I hope I had going for me is that Bad Girls are more interesting than Good ones. The Bible has an enchantment with them – Delilah, Bathsheba, Jezebel, Salome and then some. It does them proud. The nineteenth-century Bad Girls – Hedda Gabler, Becky Sharp and Scarlett O'Hara, whose bad girl deeds and misdeeds burst upon the world in 1936 but was yet a nineteenth-century woman – all live on in iconic glory. My narrator who plans to kill the Englishman because he has the money is thoroughly bad.

The time frame is 1962, with England not-yet-but-on-the-verge-of Swinging. London was not the Mecca for tourists it has become. It was however regrouping itself for its cultural explosion, its fashions of Carnaby Street, its playwrights' invasion of Broadway, to say nothing of the Liverpool sound of The Beatles and the Glaswegian sound of James Bond. But in the '60s, all good Americans skipped bombed-out London and rushed to

Paris. I myself went straight from New York to Paris where I stayed happily for a while surrounded by new American friends. I didn't have any in London and it occurs to me now that this feeling of isolation rubbed off onto the novel. Then too, America at the end of WWII was the richest country in the world, however much of its money went to rebuilding Germany and Japan, the defeated enemy, and none to brave England. Which, as my novel also reflects, didn't make Americans very popular with the English.

Short digression – It didn't work the other way around! The English coming to America were unequivocally ecstatic about everything in the New World and Americans, quick to return the compliment, rolled out the red carpet.

Another point: in the '60s, publishers were giving writers the freedom to be explicit about sex – its longings, its cravings, its orgasms, its masturbations. I took advantage of this. Sexual matters combined with self-interest activate my two leading characters who, while they think they are guided by their reason, in reality only use their logic to justify their passion.

Perhaps not surprisingly, I have also written a romance. At least according to Brewer's Dictionary of Phrase & Fable, which decrees, 'The modern application of the word "romance" pertains to a story containing incidents more or less removed from the ordinary events of life.' That seems to describe my story too as the contenders fight, flee, reconnoiter, re-engage and fight on with fresh energy to the end – to justify their out-of-control passions.

Elaine Dundy
2005

PART I

CHAPTER ONE

There is a sort of coal hole in the heart of Soho that is open every afternoon: a dark, dank, dead-ended subterranean tunnel. It is a drinking club called the Crypt and the only light to penetrate it is the shaft of golden sunlight slipping through the doorway from time to time glancing off someone's nose or hair or glass of gin, all the more poignant for its sudden revelations, in an atmosphere almost solid with failure, of pure wind-swept nostalgia, of clean airy summer houses, of the beach, of windy reefs; of the sun radiating through the clouds the instant before the clouds race back over it again – leaving the day as sad and desperate as before.

I was having a drink there one sunny afternoon last year in the midst of a futile heap of hoboesques, although wait – that isn't strictly true. I was standing there with a drink in my hand but I wasn't drinking it. I was nursing it for dear life. Hovering over it, as we used to say at dear ole Bullsht Hall, where I was so gently schooled for four boarding-school years, and I was feeling utterly and completely demoralized – treading water and tiring fast.

The sun suddenly went out – in, that is – and the ensuing darkness tearing me from my vision of the outside world was claustrophobing me up with the Crypt and its inhabitants; ensnaring me in their knotted hair, hooking me on to their ravelled sweaters, leaving me haggard with concern for their buttonless jackets, their flapping shoes, their bent, bruised cigarettes smoked down to the nub. The Soho scene. I looked around and shuddered. I had nothing personally against these people, quite the opposite; I was most awe-fully impressed. It was simply, when I analysed it, my distress at finding myself in a room where I seemed to have more money than anyone else and this condition was especially intensified by the fact that though I was probably richer than anyone there, I was virtually broke. Not flop-house-lower-depths broke. But what I'd managed to save over the two years working on one of the better Quality Mags in New York was trickling through my hands at a terrifying rate.

And the irony was that I was in there suffering the poor only on the highly improbable off-chance of running into the very rich! I mean, precisely, C. D. McKee. For, in the entire month that I had been searching London for him, this was the only place I had heard his name even mentioned.

London had been alarming, distinctly alarming, in the way it could force me – a not unpresentable young woman – to spend one whole month in it and meet only the following people: two Portuguese (pick-ups, staying at my hotel), two Hungarians (pick-ups, not staying at my hotel) and two American boys (queer; exchange students at Oxford; on the plane coming over). The Portuguese had taken me on an excursion trip up the Thames. The Tower of London had been our original goal but when we got to the spot on the map where it was supposed to be and it wasn't and nobody around knew anything about it, they eventually became too embarrassed to keep on asking about so large and obvious a landmark, gave up and took me on an excursion boat (there in plain sight though not on our map) in order to prevent the outing from being a complete bust.

I took the same boat up the Thames again about two weeks later with one of the American boys. I forget why. It was a

Sunday, I think, and everything was closed. It was a hideous ride with warehouses and smokestacks on one side of the river and Bovril and Milk advertisements on the other but by then I wasn't particularly in the mood to get upset about the looks of a river. It had rained almost steadily since I arrived and I thought London the ugliest city on earth. Marble Arch and Piccadilly Circus. Ugh. The dirty-green grass patch called Leicester Square surrounded by Movie Palaces, restaurant windows full of chickens revolving on their spits and the new Automobile Association Building – hardly Art Nouveau. Oxford Street. Ugh, ugh.

There had, of course, been that brief enchanted glimpse of the beautiful square at the end of which stood C. D.'s house where I arrived one morning, his address still clutched in my hand, steadied for the big confrontation scene only to be stopped dead in my tracks and swiftly brought to rout by nothing more than the sight of his butler ordering a delivery boy round to the tradesmen's entrance.

The Hungarians took me to meet some more Hungarians in an Hungarian restaurant run by other Hungarians.

And then there were those few salty exchanges between me and various Espresso Bar attendants.

Anyway here I was back again in Soho in this terrible dive the Crypt because what had happened was that the night before one of the Americans, down from Oxford, had said, 'Hey, someone gave me a list of literary pubs, did you ever? Isn't it straight out of Shakespearian times? They're in Soho, see, that's where all the you know, sort of odd-ball Greenwich Villagey Left Banky off-beat In-group types' – (that was the way he talked) – 'oh, artists and painters and all that jazz are supposed to hang out. So why don't we give it a whirl, hey? Might be a fun thing.'

So I went. I had nothing better to do, had I, except recount my money and repaint my finger-nails and die of frustration?

The Crypt had been the place we'd decided to start at and it was here, at this very bar, that I overheard for the first time in England the magic Name.

'I say, Bollie, you were very smart last night. Very smart indeed. C. D. McKee, big as life! How did you manage to pull that off?'

'My dear, he came along with Alex who hates me of course but—'

'Alex? What was C. D. McKee doing with Alex?'

'Oh but McKee is *sweet*. You simply don't understand him,' said Bollie, an enormous boy-shaped man with large sorrowful eyes and a headful of greasy curls, hermaphrodite breasts showing through his torn pullover. 'I tell you he's sweet. Not a bit frightening really. No side at all, when you get to know him. He and Alex were staying in Scotland at Perdita Gallow's and I gather they both ended up in the Passing Out Room and then decided to motor back to London together the next day.' His voice was high and wavy and very loud and he had a delicate way of running his fingers through his greasy black ringlets as he spoke and patting them again fondly as they bounced back.

'Let's get a drink and stay here,' I whispered to my friend. 'I want to take this all in.' I pressed into the crowd that had collected around Bollie.

'Ah, the Honourable Perdita. How is she? Still mad as ever?' asked a youngish man with grey hair, his mouth twisted into an affectionate toothless grimace.

'As a hatter,' Bollie confided cosily to the whole crowd. 'Alex says she came down to dinner one night all splendidly got up in lavender satin except for one breast hanging out, my dear, quite *casually*. He did wonder whether to spoon it back in. Not that she was in any state to mind one way or another, poor old bod. She's been frightfully sad since Adrian left.'

Bollie was a sort of chain-talker, lighting one end of a conversation to another without letting the first go out. The ladies – God bless 'em – Kitty and Clarissa and Chloe and Cassandra –

were all in pretty bad shape, I gathered. All mad, all poor, all sad.

A tall emphatically sloshed young woman whose hair entirely hid the upper part of her face was lurching around clutching a large drawing-folder which kept jabbing everyone in the stomach. She lurched up to Bollie demanding to know when he was going to paint her. 'You said you would. You know you did.'

'I did not. Get away, you dreary old mizbag,' said Bollie indignant at the interruption.

'But you did. You promised. You swore on your mother's grave.'

'Really? Well, that must make me Miss-I-Don't-Care of this month because I'm not going to do it,' and he turned away from her and got back down to business. 'No, about C. D. C. D. *McKee*. He was in here last night, you know, standing right where you are, and he said to Alex – I heard him, Alex will deny it of course, he's so jealous of me – he *said*, "But I'm delighted to see Bollie, he always makes me laugh." Oh Alex was *livid*. That Alex. He's madly jealous of me – of everything I do. For instance, the other day—'

'A *very* angry young man. He tells me his latest epic is going to be called B— the Duke.'

'How delicious. And I bet he'd love to.'

'So what's *your* big ambition in life?'

'Seriously?'

'Of course.'

'To sleep with a sailor.'

'You mean you've never? How quaint.'

'I've been meaning to ask – who gave you that black eye?'

'My dear, it was the most . . .'

'Sordid, isn't it?' said a voice in my ear. I looked around and saw that it came from a handsome, fierce-looking young man who managed to grin and glower at the same time, his scowling white face emoting beneath thunderous black hair. 'Sordid Soho.

7

Failed Soho. Failures. Yes you, I'm talking to you,' he went on, staring me straight in the eye. 'You know what gives it its special mouldy atmosphere? These phonies have no connection with money. That's all. Simple as that. Never touch the stuff. No contact between art and money for them, thank you very much. A shade unrealistic, *n'est-ce pas?* And what, do you imagine, brings these cretins converging from all corners of London together? Art? Literature? Painting? Don't you believe it. You'll never hear a bloody word about a book or painting or even a film pronounced by these prize stoics. Gossip, yes, that's the stuff – that's what brings them here, that and a common lack of money and a common desire to get drunk. I'm drunk,' he continued, leering a little, 'but I've made the connection between art and money. I'm Scotty Schooner – ever heard of me? Highest paid script-writer in British films. God what an epitaph!' He giggled and then scowled again. 'You can't get drunk in London. Where can I go to drink? I've got my bloody principles. What do they want me to do? Join one of those jolly men's clubs with all the other jolly clubmen slumped against the bar wading through each other's anecdotes marking time till their next chance to blackball some prospective member? I'm not hanging around this country any longer, thank God. I'm off to India. That's where the future lies. I leave tomorrow. Want to come with me?' he asked me suddenly. 'Come on. I'm not taking my wife, either. She thinks there's something sexual about my Indian kick. She's damn right there's something sexual. Matter of fact there's something sexual about you too.'

'Schooner, old cock,' said Bollie, drawn away from his own group by the mounting ferocity of the other's diatribe, 'we all feel the untimely departure of your well-loved genius from these shores calls for a tiny stirrup cupette or two – a bijou drinkette . . .'

'Oh all right, all right,' said Scotty wearily. 'Next round on me.

Only ask for it like a man. Treat me like a person, will you, not some goddam celebrity.'

Bollie, a large whisky waving dreamily in the air, was toasting Scotty from a distance. And when I spotted him again the piano was playing *Avalon* and Bollie, his arms around the barman who was also trying to hold him up, was slowly and solemnly waltzing him round and round the tables.

Scotty Schooner closed his eyes against the sight. 'Dear Christ, what whimsy. What typical English whimsy. It goes straight into my next Peter Sellers film. God how I hate the English! This is a wonderful place to hate the English in, isn't it?' he added with relish. 'Wait till you hear some of our bar chatter. Very sophisticated we are. Real Coffee House stuff. The journalists have their John Huston and the-late-Mike-Todd stories, the poets and painters their social swim stories, and each and every one, down to the last sod, his Dylan Thomas ones. It's a bloody marvel. It's like clockwork. Wait and see—'

Scotty had pushed his face into mine to see how I was taking all this. I had noted from the beginning, of course, that he was drunk but had decided that as it was the least important thing about him, I could ignore it. Quite suddenly it had become the most important thing.

'Well, what do you make of us? Don't just stand there gawping.' His general truculence was focusing itself on me. 'Haven't you anything to say?'

I'd smiled a gracious Social Worker's smile and the bloody drunk (as he no doubt would have referred to himself) saw right through it.

'What did you say your name was?' I asked nicely. 'I'm afraid I didn't . . .'

'Scotty Schooner, your ladyship. And don't you be putting on airs. You're an aggressive little bitch on the make if I ever saw

9

one. I know your type, I could recognize it a mile away. I've been watching you ever since you came in. Slumming, eh? But you're panting to get inside the circle. What goes on with you, anyway? What's it all about? Come on, what have you got to say for yourself?'

'Hey, now look here. Now you look here just a moment. Now you apologize to this lady.' My nice little American friend was shocked and indignant and – in the circumstances – very brave.

'No, let me answer him,' I'd said, and I turned to Scotty Schooner. 'I won't talk to you because you won't listen. You just want to fight. The only reason you attack people is because you want to be attacked back, isn't it?' And taking advantage of his uncertain grin as he tried to reshape my words into some coherent meaning, I walked out.

'Gee, you were great,' said the American. 'You really handled him. I should have punched him though,' he added wistfully, 'shouldn't I?'

'Not at all,' I said hugging him soothingly. 'You can't win with a drunk. But I was terribly touched that you sprang to my rescue.' I patted him on the head. 'You're a good little boy.'

'Thanks,' he said gratefully, 'I like being mothered.' And then, a shade regretfully as he moved away, 'Of course, I like being fathered too.'

* * *

It made me laugh all over again thinking of that remark as I stood sentinel at the bar of the Crypt the following afternoon ready to leap at the next whisper of C. D. McKee's name. The inmates were all there as I had left them the night before: same clothes, same positions, same conversations.

Bollie, one elbow on the bar, his hand cupping his cheek, swung gently from side to side in an arc, delicate and dainty of gesture as ever, his greasy curls still bouncing gaily back through nicotine-stained fingers, his voice still contentedly singing to itself something about a Gate House and the Marquis of Oxall who was a duck. And then from his unspeakable trousers he pulled out two dog-eared Kodak snaps and went on about *Lady* Doone Leap Falls, aged seven, if you please, holding court in the bathtub. And then more about Alex who was furious, simply fiyur-ious, Bollie's eyes flirtatiously rolling upwards over the dry rot marks in the ceiling as if to entice them to come down and play with him. '. . . and the Marquis let out a *whoop*! Oh would we stay to dinner, what a wonderful idea, and we all got tiddly in the nicest way of course . . .'

Oh damn. Something would have to be done. He was my one hope. I'd have to offer to buy him a drink.

I had stepped forward when an unexpectedly hard bump jolted my arm and flung both my drink and my handbag to the ground. Stooping down to retrieve them I came face to face with a short red-faced man.

'I say, I'm sorry.' His smile quickly slipped into a quaver. He handed me back my bag and glass, now of course empty, and then he said, 'Thank you!' in that baffling way the English have upon completing an act of politeness you would logically be expected to thank them for, like giving up their seat on a bus or helping you on with your coat.

'You're welcome,' I replied anyway.

It had a startling effect on him.

'You're welcome? Yurr wa-alcome?' He caricatured an American drawl. 'A Yank, eh?'

'Why yes. How did you know?'

'*You're welcome*. We simply don't say it over here.'

'What do you say?'

'We doan say nothin'. We jes' skip it.' And holding his pint aloft, his elbow pointing straight out, he took a large swig of his beer.

I now realized what had caused the handbag-and-glass incident for this elbow-in-the-air style of drinking immediately sloshed the drink in his neighbour's hand.

I decided to go to work on him. I needed all the help I could get.

'That's fascinating about "you're welcome." How clever of you to have spotted it. You must be a writer.'

'Well, yes. Or perhaps no. I'm a journalist. I work for the *Piccadilly*. Very posh picture rag.'

'Oh, yes. I read it all the time.' I did. I read all the magazines and papers I could get, vainly hoping to come across some mention of C. D. 'What's your name?' I asked him.

'Hal Smithers. Smitty,' he added as if hating it.

'As a matter of fact I remember an article you wrote. It was very interesting. I liked it very much.'

He shrugged it off. 'Nothing to it. Get an angle. All you need's a gimmick. Or a gismo as they say Stateside, heh, heh. Now what about you? What's a lovely girl like you doing here? Bumming around. I believe that's the elegant American expression?'

I was taking against Smitty fast. But then I realized from his defensive manner that he probably expected to be disliked and I really disliked him too much to do what he expected. So I persevered.

'Not at all. I'm looking for a job. In fact,' I said, thinking to win him over, 'I need one.'

'A-*ha*. The Career Girl. The typical hard-boiled I-know-where-I'm-going American career girl.'

'No,' I corrected him soberly. 'A working girl.'

I felt his antagonism drop, and with it – and this really confused me – his interest. Even in the dark cool atmosphere I could feel him cooling off.

'I'll . . . um . . . get you that drink I spilled,' he said backing away. 'What was it, beer?'

So there was no pleasing him. So the hell with it. 'Scotch and soda,' I replied calmly and he slunk off to get it.

Out of the corner of my eye I saw that a girl was watching me. She smiled as he left.

'Tried to make an impression but I'm not doing too well, am I?' I said to her.

'Heavens, do you really want to?' She was an attractive-looking girl with a warm smile. And then the vagrant shaft of sunlight settled on her head and transformed her into a real beauty; a dappled girl with dappled eyes, all flecks and freckles and soft brown hair shining silver in the sun. And best of all she looked so clean and starched and freshly laundered against the grime. It was such a friendly face, holding out such hope. My angel of the sun-shaft. And oh, I thought, you are in time to save my life.

'I mean do you really want to impress Smitty?' she was asking incredulously. 'Why?'

'Well, for one thing, so he'll pay for my drinks.'

'Then you're going about it in the wrong way.'

'Because I said I wanted a job?'

'Wronger. You said you needed one.'

'Well I thought he'd prefer me poor to rich. You know, we rich Americans and all that.'

'Oh no. You've got it all wrong. The main point about this lot is that they're probably the snobbiest in the world. The shabbier the snobbier. Or so my dear husband keeps assuring me. So if you want to get anywhere with them you'd better stop being poor.'

'So what'll I be?'

She thought for a moment. 'An heiress,' she said. 'It's all right, you know. They'll believe anything.'

Smitty came back and handed me my drink. 'Cheers,' he said and took a handsome swig of his own, automatically turning around to see what damage his elbow had caused. 'I say, Dody, sorry. Didn't see you standing there.' Then he introduced me to the girl I'd been talking with.

'This is Dody Schooner,' he said. I registered the Schooner immediately and wondered if she was anything to do with the angry Schooner of last night.

'And by the way, what's your name?' he asked me.

'Honey Flood,' I heard myself saying out of the blue. And the lying had started.

'What brings you out so early?' Smitty asked Dody. 'You and Scotty don't generally turn up till much later on at night.'

Dody leaned against the wall elaborately languid. 'Me? I haven't any better place to go. Not for the moment. Have you? Do let me know if you find one.' Quite suddenly her face had become strained and there were tears in her eyes.

'So he wasn't kidding when he said he was going to India!' It burst out of me before I could stop myself.

She looked at me. 'That's very interesting,' she said quietly. 'And what did you say your name was again?'

'Honey Flood. But look, I only met your husband for a second for the very first time last night. Only he mentioned something about going to India and he was awfully drunk at the time and I didn't believe it. I thought he was just talking.'

'He was just talking all right but he's gone to India too all right. That's why I'm here. To annoy him. He hates Soho so much he hates it more than anything in the world except me of course. And the electric fire in our bedroom. And the tea break at Shepperton Studios. And . . . oh I forget . . . the list is so endless.' Her voice was skidding out of control in the most alarming manner. 'The Soho game is up, you see, that's what he keeps saying. And then there's this girl of course, this Indian girl. I really would give a lot to annoy him. Excuse me.' The tears were unstoppable. 'Don't go away, please, I'll be back,' she called over her shoulder as Smitty and I watched her work her way to the john.

14

'Well,' he said lamely after a while. 'Hope you find yourself a job.'

I came in with a rush. I looked him straight in the eye and gave him my pitch. 'I must stop lying,' I said. 'My doctor says it's bad for me. I'm not really looking for a job. The truth is I'm in England because I'm recovering from a nervous breakdown. They thought I'd have a better chance starting fresh over here. Away from the pressures. I'm being psychoanalysed as a matter of fact. It's not *not* having enough money that's the trouble. I've got to face that. It's, oh dear. It's having too much. It can be just as upsetting.'

'Yeah.' He nodded wisely. 'Just a crazy mixed-up kid, eh?' he added in what – had my tale been true – would certainly have been the bad-taste phrase of the century, 'I say, this is fascinating. Where are you staying in London?'

I gave him the name of my hotel, saw by his reaction that it was by no means an O.K. one and added with agility, 'It's part of my cure. From having too much money. I'm to try to live like an ordinary person, for a time.'

As Dody predicted he swallowed it whole. 'Drink up,' he said. 'I'll buy us another round.'

'Oh please let me.'

'Don't be silly.' He was firm.

'Okie dokes.'

'*Okie dokes.*' He shook his head. 'Wunnerful. You crazy cats.'

While he was gone Dody returned looking all pretty again. 'Don't pay any attention to me today,' she said. 'I've gone a little mad. I'm over the worst of it, I think.'

'It worked,' I crowed. 'It worked. I am an heiress and he's fallen for it and I can't thank you enough.'

'What are you up to? I'm so intrigued.' Her eyes were glowing. Aha, I thought, here is a moon-girl – I knew the type well from school – a moon-girl travels around in orbit reflecting her particular sun of the moment. And in her eye a silvery tear, a pale moonstone dissolved down her cheek. But she was smiling with interest.

'It's too long a story to go into now,' I told her, 'but if I haven't met a certain Englishman soon *my* Soho game will be all over too.'

'Oh – can I help?' That said something about her character too. Something useful to me. The sisterhood of women. For there had been that moment's suspicion over me and her husband but it had passed. And she trusted me.

Smitty was coming over to us. And so – wonder of all – was Bollie, the Prime Object. 'Why didn't you come for your sitting yesterday, Dody?' he complained. 'I waited hours. I wouldn't have got out of bed at all if I'd known you weren't. As it turned out it was a great mistake. Nearly broke my neck over the milk bottles in the passageway.'

'I'm sorry,' said Dody. 'I wanted to telephone you but Alex said he didn't think you had one.'

'Ooooooh!' Bollie let out a scream like a siren. 'Of *course* Alex wouldn't give you my telephone number. He's madly jealous that's why. The other day when C. D. McKee – my dear – C. D. – Hello my dear. How are you feeling this afternoon?'

Quite suddenly he had spoken to me. At last.

'I'm fine,' I replied and I slithered up beside him. 'Look you're a painter so maybe you can help me,' I began, wasting no time, 'I want to buy some paintings while I'm over here. Preferably new artists – unknowns. You know how prices skyrocket once an artist's reputation is made in New York. What are the good galleries? I don't know where to start.' There, that ought to strike the right tone: rich and gullible.

'You've come to the right person. I'll begin by steering you away from the bogus ones. Freddie Baron's for instance. Don't even stop to fix your hair in his window. He really is the most awful fraud and a crook to boot. Specialises in studies of children sucking their toes. That sort of thing.'

'My round next I suppose,' sighed Bollie straightening up to face it. 'Has anyone got a fag? Gold Flake – Smithers, dear chap, how very rough and ready.'

I caught Dody's eye. It was apparent that there was no love lost between these two old friends. Yet neither was going to leave. And all because of lil ole me.

'Now you won't, promise me you won't *dream* of doing the galleries by yourself,' Bollie was imploring me. 'They'll only cheat you. You must let me take you round myself. They all *know* me, you see. They wouldn't dare pull a fast one with me around.'

'Oh would you? Oh gosh, I'd appreciate it,' I gushed.

'She is pretty, isn't she,' he said of me, cocking his head to one side. 'She looks so like Rosemary Smite-Oakes it's uncanny. Of course now Rosie's become Lady—'

'To the duchess!' shouted Smitty suddenly raising his tankard, his elbow perkier and more dangerous than ever.

'Which duchess?' Bollie looked at him with suspicion.

'*Any* duchess,' replied Smitty, smiling maliciously.

'Oh. I thought you meant Lucinda. She was around with John Huston not long ago. He was off to dine at Wheeler's. He was telling us . . .'

'Hey, what about eating?' I said. I was starving.

'This place's got a restaurant upstairs. Good cheap food,' said Smitty. 'What's wrong with it?' he wanted to know as Bollie began his eye-rolling again.

'Nothing if you've got a nasty cold.'

'Oh, for God's sake, I give up,' said Smitty in exasperation. 'I couldn't care less where or what we eat. I've got to get back to the office to correct my proofs in a couple of hours anyway. What about you, Dody? Any place you fancy around here?'

'I'm awful at choosing. My mind goes blank. Let Honey decide. After all, she's the guest.'

I turned to Bollie. He was my man. It was from his lips I had first heard the fatal name of McKee. 'Where would *you* like to go? Where would we be most likely to see interesting people?' I asked him. 'I'm still a tourist.'

'There's only one place *everyone* goes,' said our social arbiter decisively. 'The Truite Bleue. Unfortunately I'm a bit low on funds this evening.'

'Then upstairs it is,' cut in Smitty.

'No, no,' I broke in risking all. 'Please. And it's on me. I'm one of those rich Americans, you know. I can afford it.'

CHAPTER TWO

From my very first glimpse of the battered neon trout sign that hung outside the entrance with its fish-eye winking and sputtering and every now and then slowly dying away, the Truite Bleue impressed me with its air of frank senility. Passing through the shabby entrance hall and coming upon a cubicle in which a few coat-hooks and hat-shelves had been improvised I started to hand my coat over to an old trout-shaped waiter who had been standing there staring into space but at that precise moment another more attractive action presented itself to him and he teetered off out of my reach to grope among the hats for his glass of beer. My coat, suspended in midair, fell to the ground; it was none the less three full sips later before he bothered to pick it up. You had to admire that kind of professional slackness.

We walked through one room of the restaurant and into another, which though of identical size and squalor Bollie insisted on remaining in. We were shown to a table and sat down. The dilapidation surrounding us was extraordinary. The walls were a rich Rembrandt brown-soup colour, the ceiling a yellow scrubbed-in-mud tin composition imprinted with a delicate tracery of a fleur-de-lys pattern just discernible through the dirt. As with most rooms without windows and a kitchen nearby, the atmosphere was hot and stuffy. In a corner a clumsy old-fashioned iron fan had been thoughtfully turned on but, as it was tipped inches too high to be of any functional value, the only thing it cooled was an overhanging light fixture on the ceiling dressed up in red tassels which swung crazily about under its full blast. As a matter of fact all the lighting fixtures in the room were of a fascinating eccentricity of period and style. The wall brackets above us, broken and askew, appeared to have been shot off in some Wild West saloon brawl.

The waiters looked as if they'd staggered out of an old dark hole. They creaked and wobbled and limped and trembled under their loads, their turkey-gobbler necks rising pink from their stiff wing collars. They rattled and shuffled to and fro groaning, 'Yen a plus!' in hoarse strangled Cockney-French to customers' requests, laughing toothlessly at the very idea of their clients' presumption. And yet, looking around, I saw that the restaurant was crowded with contented-looking people. In spite of everything they were eating with gusto. No doubt about it, the place had atmosphere. The genuinely old-fashioned bad service that was being meted out impartially was instantly recognizable as the real thing: a subtle sophisticated Old World incompetence we Americans can never hope to emulate, the best our rustic efforts can produce being a superficial smart-alec surliness not to be spoken of in the same breath as this lofty disdain which was both thoughtful and thorough and would not disintegrate suddenly under a pleading word, a plaintive gesture, or a large tip. These waiters were hand-picked for pleurisy, deafness, and a variety of speech defects. They were flushed of skin, gnarled of hand. The dishes that jumped on to the floor from their palsied hands were never referred to again, as it were, but just lay there for the rest of the evening to be ground under foot by passers-by.

I studied the menu. It was full of things that made my antiseptic American palate squeam. Tête de veau? . . . Boudin? . . . ('What's *that*?' I asked. 'Blood sausage,' said Bollie. 'Oh.') Tripe a la mode de Caen? . . . ('Never mind how it's made, no thank you anyway.') Fried sweetbreads? . . . Fried brains? . . . Sautéd kidneys? . . . Stuffed heart? . . . (*'Yen a plus!'*) . . . Well, what about a rabbit stew? Yuk! What about the trout? I'd just seen it plopped into a plate at a neighbouring table with its head on. Even besides the head and fish-eye there seemed far too much detail to it. It looked far too realistic.

'Hurry up, loove, haven't got all day,' teased Smitty. 'We should have stayed at the Crypt.'

'You all order first, please,' I said. 'I'm deciding.'

I searched around the restaurant to see what other people were eating that didn't look so very much like itself.

And so at last it came about that there, directly opposite me against the Rembrandt-coloured wall, my gaze landed upon a Rembrandt-looking man smiling lovingly at me with a pair of merry blue eyes. The moment, so initially intense, continued to intensify itself until it seemed frozen in space, apart from all the other moments that went before it, prickling my spine, reaching up into my mind and splitting it asunder, causing it to skid about arguing with itself. *'It isn't; it can't be—'* was my first thought. *'But you knew it; you predicted it,'* was the answer. *'That's why you must be wrong.'* And back over it again. For the man I was looking at wasn't the terrible-tempered ogre I'd expected from the photographs and descriptions: was it merely my own fearful imagination that had misled me to the false image of precise attire and a sneer instead of the reality of a crumpled collar and a delightful leer?

The man looking at me was in his late fifties. Stout and rumpled. Comfortably cushioned. Grey-haired, with a lock that fell across his forehead. A fleshy sensual mouth and a podgy mobile nose. A good coarse face full of robust health and a lustiness one could tell at a glance owed nothing to outdoor life. And those blue eyes – but they were exactly the colour of mine! Not taking his love-glance off me he began talking to his companion. I saw his plump well-padded paws, the fingers lying quietly together like mittens, move forward and sort of hug himself while he sat there still smiling at me as if I were the best thing he'd ever seen in his life. He looked so – what was it that gave him his irresistible charm? He looked so *accessible*. That was it. A great simple truth struck me with surprise: charm is availability. How had I ever thought otherwise?

'Who is that – just across from us?' My voice sounded funny, as if I hadn't used it for a long time.

'Well I'll be damned,' said one of them. 'There's C. D. McKee.'

I felt myself calm, almost passive now that it had happened, watching objectively the others shifting around into position to get a good look. C. D. and the man he was with looked back. And then everyone fell to recognizing everyone else. Especially McKee. First, very pointedly, he took his eyes away from mine and bestowed upon each of us a special attention that registered like a rating: a kindly, tolerant, somewhat reminiscent smile for Bollie; a softer, more courtly one for Dody; and then – something I'd never seen before – his face unchanging, still wearing the same expression, the leftover one from Dody – he let his eyes flicker past Smitty so that, while the impression remained friendly, the impact was that of a direct cut. Finally, as if to underline it all, he came back to me again, allowing his face to break into a series of dazzling and worshipful glances. The whole performance was masterly. I smiled back my applause. Well done. Got it. Every nuance.

We resumed our foursome. The meal got ordered. God knows what I ate or what it tasted like. Bollie and Smitty picked up the conversation with redoubled energy, McKee's presence in the room stimulating them to even dizzier heights of anecdote. Dody renewed her attack on her husband. The man with C. D. was someone Scotty had forbidden her to like because he was a snob and a member of White's or something, but as a matter of fact why shouldn't she and she was deciding right now to like him anyway. He was giving a party next week and they'd been invited and Scotty had said he wouldn't be seen dead at it. So she was going. Then, with Bollie's Stately Homes still tumbling down around us, Smitty turned quite serious and professional and confided to me that he'd been trying to approach C. D. for the past year to interview him for a series of articles for his magazine.

'Oh and I want to meet him,' I declared passionately, 'I simply must!'

'Whatever for?' Dody looked at me in amazement. 'I mean apart from the thrill of pure terror that runs through me at the sight of him I don't get his point. I mean he doesn't do anything, does he? What did he do anyway? I always forget.'

'He's had many lives,' said Bollie. 'He's what's known as a Significant Figure. He was a poet once, did you know? Several distinguished vols of verse long ago. Then there was the madly revered Oxford-don-of-staggering-intellect period. Philosophy I think. Of course. He was the School of Philosophy. Fellow of Christ Church and all that. And following upon its heels a Brigadier General if you please during the last war. A disastrous scuffle with big business. A rich wife. A widower. Patron of the Arts. Very generous. He doesn't have to do anything, silly child, he simply is.'

'It's the Brigadier General part that interests me,' said Smitty. 'It's for a series of profiles, Famous Faces that Saved England. From what, ha, ha. Dear old-fashioned World War II is all the rage now. Nostalgia. What really happened at Invergordon when the Fleet mutinied. The Fleet if you please. And foot soldiers and all that lark. Anyway rumour runs that the old boy across from us single-handed broke the Jap naval code so all the Allies knew what our little yellow brothers were up to way before they did. He was a bright bloke, McKee, I'll give you that. I think it's a shame he's gone to seed playing at idle rich.'

'Well I don't care. I think he's a horror,' insisted Dody.

'How long since you last saw him?' asked Bollie. 'I assure you he's altered so in the past year you'd scarcely recognize him. Positively mellow, my dear. Not a trace of the old irascibility. Sad in a way.'

'Not for the rest of the world,' said Dody. 'Every time I've run across him at a party he's been in the middle of some awful remark. I once overheard – well, overheard is hardly the word his voice carries so – I once heard him advising someone to get rid of his wife if he wanted to be taken up by the right people. He wasn't joking. Can you imagine? The spite and malice. I think he's a dangerous nut. Like my husband,' she added bitterly.

He was still smiling at me from across his table. I smiled back. I was beginning to feel his danger and excitement. 'He is a nut,' I said exultantly, 'and I am a nutcracker. I am going to crack him! Well, why not?' I added calming down. 'I mean he's got the reputation for being a lady's man, hasn't he?'

'How would you know that?' asked Smitty. 'I thought he was strictly an English product. Home-grown. I shouldn't have thought his special kind of snob-appeal had travelled across the ocean.'

'As a matter of fact I've been interested in him ever since I read one of his books of poetry. We do have books in America you know. It was beautiful.'

'Well, you may be right,' said Smitty doubtfully. 'I hope you are. Maybe I can sell my series to some Yank paper.'

And then, I suppose, we continued eating. Luckily I was seated next to Smitty. I leaned over to him. 'You do want to talk to him about it, don't you?'

'Rather.'

'I think I can arrange it.'

'I think you can too. He's really giving you the eye.'

'O.K. Leave it to me. Only watch the progress of our meal so that he doesn't leave before us.'

'Rightyho. No fear. We'll skip the coffee if necessary.'

It wasn't. C. D. had no intention of leaving before us. He lingered and lingered; drinking his brandy and drinking in me.

We finished the meal. We were ready to go. The waiter, being no fool, presented Smitty with the check. I offered to pay it. I caught him hesitate for a minute and then decide against it. Too tricky in front of C. D. So he let me off the hook and we got up to go. Bollie and Dody walked through the restaurant, paused to pay their respects to C. D. and walked on. I pulled Smitty back pretending to have mislaid my purse so that the coast would be clear. I checked my face in my pocket mirror and wet my lips to make them glisten. C. D.'s eyes were on me again, practically rolling me up to his side. I took a deep breath. Give, I told myself, with evvverrrrrything you've got. I advanced the necessary steps and parked myself right smack in front of him. He rose. Smitty poked around from behind me and quickly spoke his piece. They'd met several times. Mr. McKee wouldn't remember. At a Whitechapel Gallery exhibition last. Ah, yes. Well, he Smithers was a journalist on the so on and so forth and doing a series called and so on and so forth and most anxious if McKee could spare the time for a few minutes chat with him – just a half-hour would do – at his home if possible to get the atmosphere, that sort of nonsense, for our readers, you know? C. D. looked down at the table-cloth. It was a tense moment for us all. Then he looked up again and speaking slowly and with an incredibly musical voice he said that it probably could be arranged. Mr. – Smithers was it? was to telephone him in the morning. 'And?' he continued, his eyes sliding over to me, his musical voice rising up into an insistent question mark. 'And?'

'Oh. Oh, Miss Flood. Allow me to present Miss Flood. Just over from the States.'

'How do you do, my dear?' C. D. asked me, gravely offering his paw.

'Hello,' I answered as gravely, taking it, and we smiled at each other as if sharing some private joke. Abruptly he switched and began quizzing me. Was it my first time in England? Yes. How did I like it? Oh, fine. Hmmm. There was a faint withdrawal, a faint frown. Yes, I had disappointed him, he had expected more. And what did I think of this restaurant? he continued almost sternly: 'Like eating in a dining car en route to Lyons, wasn't it?'

I looked around in panic. The eerie yellow low voltage electricity combined with the long narrow shape of the room and the swaying light fixture with its peculiar handkerchief-covering fluttering in the iron fan's breeze certainly gave off an atmosphere of old trains at night. But Lyons? Christ, I'd never been out of America. Then a waiter, eight clacking coffee-cups balanced on a tray on one arm, a purple-stained napkin under his other, swerved unexpectedly close to me. I backed away as a flash of one-two-three studs on his shirt front loomed in front of me and then sighed with relief as, with a whirl of his shabby swallow tails, he spun away from me, neatly avoiding disaster by some very fancy manoeuvring of his game leg. It was terrible, all I could think of was that religious movie short I'd seen a couple of days before. 'It's more like Miracle Day at Lourdes,' I heard myself say.

C.D.'s laughter gurgled and gushed and squeaked and squealed. It was the laughter of a child – free and unfettered. His head rolled back and his belly fairly shook, the old jelly. And every time he looked at the waiter it started up again. Hiss – giggle.

'Delicious,' he said when he could. 'You must come with ah . . .' indicating Smitty, 'both of you. Day after tomorrow. Drinks.' A touch of the paw again. A passionate appeal in his eye. 'You won't let me down, will you? I'm so looking forward to it. Do bring her, please.' And the audience was over. But not for the rest of the audience, I noticed, which was a good part of the restaurant. The Patron flew to my side with a great snapping of fingers for my coat, my coat, '*le manteau de Madame la Princesse!*' I gave him a look. Was he putting me on? Not especially. Fall-out from the presence of C. D. McKee.

I felt suddenly very tired. Outside, I said goodnight to my new friends and exchanged telephone numbers and promises and hopped in a cab for my hotel.

I went up to my room and got undressed, carefully avoiding the great clumps of hotel furniture rising like sharp rocks from the hysterically patterned carpet in the tiny room. I made my way to the even tinier bathroom and stared at myself in the mirror. Then I began combing my hair, admiring its shining blondness. I put on my white silk pyjamas, snapped the elastic waistband twice hard against my stomach and rubbed my hand under it. I wandered over to the window and looked down at the lonely noisy traffic-filled street below. How ugly it looked under the arc light. I tried to think of the evening with pleasure. It had been an unqualified triumph. Why was I so angry? Then I knew. It had been practically the first time in a whole month that I'd held a conversation with English people that didn't involve asking for a direction or paying for a cheque. One whole long lonely month. Damn them, how dare they? I opened the window and leaning out thumbed my nose at the traffic below.

CHAPTER THREE

I called up Dody next day as soon as I awoke.

'Honey, thank goodness,' she exclaimed when she heard who it was. 'Such dramas at your hotel. They refuse to believe you're staying there. I've been on to them all – desk clerk, hall porter, manager and back again each swearing you're no such person. You're not incognito by any chance?'

I wonder now why I didn't tell her I was. Of course it would have taken too long to explain. And I didn't know her well enough. And I wasn't clear myself why I was doing it. I suppose that's enough reasons. Anyway I said that I hardly ever got messages (too true) and that there was doubtless some conspiracy at the switchboard.

'Oh dear, English hotels,' she moaned, 'I feel I should be apologizing for their inefficiency. Scotty would be I'm sure – but never mind about that. Listen, what are you doing this very minute? Could you come over as soon as possible. I've got to see you. I've something rather important to ask you.'

I got a cab to her address in Mayfair. There were four bottles of milk standing outside her door when I rang Dody's bell. And her husband had been gone less than two days. Dody was still in her dressing gown. She had lost her husband only two days ago and already she was a lost soul. She led me first into her bedroom and then apologized for the mistake and took me into the dining-room for no reason and finally into the living-room where it occurred to me watching her wandering aimlessly about picking up things and putting them down elsewhere that retracing her exact footsteps on paper would yield the blueprint of a rather interesting tango. She looked for cigarettes and all the boxes were empty. She stared at the goldfish bowl uncertainly. 'I can never remember whether I've fed him or not,' she said suddenly. 'I kept on feeding them and they kept on dying all the time. All but one. So I don't know if he killed the rest or if I was over-feeding them or starving them or what. You're supposed to give them a pinch of food every day. But how big is a pinch anyway? I don't know, I—' It was an awful sight, someone so bang in the middle of suffering she didn't even know it. 'Oh goodness,' she sighed, 'I haven't even offered you anything to drink.'

'There's some milk outside,' I said.

'Oh is there? Let's see.' We went to the front door and picked up the bottles. 'So that's where it's been,' she said. 'No wonder there wasn't any in the fridge.'

The ice-box was empty except for five eggs, two tins of sardines (one opened), half a packet of butter and a withered head of lettuce. We put in the milk and Dody looked thoughtfully at its contents. 'What with one thing and another we didn't eat in at all during the last fortnight and I suppose I haven't been eating much since. I always try to get some milk down though.' She poured out two glasses with shaking hands and we sat down at the kitchen table and drank them in silence.

'It's about this flat,' she finally said. 'Don't look at it now, it's a mess.' She flew to a corner and picked up a pair of her shoes which had been left there and then she didn't know what to do with them. She sank back into her chair and still clutching them blurted out the whole story. She was going to get a divorce. She was consulting lawyers. It was clear that he'd gone off with this other woman, this Indian woman. But there mustn't be the slightest chance of a counter-suit said the lawyers. For instance, unless another girl came to stay with her it would be quite inadvisable for her to entertain men alone in her flat, and so she must get herself a flat-mate. And she didn't know who to ask. She had the feeling all the girls who'd been their friends had also been his mistresses. She supposed she was being foolish, but there it was. What she wanted to ask of me was, would I – could I – possibly move in with her?

But she wouldn't stop for my answer. Nervously she was dragging me by the arm flinging open doors and getting in their way as she tried to push us past them in her eagerness to show me the various rooms.

'Now you're not to say a thing, not a word till you've seen the whole flat. It's really quite decent – at least it will be when I've tidied it up. And look – masses of space. I shan't be in your way at all. Two bedrooms, see? One for each of us. Of course you come and go as you please, that's understood. I mean it's better than living in some dreary hotel. Oh, Honey, if you would, it'd be such a help. He must not come back here, you see. Not to this flat anyway. It's called condoning. It's very serious. In fact I'm supposed to change the lock on the door so he can't. I like that part of it,' she said all of a sudden laughing quite genuinely, 'I don't know why but it absolutely appeals to me. I must get it done first thing in the morning. And his clothes. I don't know what to do about them. His lawyers said send them to his club. Of course he hasn't got one. Perhaps I'd better send them to his mother. She drinks.'

We were in their bedroom by now, Dody finally silent as she stared at her bed table: empty match covers, aspirin, vitamin tablets, glucose, cough drops, nail polish, nail polish remover and a half-full glass of water. 'None of it does any good,' she said frowning at the display, 'except maybe the nail polish remover taken internally. Oh God. His mother. He says it's all her fault. His father was an explorer and away all the time and his mother was too busy drinking to love him properly so he needs more love than ordinary people do.' The Indian girl had taught him all about Vedanta, an Indian religion where, as near as she could gather, everything is One, which meant it was O.K. to do anything you like whenever you like. Anyway, this Indian girl had got him very interested in it. He was always reading books about it. Her trouble, Dody's trouble, was that she'd been happy all the first year of their marriage just being in love with him. It was true she didn't care – didn't even think much about anything else. Then he began getting nuttier and shouting at her all the time that she was living in a dream world and he was determined to crash it. Look around you, he kept yelling, feel, feel something about what you see. Something, anything. Hate! Hate well and maybe you'll be able to love well.

Dody had never asked herself a lot of personal questions. Three days after they'd met he had declared himself violently in love with her, and then they'd gotten married. He was strong. He had a lot of opinions. Dody sighed and her head made a slight movement as if buffeted by a particularly strong opinion. It was easy to imagine her going into orbit, a dreamy satellite content to revolve eternally around her sun except the sun's course had become too erratic causing her to crash into reality. But now, said Dody shaking herself out of her trance, she was going to hate. Because he was right. It was stupid to be the way she'd been – passive and trusting; it meant getting stepped on. Her defiance was springing up at last. She would do all the things he hated. She would like all the things he hated. That was easy of course – he hated everything. She'd go to that man's party. He hated him. She'd get a job. He never wanted her to have a job. And she'd get a divorce.

Dody flopped on to the bed. I did think she was right about getting a divorce, didn't I? I sat down on the chaise longue facing her and lit a cigarette. I recognized that this was going to be one of those exchanges where, under the guise of seeking advice, in fact she merely wished to be agreed with. I began agreeing.

I said yes, I thought she was right about getting a divorce.

'I mean it would be silly to continue like this.'

'Absolutely.'

'Because it means he can go on behaving the way he has.'

'Yes, and on and on.'

'On the other hand a divorce is so expensive what with lawyers' fees and detectives and everything.'

'It probably adds up.'

'And it's not as if there was someone else I wanted to marry. He hated so many people I hardly know anyone any more.'

'It'll probably take time.'

'So perhaps I ought to call the whole thing off, see what happens when he comes back. He's coming back in three months. Not rush into anything.'

'That might be sensible.'

'But look – why the hell should he get away with it? Off with another woman – it's humiliating!'

I sighed my sympathy.

'And of course he doesn't love me or he wouldn't have gone off like that, would he?'

I said it was not my idea of love.

Dody wandered over to the bureau. 'This is his photograph. It's not really a good likeness. You've met him – he's much better looking than that, isn't he?'

'Yes, that was my impression.'

'He is good looking. And fun. And well known. I suppose he can't help it if girls go for him. Everyone else I know bores me.'

'There certainly are a lot of boring people in the world.'

'It really was all his mother's fault. For being so drunk all the time. And his father always off to the North Pole or somewhere.

He had a horrible childhood. He said she never even gave him a bath herself. You know, perhaps I should have shown more that I loved him.'

'Yes.'

'A man like that needs someone possessive – even aggressive. Like that Indian girl.'

'Mmnnn.'

'But you think I should?'

'Yes. I mean no. I mean should what?'

'Go on with the divorce as planned.'

'Well what do *you* think?'

'I think I should.'

'So do I.'

'Good.'

I looked at my watch. It was twelve noon and I was wondering if I was going to be able to get away with not paying for that night's hotel room or if it was already too late. 'I'd better be getting back,' I said rising.

Dody looked at me in terror. 'What's the matter? Is it something I've said?'

'Why no. It's to get my clothes.'

She looked at me stupidly. 'Your clothes?'

'To pack. To pack my clothes. Oh and before I forget' – I had forgotten; and the ugly thought struck me with considerable force – 'how much rent do you want me to pay?'

'But I wouldn't dream of it. I couldn't possibly take any money from you. It's already been paid in advance by him. And you'll be doing me such a fav . . .' She stopped in mid-track. 'You mean you'll come and live here?' she asked incredulously. 'You really will? Oh Honey, I can't tell you – I'm so relieved – why didn't you say so straight off?'

I closed my eyes and counted ten. 'I've been trying to all this time,' I said, as gently as I could.

CHAPTER FOUR

After I checked out of my hotel and moved myself into Dody's flat I telephoned Smitty at his office.

'Have you got a file on C. D. McKee in your morgue?' I asked.

'Yes, what for?'

'So that I may sparkle perceptively over drinks tomorrow night.'

'You Yanks—' I could imagine the look he was giving the phone. 'You Yanks; thorough.'

I stuck out my tongue at him from my end but merely said, 'Bye, bye. Be right down,' and caught a series of buses to Fleet Street.

Smitty got out the file and I flipped through. C. D. McKee. Cosmo Darwin McKee. Nothing at all about his early life. A few short paragraphs in which he was included in lists of academic honours conferred on him by various foreign universities while at Oxford. The war, his Generalship, meetings with Heads of Staff, etc., etc. Then a sort of social butterfly series – photographs mainly – old Porky leering out from glossy groups at Hunt Balls and deb parties and art exhibitions. I was flipping through faster when suddenly, wedged in between the Hunt Balls and his marriage to the wealthy American widow Mrs. Pauline Saegessor, and on newsprint instead of slick paper – wham – a pile of clips on the Bosworth Clute Securities case. A public scandal; a great big fat juicy business scandal. I caught my breath and studied them closely. What startled me at first was that I knew the name – Bosworth Clute. By, I suppose, a not very wild coincidence, this much married, much divorced English business tycoon was the father of one of the girls I'd been at school with. I ploughed through reams of almost incomprehensible testimony. Something about the firm being hammered on the Stock Exchange. Something about sharepushing. Something about Clute concealing his snowballing losses by using his clients' securities without their knowledge. Something about gambling on a successful Suez action by Britain that would cause a boom in oil shares. Something about Clute being sentenced to six years in jail having been found guilty on sixteen counts of conspiracy, fraud and false pretences involving £300,000. But what had all this to do with McKee? Oh – oh. There it was. A little bit tucked away at the end. Clute's Board of Directors, amongst whom C. D. was singled out for special mention by the Judge. 'As to General McKee I have satisfied myself that he was at no time aware of the transactions Clute was conducting though I should like to record my amazement at his lack of interest in the enterprise whether by naïvety or design and the lack of business qualifications which Clute seemed to feel appropriate to the selection of his Board of Directors on the whole and to General McKee in particular'. Hmm. Spot of trouble there.

C. D.'s house was in one of the prettier squares in Knightsbridge. I was especially struck by the way the front windows were lined up with the back ones so that from the approach his lovely green garden seemed to shine right through the house; green foliage through stone. In the midst of busy London the square was quiet, hushed, unrushed. His man opened the door, took our coats, showed us in. I listened to the expensive tinkle of crystal and china we set off as we crossed the hall and mounted the stairs into a long graceful drawing-room. C. D. rose and came towards us, shook Smitty's hand and then received mine in his nest of paws breathing, 'Good. You're here. I was so afraid you wouldn't come.' His man pussy-footed around giving us drinks and Smitty began the interview. They talked about cryptology for a while and then launched into a flood of war reminiscence about who didn't do what and who should have done what and what would have happened if they had. I stopped listening and looked around me. The room was exquisite. Magnificent. He lived well, old Fatso, he did himself proud. He wanted for nothing. He didn't hold back. I watched the two of them utterly absorbed in their discussion, oblivious of me, and I began to feel resentful, angry. It had begun so well. 'Good. You're here. I was so afraid you wouldn't come.' Well, what difference was it making that I had come? His man entered pussy-footing in again, whispered some message to him, and I seemed to detect in the sudden briskness with which C. D. resumed the conversation that our time was almost up. I sat there twirling my glass thinking I *must* speak; I must make my presence felt.

'Listen, I'm dying to know about this man Bosworth Clute,' I heard myself interrupting them.

C. D. turned completely around in my direction, I'd never seen a face change so fast. 'What about him?' he asked, finally.

'Well, I mean is he still in jail? Or what . . .?' Acting puzzled, I foundered about in the dead silence and then, seeming to have no choice, pushed on. 'You see, it's the weirdest coincidence but I went to school with . . . I went to school with one of his . . . his . . .' I stopped, hypnotized by the sheer disagreeableness of his expression.

C. D. put down his drink and then released me from his gaze. 'I see,' he said turning to Smitty. 'Now, I understand. You haven't come to interview me about the war at all. What you're really

36

interested in is raking up old muck. How clever of you using Miss Whatever-her-name-is as a decoy. Tell me, is it to be for one of those American scandal sheets? I'm quite curious to know.'

'What are you talking about?' I gasped.

His expression had become even more disagreeable if possible. 'It's obvious, isn't it? He begins with the respectable approach and you come in for the dirt. Quite a team. Sorry, I'm not playing.'

'How dare you!' I sprang to my feet, one part of me surprised at the surge of rage I was allowing myself to show, I who had so carefully schooled myself always to keep my feelings under outward control. 'How dare you,' I said again and got a grip on myself and went on more carefully. 'I never heard of you in my life until the other night if you want to know. Then when you asked me over for drinks Smitty told me you were famous so I looked at some old clippings at his office to see what you were famous for. And I came across Bosworth Clute's name. And I went to school with one of his daughters. At Braxton Hall if you want to check. And I want my coat and I want to leave.' And I flounced out a picture of righteous indignation.

C. D. followed me down the stairs. 'I say, please Miss Flood. Please. I am sorry. I see I've misjudged you. Do come back. At least till your friend finishes our interview. Pay no attention to the ravings of a tiresome old man. I've always been much too sensitive about the Clute thing. I've an idea. Why don't you come and sit in my study until I'm finished with Mr. Smithers? I'm sure it's all very boring for you. Then we can have a friendly drink and talk of pleasanter things. Say yes,' he implored.

'All right,' I conceded as he led me upstairs to it. 'But because I don't want to mess up Smitty's interview.'

'No, I'm sure you don't,' he murmured and he closed the door on me before I had time to react.

I wandered around for a while. A door of the study led to his

37

bedroom, then to his bathroom. I didn't quite dare explore his bedroom so I went to the bathroom and opened his medicine chest. A man is known by the medicine in his chest, I told myself, and suddenly I grabbed two small pill bottles out of it and stuffed them in my handbag and returned to the study.

Some fifteen minutes later I heard a soft knock. 'Yes?' I said.

'Miss Flood?' purred C. D. 'We're finished now. Do come and join us.' He entered and stood over me beaming. 'And what have you been doing all this time?' he asked.

'Reading your mail,' I replied coolly.

He laughed his hiss-giggle and began leading me down the stairs to the drawing-room again. Midway he paused and turned to me all charm and suavity. 'I am sorry to have behaved like that. Especially when really the whole thing is so unimportant. But—' the old loon's eyes were brimming with mischief, 'but tell the truth, Miss Flood, I assure you it won't make the slightest difference – they did put you up to it, didn't they?'

This time I marched straight down the stairs almost knocking him over, demanded my coat from his man and, without backward word or glance, left.

So that was that, I thought glumly, huddled in the corner of the taxi that was taking me back to Dody's. I mean gosh, I mean gee, I mean golly, I'd known he wasn't going to be one of your ordinary kindly everyday run-of-the-mill old gents, I hadn't expected him to be – but all this mercurial jazz, one minute one way, one minute the next – he was too much for me. I would never have gotten around him; would never have gotten him to fork over the money. Well, that was that. And now what? Back to America and forget the whole wild project?

The phone was ringing when I let myself into Dody's flat. It was C. D. The apologetic full-of-contrition C. D. He'd got my number from Smitty. He wanted my address so that he could send me flowers.

'That won't be necessary,' I said primly.

'No, but it's essential,' he replied. And could he give lunch tomorrow? And would I accept his word that this evening would never be referred to again?

What had I got to lose? I thought. Nothing. And maybe the world to gain. And so I accepted with pleasure his invitation to lunch.

CHAPTER FIVE

'Funny menus seem to be my fate in England,' I remarked, studying the one at the Half Moon Hotel in Abbington Lane near Shepherd Market where C. D. had decided to take me to lunch that day.

It was a decision that had not been lightly reached, artist at living that he was – all possibilities had been thoroughly explored and exhausted before arriving at it. It would have been too soon, for instance, for us to lunch again in Soho. And too soon for him ever to lunch again in one of those little Chelsea restaurants where, according to C. D., on top of the outward physical discomfort of sharing half a seat and being forced to choose between the roles of performer or audience (impossible, said he, with strangers virtually in one's lap to be both) was the inward one of trying to digest the globs of tomato-and-garlic sauce invariably used to cover the mediocre food. Especially for one whose digestion, as he confessed, was not presently at its most robust. There were always, of course, the grand restaurants: the Reserve, the Mirabelle, the Ritz but as an American I'd no doubt seen dozens like them in my country. And the City had excellent food too, but the atmosphere of the business man's lunch depressed him. We would begin fresh. We would lunch at a place neither of us had before. He remembered the Half Moon

Hotel. It was small and quiet. He'd never lunched there but he liked the look of it and had heard good things about it.

We were sitting in its pleasant high-ceilinged dining-room at a table near a window overlooking the winding street with its enchanting view of flower boxes and flower barrows and fruit stalls, of gaily painted doors and glistening bay windows and highly polished brass; a view so quaintly, unmistakably, *aggressively* Olde London – a miniature Nation of Shopkeepers going on at one of the corners, shopkeeping old English antiques and old English First Editions and old English shoe-repairs and old English butcherings and bakings. And then picking up the menu I read: *Toast Radjar, Toast Ivanhoe, Ogorki Demi-sel ... Crème Waldeze ... Consommé Ecolière ... Filet de Plie Orly ... Poulet Braconniers ...* something else *Champvallon ... Charlotte Printanière ...*

'What's so funny about it?' asked C. D.

'Only that I can't make head or tail of it. In America we generally get to know in advance what we're eating. Like that menu at the Truite Bleue with all that offal. Ugh, it was *offal*,' I added wittily.

C. D. looked at me unsmiling. 'You find it so odd? You must tell me about yourself. I really know so little about Americans – although I had an American wife. Did you know that I had an American wife? She died last Spring.' He seemed in a rush to get it all out. 'It was very sad. We were only married four years. Pauly Saegessor was her name before. Perhaps you knew her?'

'No,' I said lying.

'I didn't think you would. How did I get on to her anyway?'

'Something about food.'

'Oh, yes. I was wondering if all Americans shared the same lack of enthusiasm for food experimentation. Am I to conclude that civilized American eating habits are so very dissimilar to European or English ones?'

'We tend to stick to what we like. I'd never dream of having anything but a hamburger for lunch back home,' I assured him.

He smiled, thinking I was kidding. I wasn't.

'Oh, sometimes maybe a couple of hot dogs with an orange drink for a change if I'm near a Nedicks. *Delicious*.'

This made him less sure and he hid behind the menu. Suddenly he let out a bray. 'I say, I hadn't studied the thing very closely, it is pretty marvellous, isn't it? Look at this sequence – down here on the right: Savarin Biscay – very exotic I'm sure – Coupe Othello – whatever *that* is – Pouding au Riz – now we're getting closer – and plain old Baked Marmalade Roll. I simply must get some of this degarbled. Waiter,' he called, 'waiter, what can the Coupe Othello possibly be?'

'Coupe Othello, sir? A scoop of vanilla ice cream with a scoop of chocolate,' came the answer deadpan.

'How charming. Mes compliments au chef,' purred C. D. 'I think we'll stop right there,' he said to me. 'I suggest we order only the items we can't guess at. I have a feeling suspense will be the better part of this experience. And a drink first. What would you like?'

I ordered a plain old dry martini adding that I wanted it very dry and with a twist of lemon instead of an olive to show that we Americans too can enter the gourmet ring.

C. D. ordered himself a Cinzano and we went ahead and chose our meal. I decided to start with Ogorki Demi-sel and go on to the Filet de Plie Orly while C. D. plumped for the Crème Waldeze followed by a Poulet Braconniers.

The waiter returned with our drinks and began placing them in front of us wrong way round. I'd noticed a kind of mad, satisfied gleam come into C. D.'s eye as he sat silently, watching the mistake to its completion, but nothing to prepare me for the explosion by which he let the waiter – and everyone else in the room – in on his view of the matter. 'May I recommend that a little ordinary commonsense brought to your job might help you in overcoming your either real or psychological deafness, young man.' he bellowed. 'Who at this table looks *young* enough to risk a midday martini? Who looks *wise* enough to choose an aperitif?' It was unexpected to say the least.

From every corner of the dining-room heads spun round on their swivels to get a good look at the extraordinary spectacle of someone raising his voice indoors.

'Yes, sir. Thank you, sir,' mumbled the waiter as he skulked away.

'I always think it helps the class war to insult a waiter while wearing an expensive suit, don't you?' C. D. was saying to me blandly, not in the least discomforted by his moment in the spotlight. 'Now, tell me about yourself. I want to know all about you. I've decided you could be a great success over here. I'm seriously thinking of launching you.'

'I might have launched myself last night only I had to whisk myself away before I could really get started.'

'If you mean Smithers—' he paused and gave a dismissive shrug. 'I don't think – your true happiness lies in that direction.'

'Oh? Then where does it lie?'

'Frankly, I had something much grander in view. A Brewery Baron or a Bookstall Earl. Doesn't that appeal to you more? But I must know everything about you first,' a wicked smile. 'Better come clean.'

Now, funnily enough – and this was a surprise even to myself – I found I was seriously considering doing just that. Coming clean, I mean, and throwing myself on his mercy. There was something to be said for the policy of honesty if only on such obvious grounds as wear and tear. Further considerations: Better a conscious friend than an unconscious adversary. Wasn't it worth the risk appealing to his better nature? Or at any rate wasn't it safe to assume by now that he liked me; that he could be – by his own confession – sufficiently interested in helping me at least as generously as he apparently helped other people, in his Patron of the Arts role, I who, as he would see, had far more claim upon his money? Logic upon logic, it swept my heart along and my head with it.

'All right,' I said. 'All right! I'll come clean. Only brace yourself because you're in for the surprise of your life—'

But – 'Waiter!' he barked suddenly, setting the English heads swirling again. 'Waiter!'

'Sir?' He stood before us in dread.

'I wonder if you would be kind enough to break this bread roll for me.' C. D.'s voice was soft but ominous as he selected one from the bread basket at contemptuous random.

'I – I can't sir,' said the poor thing finally, red in the face from trying.

'No. Of course you can't.' C. D. carefully took the roll from him and threw it back in the bread basket in disgust. 'Shall I tell you why? Because it's stale, that's why.'

'Yes, sir.'

'Is that all you have to say?'

'I might be able to cut it with a bread knife. Shall I get one, sir?'

'Certainly not. What you can do is go back to the kitchen at once and get us a basket of fresh rolls.'

'I don't think it's any use, sir,' replied the waiter with dull honesty. 'I mean, sir, they'll be just the same as these. It's getting late, sir,' he added by way of explanation.

'But the Patron has not yet begun his siesta, I trust?'

'His what, sir? . . . No, sir.'

'Get him for me, then.'

'Yes, sir.' The waiter fled overjoyed at release.

The head waiter came, shrewdly appraised C. D., the age, the weight, the heaven knows what in the eye, and wisely conceded defeat, and the upshot of the matter was that someone – I don't know who, a bellboy, maybe even the chef – was sent down the Lane to the bakery at the corner for fresh rolls.

By the time things had quietened down however and C. D. had turned back to me and was wanting to know what I meant by the 'surprise of his life' as if nothing had happened, I'd had plenty of time to consider the monstrous dangers attendant on my projected decision to testify against myself. To consider and to reconsider and to reverse that decision. Those stale rolls, as I saw it, were manna from heaven plonked down upon our table as a warning for me to proceed with caution.

So, how to get out of it? The only thing to do seemed to be to track back to that other story, the one I'd invented in Soho of the sick chick.

'I mean that I'm sort of a nut,' I said with commendable forthrightness. 'At any rate I've had a nervous breakdown. That's why I came over here, you see. To get away from everything. And to be analysed.'

'By whom?'

'Huh?'

'Who is it? The name of your analyst.'

Wonderful how the unexpected always throws us. I was prepared for anything but a simple question like that. I had equipped myself with all possible kinds of false identifications and labels but the name of an analyst wasn't amongst them. It had never occurred to me that anyone would come out like that and demand the name of an analyst; it was too terribly personal. On top of the confusion I was shocked, really shocked, and I indicated as much.

'I – I don't think I ought to tell, should I? Isn't it sort of like breaking the Hipocratic oath? You know, like if it's all right for me to go around blabbing his name, then it's all right for him to go around blabbing mine. And everything about me. See what I mean?'

'But my dear girl, I assure you this isn't idle curiosity, you must know there are as many quacks in that field as there are in any other. I happen to be familiar with most of the good psychoanalysts practising in London. A health service I perform for my friends. Don't laugh. I mean it seriously. It's for your own good. I want to make sure you're going to the very best.'

Well that was that. It meant I'd not only have to invent a name but a School to which he belonged and maybe even an address. Better start all over again. My Ogorki Demi-sel arrived and I was flabbergasted to see that it consisted of a dish of pickles – those baby cucumbers, the kind I hate, and a bit of cream cheese, the demi-sel – that had somehow, God knew how, detached itself from the hors-d'oeuvres proper and was masquerading as a first course. Nevertheless I nibbled away brooding over which tack to take.

'I haven't actually started going to an analyst yet,' I said finally. 'To tell you the truth, I'm afraid to. All my friends that go seem to get so much wackier' – this at least was true— 'and I feel so much better now. You know, now that I'm over here and away from it all.'

'I do wish you'd tell me what happened,' he prodded me gently. 'I'm very good with stretcher cases.' He had, I noticed, stopped eating his Crème Waldeze, a flat grey soup – to give me his undivided attention.

Now I had chosen the name Honey Flood in the first place because it was the name of the girl who had been my roommate at boarding school and at college, my best friend, in short, the person I had known best. I knew her home and her family inside out. I knew her address in the East Seventies and her telephone number and the colour of her bedspread. I knew her mother's first name and that of her father, and what her father did. But I had intended only to make use of her externals; her statistics, that is. It had never occurred to me until right then

46

that I might find myself using her *story* as well: her breakdown as well as her hometown. Yet there it was, I realized, all set up – a real live nervous breakdown as right and ready-made for me as the rest of her.

However, as I embarked upon her story the strangest change came over me. I discovered that it was possible to be the sort of liar who comes to believe her lies almost the instant they spring from her lips. For no sooner had I begun to talk about myself as Honey Flood than I felt myself mysteriously osmosing into her: a harrowing experience.

Try telling a story in which you behaved in a somewhat less than exemplary fashion and try telling it from the point of view of the person you behaved that way towards *and* try laying it on thick for the sympathy of your listener, and see if you don't find your real self in the disagreeable position of standing by and watching you becoming an absolute fiend.

I gave up the pickles, downed the dregs of my mouldy martini and began to recall events I had not thought once of for at least three years. Honey, visiting in Texas that summer she fell in love. I painted a large lush canvas and flung myself into it. I pictured us moonstruck, the boy and I, languishing in a tree-strung hammock under star-hung nights. And all her desperate, dangerous wonders of requited first love slipped in suddenly as if it were my real past. A hot wind blew through parched western plains, swimming pools glittered in the afternoon sun, organdie dance dresses crushed softly into the night. The summer passed, spun golden. How vividly it had all remained in Honey's memory, so that I, who had never even been in Texas, could feel it flowing through me, could feel especially the boy, the silky, skinny, highstrung boy – who happened to be a multi-multi-multi-oilmillionaire as well.

And then, back to college in the autumn. It was, Honey remembers, Junior Year. A snow-storm of love letters from the boy. Some of them, says Honey, I show to my roommate, for we've always been so close, and she seems so happy for me. Oh, and a little amused as well, I know – she's a bit of a cynic, this roommate. Well, not exactly a cynic, perhaps that's the wrong word, but so sophisticated, and cool, and knowing. I can't imagine, says Honey, what *she'd* ever be like head over heels in love so I don't show her all the letters of course but enough, unquestionably enough that she can see how much we matter to each other, the boy and I.

Weekends through October and November all spent with him at his college, and finally, the engagement ring. The diamond big as the Ritz, my roommate had called it. She always referred to it in that way. It caught on, became a kind of campus joke. That was a couple of weeks before Christmas vacation. And before the vacation came the Junior Prom at our college. And after that came the end.

I was all wound up now, carried away. I hardly noticed the changing of the plates.

'What do you mean the end?' interrupted C. D. 'What happened?'

'My roommate. She stole him away from me. And it was easy as pie! It was Friday afternoon and she'd met him for the first time. She picked a fight with her own date, saw to it that he left in a huff, and then she flung herself upon the mercy of mine and that kept the three of us stuck together like glue for the rest of the weekend. That apparently was all the time she needed—'

(*Fascinating, but fascinating! I, the me, the real me, had forgotten all this until now. Wiped it out of my mind completely.*)

'It was the ring that got her!' exclaimed Honey to C.D. now with a sudden flash of perception. 'My diamond ring – you know, as big as the Ritz? Up till that she'd been – well, as I said, she seemed so happy for me. But that ring changed everything.

She couldn't bear the sight of it. She kept on and on about it. She wanted to know how I could stand someone with such vulgar taste. She said she'd expected more of me than that I'd throw myself away on one of those joke Texans with a ten gallon hat and spurs and twelve identical sports cars. Every time I tried to defend him she'd point to the ring and say that anyone who would give me a present as vulgar as that must be vulgar himself.

'So you can imagine my astonishment when, upon finally meeting him, she managed to twist the whole thing around against *me*. I stood there, stupidly rooted to the spot, listening to her going on to him about how utterly unlike my description of him he was, how she'd been led to expect one of those joke Texans with a ten gallon hat and spurs and twelve of everything. I tell you I couldn't believe what was happening. I didn't know how to handle it. I tried denying it and I tried laughing it off but it was no use. She was on to something – something she'd caught from his letters: he was a big man in the West but he still felt like a little boy in the East. He could still be thrown by remarks like that. Well – that was the kick off, and somehow after that everything collapsed around me—' (I paused, half for effect, half to re-savour this extraordinary experience of someone else's pain so completely taking over my own emotions. It was like being on both ends of a see-saw: half-for-effect, ping! Honey's pain, pong! Ping! Pong! Ping!

'I don't understand,' C. D. was saying. 'What possible motive did she have for behaving that way?'

'None really, that was what was so awful. Or, at least, none that made any sense. Simply that she was seized with an overpowering urge to spend some time with a man who had that much money. Anyway, that's what she said. Not that she even wanted to spend the money herself. She didn't want anything. She just wanted to see how it was spent. It was apparently spent that Christmas, the two of them together, on dining and dancing at the El Morocco and the Stork Club and a string of orchids and she got disappointed – or disillusioned. Or bored. It didn't last long, the two of them together. It meant so little to them both. I think that finally was what flipped me. That she did it out of idle curiosity And the last letter I got from him – it almost killed me – saying what he'd done to me had at last made him realize the sort of person he really was, that maybe he was never meant to be anything but a rich Texas playboy. Well, maybe it was true – you can see his picture in the papers every day now with a different movie starlet but the thing is we never got a chance to find out. Such a waste. And I loved him so much. You see, he was only *half* spoiled when I knew him.' Tears sprang to my mind, seeped down into my eyes and ran warmly along my cheeks. I didn't brush them away until they began to tickle.

'So I went home for Easter vacation and I slept all day and I cried all night and somehow I never got around to returning to college. In fact I didn't do anything for the next two years except sit around the house. And mope. Until finally I got myself up. And I came over here.'

(*Only you didn't, Honey, I thought sadly. I came. And whatever became of you? Are you sitting there still?*)

Listen, dear reader, I know what you must be thinking, I can almost hear you now. 'What's going *on* for chrisakes? Stories within stories and about her roommate yet. I mean Jeez, who *needs* it? Flashbacks are bad enough, but stories about stories, man, **w**hat is *that*?'

And I know, I know, but what can I do? That's the way it was that sunny day in the rich, red-carpeted, high white-ceilinged dining-room of the Half Moon Hotel at 2.15 p.m. in the afternoon. I told my little tale and I swear, out of the corner of one eye – cunningly aslant (the other fixed sturdily but uninterestedly on the Filet de Plie Orly which discovered itself to be an old piece of fish with some white stuff on it), I gleaned a glimmering of one solid fact: the Old Man was definitely picking up on me, you dig? I mean he was flapping around. Half hooked.

Look: all I'm trying to say is that there comes a crucial moment in a relationship in which one person is moving towards the other – passing from stranger to acquaintance to something else – when (to be precisely *Précieuse* for the moment and get out Mademoiselle Scudéry's *Carte de Tendre* that I used to study in French class) when one must make the perilous journey from, let us say, the *Ville de la Curiosité* to the *Ville de la Compassion* without falling into the *Lac d'Indifférence*, and C. D. made it via the tale I spun. No question about it, it was the Main Event of that lunch (far more than his waiter-baiting, for instance, of which there was a great deal more, like his handing his umbrella to the cloakroom attendant with a lordly 'And refurl it for me, please'). And the reason it was the main event was because the guilt and confusion and melancholy I had felt in the telling, being genuine, added immeasurably to the quality of my performance, enabling us both to melt into an ecstasy of sympathy for the betrayed Honey.

C. D. was staring into space unconsciously tearing at the soft insides of the fresh new rolls, kneading them into pellets.

'Two whole years to get over someone as worthless as that. What folly.' His eyes trailed across the tables as though with a view to rearranging them. But it was his thoughts he was re-arranging, for when he finally spoke again it was from the depths of one troubled soul to what I am sure he felt to be another. 'It is possible,' he said with soft emotion, 'that before our paths separate I shall owe you many things, not the least being the salutary effect you've had today of reminding me of my age—'

'Oh but I don't think of you as being—' I began protesting.

'I mean, you remind me for how many layers of years the habit of cynicism has been drying and encrusting my sensibilities. I had forgotten that the young are still young where it matters most – in years. They are still new to experience.' He broke off and gave me his burst-of-sunshine smile. 'How strange and delightful to be new to experience! But that isn't very helpful to you, is it? I'm expressing myself badly. I'm trying to explain my shock – and mind, I'm saying this against myself, not you – my shock at having caught a glimpse of what lies underneath a nature I had thought remarkable mainly for its self-possession. As I say, the habit of years, my dear, can you forgive me? I'm truly touched by your rotten luck, believe me. You're not eating?'

'Guess I don't feel very much like it,' I said wanly. How did he think I could talk as much as that and eat at the same time?

'Mightn't the Coupe Othello cheer you up? Have it, do. All children love ices for a treat, don't they?'

I managed a smile and accepted.

'Good. Meanwhile I shall feed you up on quotations. How about "He that made you bitter made you wise"?'

'Who said that?'

'Can't remember right now. Or, to paraphrase poor Dylan, "After the first deception there is no other"?'

I managed another smile less wan and looked away. Oh isn't there, Old Man, oh isn't there? Wait and see – the hostile thought had forced itself upon me but I pushed it firmly to the side before it was able to do any harm, gazed gratefully into his eyes, and our sympathy continued.

'The perfidy of roommates, the treachery of best friends,' C. D. spoke almost wistfully, looking down at the spoonful of chocolate ice-cream halfway to his mouth as if coming across some long-forgotten nursery rhyme. 'Does it still go on?'

I thought of Jungle-gyms and slides on the school roof, of milk and crackers at eleven, lost mittens and a tiny little girl in a green jacket, my 'best friend' in first grade, and laughed outright.

'You were right about one thing,' I said with absolute sincerity. 'You are wonderful with stretcher cases.'

And when we rose to leave there was a rapport as warm and comforting as my tears enfolding us. I felt for the first time since I'd met him a complete calm; the sublimely passive action of being borne unresisting along (back to the *Carte de Tendre*) the *Fleuve d'Inclination* into – ah but wait – into the *Mer Dangereuse*! For without warning, as we were passing through the lobby, he swerved us abruptly off course with so brusque a pressure of arm and body that I broke step and almost fell flat on my face as he hurtled me towards a side door where we gained a breathless exit into the street.

'What in the world—?'

'Someone I wished to avoid.'

'Who is she?' Out of its corner my eye had caught the striking image of a woman, tall, pale, and brooding, seated by herself along our intended path in the lobby.

He looked at me but quite without surprise, as if to show again how totally he was accepting me into his life. 'Lady Mary Hare-Vermelli. I couldn't let her see me because I'm not to know that she's back in England. I didn't,' he added, holding back nothing.

We walked along the pretty lane in silence for a while, and then I said, for there was no need to ask, 'You're in love with her.'

'Oh, everyone is!' he replied with a touch of exasperation. 'Has been since her sixteenth birthday. She's a Hare.'

'A what?'

'One of our great families. Old but impoverished. And so—'

'And so?' I encouraged him for the next thought seemed to have stopped him mid-air.

'And so they married her off to the wicked Baron Vermelli. It's quite a fairy story. An enormously rich upstart whose father made shoelaces in Naples.'

'Golly, do those things really happen?'

'This is England,' he said, not without a note of pride. 'Vermelli treated her vilely, I suppose you'll be delighted to hear, ran through his money and had the appalling taste to die practically penniless. "Anyone can buy nobility," she said to me soon after, "but who can buy money?" That, she felt, was the lesson her family ought to have learned from it all and she is determined they'll not forget it. She's turned her back on what's called polite society and now takes up only with the most frightful cads, smugglers and spivs, and I don't know what, really dreadful types. Everyone's terribly worried about her but she seems bent on having her revenge. I wonder who she's—? Some gigolo, I expect. Pest!' He had stopped walking, shifted his umbrella and buttoned his portly frame into his overcoat. 'I feel like a big fat house with everybody dead inside it,' he declared suddenly, looking quite haggard.

'We must comfort each other.' I put my hand on his arm, gently reminding him of my own sad plight.

'But of course! That is the reason we have been brought together.' He responded as quickly and joyfully as a child given back its lollipop. 'I'd like another glimpse of that new Rolls I saw in one of the showrooms along Berkeley Square,' he said a minute later, quite happily tucking my arm in his as we made our way up South Audley Street, first stopping off at a National Provincial Bank (looking, I thought, more provincial than national) where he cashed a cheque I was able to count out as £50 before he pocketed the sum, and then continued onwards to Berkeley Square entering a showroom where large Rolls and Bentleys glistened and gleamed.

'Good afternoon, sir!' sang out the car salesman, springing forward zestfully, bursting with high-spirited gaiety.

'We've come for another look at that Rolls.' (*We*. So I was to be party to this extravagance too!)

'Of course, sir. Let me see. That would be our Silver Cloud, wouldn't it? If you'll step this way. We've moved her over to this corner to make way for another new Rolls,' he explained chattily as we followed. 'Ah, here we are. She's a real beauty, isn't she?'

'I wonder if we might be allowed another peek into the luggage compartment. Want to be sure there's enough room. Well, what d'you think, Honey? Come here and have a look.'

I found myself peering thoughtfully into an empty hole. What did I think? I thought nothing. I thought: this looks like an empty luggage compartment, so what? Luggage? What luggage – whose luggage?

'Umm – nice,' I said lamely. But then I realized he had actually called me Honey for the first time and I had plenty of thoughts about that.

He seemed satisfied and stepped back a pace or two the better to take in the car as a whole. 'Nice lines,' he commented.

'Oh, lovely lines,' I agreed enthusiastically. 'And lovely colours. Black and tan. Wonderful idea.'

'Let's get in. I want to get the feel of the wheel once more.'

'Certainly, sir!' exclaimed the salesman. The slightest pressure of his hand set off the suggestion of a well-oiled click and the heavy gleaming doors flew open as we climbed up on to our great leather-upholstered high horse.

'And try those springs, Madam,' the man gleefully exclaimed.

'The springs?' I looked nervously over at C. D. from my corner of the monster machine.

'Bounce!' C. D. commanded me imperiously.

I was feeling myself in a situation that left me far from confident. What was I doing so far from the ground in a strange stationary automobile staring blankly through its windshield into a roomful of similar ones? All I wanted was to get down and out.

Nevertheless I bounced. With, one hoped, a certain detachment, a certain dignity, a certain nonchalance. But I bounced.

55

Then, to my surprise, C. D. began bouncing too. Positively flinging himself into it.

After a while C. D. subsided seemingly pleased, made a few desultory passes at the wheel, encouraged our friend into a learned and lively discourse on mileage, tonnage, and bootage, with side excursions into dashboard facia gadgetry, gear shift values, the turn of the wheel, the spin of the wheel, and the lock of the wheel. He was tuning up to sing full-throated praise of that road-worthy miracle the Rolls-Royce engine when C. D. broke him off with the announcement that we were now ready for a go at the back seat.

Swift, silent and heavy swung wide the doors again as we slipped over the smoothest leather, even through clothing, that skin ever touched, out of the front and into the rear of the car.

What made me so sure all of a sudden that C. D. didn't know how to drive? Was it his abrupt dismissal of engine-talk, or something unprofessional in his stance (if I may put it that way) behind the wheel: something odd in the relationship of feet to floor pedals? Or was it simply the way he stretched with an audible sigh as he sank into the back seat? I don't know. It was one of the mysteries about him I never solved. I never could bring myself to ask him outright and he never told me. Isn't it funny? I found out about everything else about him. What pockets of resistance we keep hidden about our persons, what inexplicable shynesses, what reserves of reserves! Though what was worrying me at the time was hardly of so philosophical a bent: more specifically it was his hand which had suddenly sprung out to clasp mine. Had it sprung as the result of an uncontrollable passion, or was it merely the natural extension of his sense of well-being? I let my own hand lie in his in a sort of non-committal way – asleep you might say – while my heart raced and I pondered my feelings.

What a long way we had travelled today – were travelling still. The voice of the car salesman meandered on, babbling of foot-rests and arm-rests and ash-trays with their super-buttons. I looked idly out the window at the unknown scenery of France or maybe Italy flying past and the man's voice seemed to recede further and further into the back of my mind so that my brain was only dimly recording it as it discreetly blew the foam off the Income Tax dodge: '. . . and therefore buying it in your company's name naturally establishes its use for business purposes hence, etc., etc . . .' before it disappeared entirely, got left behind as C. D. and I went rolling across our countryside faster and faster, hand in hand, in perfect contentment.

I glanced at the old man lounging by my side taking his ease, the afternoon sun tipping his hair and features with a rare old gold so that he looked more holy, more Rembrandty than ever. Dear old man, my dear sainted unknowing benefactor-to-be. I almost squeezed his hand and stopped myself in time, my goodness me brazen hussy what was I thinking, that would never do. Time to land, I told myself. Don't go too fast. Time to check back on Earth.

'Say wouldn't this be the greatest for watching drive-in movies?' I said with a determined heartiness. 'We'd have no trouble seeing over the tops of other people's cars in this crate would we?'

C. D. looked blank. 'What are you talking about?'

'Drive-in movies. Oh, come on, don't make out you've never heard of 'em.'

Abruptly he let go of my hand, leaned forward, press – click and was on his way out. Well, I'd wanted to break the spell. Looked like I'd succeeded. Obviously he was not amused by my frivolous attitude towards that sacred machine. But his heel must have caught in something on the way down for the next thing I knew he was hurtling forward head first saved only in the nick of time by the quick reflexes of our friend who righted him with a steadying arm to the elbow.

And it was during that split second when disaster seemed imminent that I had my vision of him as Humpty Dumpty falling off the wall, crack open—! and gold coins splattering on to the floor with a sound of a thousand golden bells. But more unsettling was the fierce, triumphant exultation that accompanied this absurd vision and sent my blood thumping through my veins even as my appalled mind wrestled with its significance.

I jumped out of the car after him. 'Are you all right. Gosh you frightened me. You almost had a great fa – a nasty fall,' I corrected myself quickly but he was even quicker.

'Humpty Dumpty is quite all right and still in one piece,' the canny old bird assured me with cold dignity.

'No, I only meant it was such a great distance from the wa— from the ground. I only meant it's such a fantastically high car—' I continued doggedly but he had turned aside to the salesman and, in elaborately humble tones which somehow had the effect of underlining his displeasure at me, was wondering aloud if he might possibly dare impose further upon the man's good nature to the extent of arranging for a demonstration.

He was not kept long in the dark. 'But of course, sir. My pleasure. Perhaps you'd care to take her for a spin this afternoon?'

C. D. took his time consulting his watch, the car, the day, the shape of my face and – if I was right about his driving – possibly the need for saving his own before rendering the verdict. 'It's too lovely out,' he decided. 'We are going to sit in the park awhile.'

'Very sensible if I may say so, sir,' the man concurred. 'Such delightful weather.' He radiated a three-way beam that managed to include even himself in its approval. 'And when would you like the demonstration, sir? I'll be glad to arrange an appointment for you now.'

'I shall have to look in my book first.'

'Certainly, sir. My card, sir. If you'll telephone me the morning of whatever day is convenient.'

The card-giving ceremony, I noticed, was performed with breath-taking speed and perfunctoriness, the card landing in C. D.'s pocket without being stopped even for a second's token look.

'Goodbye, then,' cried C. D., his part of the comedy over, as with a conclusive gesture he propelled me towards the door.

'And good-day to you, sir, madam.' The man genuflected and showed us out. I studied his face carefully. Was this the tenth or ten-hundredth visit C. D. had made to that showroom? It was impossible to tell from the man's face for I saw reflected in it neither impatience nor relief but actually a kind of wistfulness, as at the departure of a good friend at the end of a pleasant evening. Come back soon, it seemed to be saying, half an hour of good clean fun, what better way to pass the day? And when I looked back it was to see him standing in front of Silver Cloud lost in admiration.

We strolled down Dover Street in the sunshine.

'I think you make him very happy,' I said at last.

C. D. eyed me quizzically. 'You wouldn't be pulling my leg, now would you?'

'How do I do that?'

'Making fun of me, I meant.'

'You wouldn't be pulling his?' I countered. 'Or mine?'

'And what makes you think I should?'

'Because you're not really thinking of buying it at all, are you?' I blurted out.

C. D. considered the question. 'Cynicism can become an ugly mannerism in the young,' he finally replied. 'I suggest you curb it before it develops into a habit. As it happens I really do need a motorcar—'

'Or choo-choo train?'

'What is the meaning of that?'

59

'Well you English are always sneering at us for saying "horse-back riding" instead of just "riding", so why "motorcar"? Why won't just "car" do?'

'I doubt that we shall pursue this battle of language with any profit,' said C. D. languidly. 'May we not declare an Anglo-American Usage truce for the day?'

'How can we,' I groaned, 'when we both *use* the same words all the time?'

'Think of something else,' he suggested. 'Think how lovely the day is. Think of all the attention you're attracting. There. Doesn't that make you happy?'

And do you know it was the strangest thing, but it was true. I, who had wandered this town for weeks desolate, friendless, almost invisible, suddenly found all sorts of people staring at me – no – staring at us, for wasn't I the same girl wearing the same clothes as before? It was decidedly the 'us' that turned the trick; we loaned each other a mystery and glamour, together we stimulated a curiosity we couldn't hope to stimulate on our own. It was truly remarkable: one would have had to be as beautiful as a movie star, as famous as a politician, to arouse the same interest that we two nobodies with only our discrepancy in forms and ages were managing to do. I couldn't resist playing up to the situation, over-playing it in fact, roguishing looks and tossing curls at him, so determined was I to let no one pass us under the mistaken impression that what they were passing was a mere Dad and Daughter team. And pausing to examine the contents in the window of a jewellery store I saw doubly illustrated the importance of the setting to the jewel; for there beside the emeralds, rubies, and pearls glowing in their nests of diamonds was our corporate image reflected in the glass. How well we went together. How we matched, balanced, set each other off: his rotundity emphasizing my slenderness; his air of portly affluence my fragility; his ruddiness my pallor. Even his very hat, a bowler, emphasized my hatlessness, seemed to make my hair shine as it never shone before, while the rough, blunt cut of his English features somehow rendered my ordinary American ones exotic.

Another thing: it would be absurd to say he brought beauty into my life, it would be carrying romantic statement to ridiculous extremes, but it was the damnedest thing the way the clearing of the weather happened to coincide with our meeting almost, as it were, at his bidding revealing all manner of pretty streets and buildings and squares. Or was it just that he was so clever about steering me through some of the best bits of London? Oxford Street splattered and soggy with rain is quite a different proposition from St. James's Park in the cool dappled sunshine, where we now took our ease reclining upon the soft grass that sloped gently down to the pond.

'Animals!' I exclaimed in surprise, looking at the pond, 'Why the place is full of animals. Look at 'em – ducks, pelicans, geese, and gosh, even a black swan. How divine.'

'Surely they're called birds.'

'In a city anything that isn't a sparrow or a pigeon is an *animal*. As a matter of fact pigeons and sparrows aren't really birds to me either; they're people. Like the poor who are always with us,' I said, looking around for the poor as I spoke but there weren't any.

'Parks are for the poor. Alas, that they haven't a chance to enjoy them. Only the very young and the time-wasters like us can.'

'That's because you hide them so well. This beauty, for instance. How d'you expect them to find it? I wouldn't if you hadn't led me to it.'

'It is pretty, isn't it?'

'Ravishing. You really do grow the most sensational trees. The ones in Central Park are spindly by comparison. Look at the huge thing we're sitting under – whatever it is.'

'Don't you know?'

'Should I?'

'Slum child.'

'Not at all,' I said haughtily. 'My father has a huge estate on Long Island, if you must know. I don't go around asking the name of every tree I come across for heaven's sake.'

'But really, not to know the simple elm—'

'No, nor probably the simple oak.'

'Nor the simple sycamore – maple, I believe you call it? Nor the simple lime?' he asked pointing them out to me.

'Lime? No kidding, is that really a lime tree? With *limes* on it?'

'You call it linden.'

'Oh.' I sat up suddenly. 'Hey, as a matter of fact I did know all the names once. There was this batty old Botany teacher we had at college who used to race her class around the campus every spring making us tear the leaves off the trees for an identification exam. I did very well, I remember, fifty out of a possible sixty. Something like that. Couldn't remember a single one by the end of a week, of course.'

'What were you doing studying Botany? Surely Science wasn't your subject?'

'God, no. It was a required course.'

'For what?'

'For anything. I happened to major in the Dance. I mean I planned to,' I corrected myself, suddenly remembering I was Honey. 'Actually I was an English major and graduated with honours.'

'The *Dance*. What an extraordinarily whimsical thing your university education is. Botany and Dance on the same curriculum.'

'Oh there were a lot of subjects you could work into your course if you wanted to. Taxonomy and Ecology, Hymnology, Public Finance.'

'To what purpose?'

'The well-rounded person, of course,' I said beginning to feel irritated.

'Well-rounded, my foot,' he snorted. 'Eclecticism run mad, that's what it is!'

'Quit picking on us.' I rose from the grass and walked slowly away towards the pond pretending to be hurt; and under the pretence I really was hurt and damned annoyed at myself for being so. What was eating me? I certainly didn't consider myself a patriot, had never considered myself an American with a capital A for that matter, and yet half our conversation that day seemed to consist in sniping at the other's country. Was I going to allow the rest of our time to be wasted in transatlantic squabbles? It was dangerous to say the least.

A little girl feeding the ducks noticed me standing there and casually offered me some bread so that I could join in. What did she care what country I came from? The act of unthinking generosity did much to restore my sense of balance.

Presently C. D. was beside me. 'I'm thinking of going along to the Antique Fair. I understand they've got some quite extraordinary pieces this time. Will you join me?'

'That would be really asking for it,' I sighed. 'If there's anything I know less about than trees it's antiques.'

'Then it's time you learned.' Something in his tone had made me turn and look at him closely, and I saw that his eyes were as grave as his voice and I understood finally that being with C. D. meant being continually under his instruction; but that it need not necessarily be meant unkindly.

'You're serious, aren't you?'

'Of course.'

'No, I mean . . . I mean . . . lime,' I said suddenly, pointing to the linden tree; and 'sycamore,' I said pointing to the maple. 'Now teach me about antiques,' and I smiled in sweet surrender and we tootled off in the general direction of Park Lane.

We were stopped on South Audley Street by the two gigantic elephant-sized elephants made entirely of china that filled the high windows of Goodes.

'What do you make of those?' asked C. D., calling my attention to them.

'Crazy,' I replied admiringly.

'Would you like to have them?'

'They're what I want most.'

C. D. considered. 'Only *one* I think though, don't you?'

'Oh yes. Two's too much.'

'We'd like to inquire about the elephants in your window,' C. D. told the startled sales clerk. 'We rather fancy something for our hall. We have a very big hall and we need something to fill it. I think one of those elephants would do nicely in our front hall, wouldn't it, my dear? Right in the centre.'

'Not perhaps the teensiest bit off centre?' I wondered.

'Dear me, no. Dead centre. Yes. Instead of a fountain.'

'Now I see. Of course, darling.'

'How much are you thinking of asking for them?' C. D. inquired.

'Why I – don't know, sir,' said the sales clerk. The thought had clearly never entered his mind. 'We don't have many – In fact, I don't even know if – A moment, sir. I'll try to find out.' He edged over to the window, standing as close as possible to the enormous pieces of crockery, and strained forward peering under their huge bellies hopefully as if they might offer up the secret. When they didn't, he wandered off.

'They come to about £3,000 each, sir,' he said returning. 'But I'm afraid they're not for sale.' He seemed greatly relieved.

'What a pity! Why not?'

'They're being shown at the next Paris Exhibition.' The man regarded them once more with total mystification. 'They're – ah – very unusual objects aren't they?' he added, before he put them safely out of his mind. 'Perhaps something else?'

'There's nothing else big enough,' complained C. D., letting his eyes flicker discontentedly over the tea-sets and greeting cards. 'No. I had my heart set on one of these elephants.'

'In any case, I'm sure we'd only sell them as a pair,' said the clerk, who was still determined to save him from his folly.

C. D. paused before receiving inspiration; then 'Perhaps we could have one copied?' he asked hopefully.

'I'll try to find out for you, sir,' sighed the clerk and dragged himself off but returned in considerably better spirits.

'I have to disappoint you again, sir,' he said cheerfully. 'They can't make 'em up nowadays.'

'Oh?'

'Haven't got the kilns!'

'Haven't got the *kilns*?'

'That's right, sir. Haven't got the kilns.'

'Ah.'

'You see, sir, you're going to need a pretty good-sized kiln to get one of those animals into, aren't you? I mean to say, sir, one of your ordinary kilns isn't going to do the trick, is it? And that's the trouble, sir, they aren't building kilns that *size* any more.' He'd gotten quite worked up about it.

'Well, well, mustn't grumble,' said C. D. soothingly. 'It's the same all over nowadays, isn't it?'

'Yes, sir, I expect it is. I am sorry.'

'Come along, my dear.'

'Good-day, Sir. Madam.'

'Goodbye.'

'I'm beginning to enjoy this,' I said back in the sunshine again. 'What shall we try to buy next – the Tower of London?'

But C. D. only murmured softly to himself, 'Always wondered what the silly things cost,' and continued majestically down the street.

The woman walking towards us was staring at us very hard. She even stopped to follow us round as we passed.

Gallantly C. D. tipped his hat. She smiled and walked on.

'Who was that?' I asked.

'Haven't the faintest idea. Thought she looked jolly pleased to know me though, what?' And he cocked a merry eyebrow in my direction. And he stepped out smartly, jauntily swinging his umbrella.

PART II

CHAPTER SIX

The antique fair, an Event of the Season, gets run off every year at a great gallop in one of those semi-official town houses of most elegant and ambitious proportions on Park Lane. Enter and ascend a billowing baroque staircase (imagine myself gravely on the arm of the Archduke, while a thousand violins swell into a Viennese waltz) and you will find yourself in no time standing directly in front of the Main Exhibition Room, a room stuffed to swarming with extravagant-looking people and extravagant-looking objects – crystal, silver, china, the paintings, the tapestries, the furniture, the carpets, chandeliers . . . antiques, antiques, antiques. Pile upon pile, one great, enormous junk shop.

C. D. paused under the archway, breathing dedicatedly. Picture if you will a C. D. gone mad. A bull in a china shop – an aesthetic bull that is – a bull run mad on aestheticism. For if American education had struck him as eclecticism run mad he was striking me as aestheticism run mad. His eyes shone and darted about ferociously coveting all they beheld. His mouth salivated (at least he licked it several times in a kind of mopping up gesture), his hands clenched and unclenched, his brow perspired; a most unnatural fever seemed to have overtaken him. And then he got a grip on himself, marched boldly into the room, took a good look around him and relaxed. And he looked upon everything and everywhere in that old man's way of his that struck me now as being also like that of a very young baby – so lovingly, so wonderingly. But with an avidity too, that avidity special to C. D. A hungry look cast upon each object of beauty as it flowed and filled and satisfied the innermost reaches of his soul. His eyes would seize upon the object with the impatience of youth, then – here was the difference – come to terms with it; set it down: the eyes avidly picking up each beloved object in salutation – putting it down gently in farewell. Eyes look your last! Strange old man, heartbreaking, heart-broken old man – to be so moved by the polish of wood, the curve of a chair-leg, the glint of crystal, the fade of Aubusson. As though he were missing it all already.

At last C. D. smiled, his communion over. 'Well, what d'you think of it all? Splendid, isn't it?'

'I'm remembering the Botany class Leaf Hunt. Am I going to have to learn all of this too?'

'You got fifty out of sixty,' he reminded me.

'But I was five years younger then.'

'And five years stupider, I should think,' he said crisply. 'Now then, look sharply and tell me where you'd like to begin.'

'At random,' I said – or rather called after him, for his enthusiasm had already plunged him into the crush.

'What have we here?' asked C. D. gaily. We had come to a clearing, a tiny oasis in the room mysteriously empty of crowds. '"Examples of pre-classic Indian peasant culture around 1500 to 300 B.C."' he read from a placard hanging directly over several glass-topped tables. 'I say, a Mexican collection – the ideal place to start, what? Mexico: your part of the wor—'

'Oh stop – oh please don't say it,' I begged. 'Can't we forget for this afternoon that an ocean divides us?'

'No, but seriously do let's take a peek anyway. We may have stumbled across something perfectly fascinating. I know next to nothing about pre-Columbian art, do you? They must be some recent excavations. This case seems to contain some excavations found along the coast from Jaleaca to Acapulco. Well we've heard of Acapulco anyway, haven't we? Diego Rivera did an excellent series of sunset paintings there. I've got them in a book over at my place. Must show them to you. Now, these stones,' he said peering into a case, 'or . . . ah *masks*, I see they're calling them – votive masks – can't think why, never mind I expect we'll find out – are in the "Olmec" style, referring to the Olmec civilization, "typified by the round face, the flat nose, the eyes and mouth absent or only suggested, and a sort of sulky expression . . ." Hmm.' We both stared for a moment at the almost smooth and supremely uninteresting-looking stones in which not only the eyes and mouth but the sulk as well had disappeared. 'Too silly, really,' C. D. finally broke out giggling. 'Listen to this: "It has not yet been established whether the artisans were trying to depict *babies* or *jaguars* (the jaguar was believed to possess supernatural powers) hence the designation Baby-faced Jaguar Votive Masks." Well. That seems to be all they've got in any of the cases. What do you make of them?'

I replied with my own version of the votive mask, especially strong in the sulk, and he backed away, closer to sheepish than I had yet encountered him. 'Not on the whole a very stimulating exhibit. Don't think you need remember any of that, you know. After all, our purpose in educating you is to make you more interesting, not less so. On the whole I think you'd be wiser to forget it.'

(But I haven't as you can see. I can't. That old eclecticism.)

'Battersea, and Bilston. How charming,' exclaimed C. D., as he suddenly pounced upon a display of tiny enamel pill-boxes, picking one up for me to see. 'And Chelsea,' he exclaimed again, picking up another. 'But what a beautiful collection! Now here's something useful for you. They're all the rage these days, and as you might expect being carted off to America as fast as they can lay hands on them,' he added laying his own mitts on another.

'What's the diff—' I started when wham! like that out of the woodwork came an ancient little gnome.

'Yes, sir? May I help you?' The suddenness of his appearance along with the gentle yet firm way he removed the whichever-it-was box from C. D.'s hand and the alertness in his eyes made us both start guiltily. And I suddenly saw us through his eyes as not exactly common pickpockets but let us say a couple of high-class shoplifters one of whose itching fingers he had stopped in the nick of time. C. D. strove to calm his fears with appropriate and expert comment, 'Really fine 18th-century enamel,' and that sort of thing.

'I see you know a great deal about these boxes, sir,' the man conceded.

'It is the finest collection I have ever seen,' C. D. declared.

'It is the finest collection in England.' The tiny sentinel smiled, pleased; his watchfulness not abating but simply elevating us to International Spy status, a sort of Mata Hari and Charlie Chan combination, I imagined, me with my hair falling concealingly over my face as I bent to examine the boxes, C. D. bland and suave; surely the suavity of his movements betrayed Eastern origins.

'But the finest collection is said to be that of the Earl of Saxenborough?'

'This is Lord Saxenborough's, sir,' exclaimed the little one triumphantly though not unkindly, C. D. having now disarmed him by his stroke of ignorance.

'Is it now? Ah, I didn't notice. What a piece of luck. I've always wanted to see it.

'That coffee-set over at the Meissen china exhibition, I don't believe I've seen one like it. I must—' C. D. broke off abruptly, his hawk-eye having ferreted it out some fifty feet away. And he drifted off sudden as a feather in the breeze.

He stood enthralled before the huge pink and gold china-set. Absurd baroque ornate, the cups were in the form of delicately sculptured blush-pink rose petals with shining gold-leaf inside. I felt my first twitch of excitement since I'd been there, my first inclination towards acquisition. I who thought I coveted nothing. The voluptuousness was stunning. On every piece of china – the cups, saucers, creamer, sugar bowl, there was so much to discover – a bee on one, a drop of dew, a bud. Flyblown petals curled delicately shaded. I held a cup in my hand.

'Too bad,' said C. D., matter-of-factly pointing to a saucer. 'Too bad this one's a replacement.'

'Oh no, sir,' the man was shocked.

'Look it up in the catalogue, I think you'll find it's at least a century later than the originals. See here?' He showed it to me as the man pored over the inventory. 'The colour's off – hold it up to the light. It wasn't the carving of the petals originally, it was the painting too – see the shading. The whole feeling is different. It's as if the man who did this one had never seen a rose: certainly had never seen it growing in a garden. The petals are regular, wooden compared with the other. Even the dewdrop is mechanical.' I was stunned for now it screamed copy. How did I miss it? 'The creamer is a copy too.'

'You're right, sir,' the clerk finally said. 'Missing saucer and creamer replaced in 1860.' We looked at C. D. in admiration.

And all of a sudden there was Lady Mary Hare-Vermelli swimming towards us through the crowd.

I was still holding a cup and I dropped it. It hit my foot first and rolled on to the carpet. The attendant picked it up, examined it for damage and put it back on the table. I stepped away tactfully and that was that. But not quite; for I had partially absented myself as one does during those moments of panic and now had to check back on what else had gone on during my absence. For one thing people around me began breathing again though I had not been conscious of them having stopped, for another I discovered at least part of my vertigo to be the direct result of having dived down after the cup myself as well as the attendant, and that the slight soreness on the side of my head was due to C. D.'s having dived down too at the same time and presumably in the same place.

And the other part of my vertigo? Lady Mary Hare-Vermelli. For there she was – a middle-aged nymphet swimming towards us as if tangled up in seaweed. I suppose that C. D. had decided that the two of us were too awkwardly placed or too chaotic in general for formal introductions; at any rate he did not attempt them so that I felt free to study Lady Mary openly as if she were an example of pre-classic Indian peasant culture or an early Meissen coffee-set. She was a flat, slender creature and the black tweed coat floating around her was of casual cut. Of even more casual cut was her hair, chewed-off, blown brown hair worn in a vague fringe. She wore vague chewed-off lipstick, a black pleated skirt, and a white blouse with a Peter Pan collar. She was easily the most effective-looking woman in the room. Effective like Garbo, I mean, like Hepburn. She had, to put it mildly, her own style, and she carried it off with her own sense of Destiny, which she wore casually, like her coat and all the rest of it. Two things besides her liquid green eyes were particularly striking: her stance, with its implied equivocation of being open and eager to engage in conversation while at the same time unfortunately at the mercy of a fierce dog straining at the end of a leash, and her expression, which, even in repose, was of a blazing transcending brightness.

'One absolutely *felt* one would run into you here,' she breathed at C. D. The breathiness was of primary importance in the delivery of her utterances and this together with her odd diction and inflections produced a manner of speech which sounded to me affected to the point of affliction, contrasting strangely with the downright carelessness of her looks.

Her presence reduced C. D. to a jelly.

'We've come from the Saxenborough Collection,' he began.

'Billy's beastly little boxes!' she breathed, stringing her gurgles and gasps and pants into arpeggios of nuance. 'They've grown quite out of hand, haven't they?'

'Grown to fetichism,' C. D. agreed, executing a graceful tack, seeing the way the wind blew.

'Oh *zac*-tly! One knows so ex-*act*-ly what one means!' Lady Mary rewarded him with a staccato of sympathetic gasps. 'Whatever can have given him the queer notion of collecting such rubbish in the first place? All those Gaiety Girls, I suppose.'

'A collection of their dancing slippers would have been more to the point.' C. D., by now, was quite willing to dump the whole Saxenborough cargo overboard for his beloved. 'What are you doing in town? Shall you be staying long?'

'Didn't I glimpse you earlier today?' She side-stepped, neatly embellishing this revelation with more gurgles of high intrigue.

'I don't think so,' he lied, thoroughly flustered.

'Surely you were lunching at the Half Moon?'

'So I was. I'd forgotten,' he backed down. 'Mayn't I see you some time? Could we have drinks tomorrow?'

'Shan't be here, alas.'

'Tonight?' he pleaded.

'Oh dear . . . I don't know . . .' The invisible leash had given a tug making us aware of a tiny dark young man in a positive fit of Votive-Mask sulks, glowering at us in the distance. 'Sean must be back in Dublin in time. Though p'haps I . . .' She shot C. D. a bright disconcerting glance which for a moment included me and suddenly swam off sideways. In time for what, I kept wondering as I watched her ripples.

C. D. regained his composure with her departure. 'She's pretending to try to bring him round to meet us,' he announced calmly. 'She won't succeed of course. Oh, the affectations of a great beauty. Look at that, will you – rubbing her elbow with one hand and stroking her hair with the other.'

We looked on in silence at the gently turbulent scene progressing between Lady Mary and the youth, until, her luminous glance sweeping back over C. D. in a final arabesque of regret, she allowed the leash to give its final tug and she was off.

'What was she doing here?'

'Why, what should she be?'

'I don't know. I thought she was supposed to be so Beat or something.'

'You wouldn't stop her from going to a museum, would you?'

'I wouldn't stop her from going anywhere. I just thought— Oh never mind. Who was that with her, her son?' I couldn't resist adding.

'Her lover,' he snapped, giving me a dirty look.

And now he surveyed the room with dissatisfaction at the spoils she had left behind. He could no longer find any pleasure in it and in his irritation he launched into a series of complaints. The place was too hot and too crowded; it was badly arranged; it was impossible to find anything.

'What is the difference between Battersea and Chelsea?' I asked, trying to distract him.

'Porcelain and enamel,' he snapped closing the subject once and for all. He stared at his watch. 'I have to leave soon. Anything you particularly want to see? Well is there?' he said.

No reply.

We started making our way out.

'Wait a sec.' I stopped dead in my tracks. Honey's engagement ring was sparkling up at me from a case of jewels. I went over and examined it closely. Yes, it was Honey's ring. Or rather its exact duplicate, even to size. I stared at it hard. Even looking at the likeness I could feel the same rage and hatred I felt towards that other ring. How ugly it was! An innocent object lying innocently in its velvet case harming no one. But it wasn't innocent. It was evil. It was a thing of evil. It stank of corruption, sorrow, and death. The sight of it released in me the same ruthless determination to get rid of it, get it out of my sight for ever, revived in me the same scheming plots and plans to remove it from her, from me, for ever at all costs – get *him* away from her even if it meant taking him away from her myself. Seeing it there shining with evil, I felt justified; reassured that my motives, whatever they looked like from the outside, had been pure. I had been a loyal friend to Honey, had not wanted to see her hurt, had wanted only her happiness. My thoughts took a sudden plunge and I remembered startlingly another diamond ring, of many, many years before, how old was I – eleven? The one my father gave me to celebrate making his first big pile. I'd worn it to the new snobby school I was attending in New York and all the children had taunted me about it. I'd thrown it away, secretly, out of the window, thrown it away in rage and shame: 'But Poppie, I lost it I tell you. I don't *know* where.' I had to smile. What children will do! And yet I'd been right. I'd known it even then. Diamonds stank of corruption. Money, money, money . . . corruption, sorrow, death. The refrain rang in my head.

'Georgian paste,' I heard C. D. saying.

I looked at him blankly.

'Eighteenth-century Georgian paste. All the jewellery in these cases.'

'You mean they're not real?' Odd, this feeling of relief.

'Another gap in your education. You have the makings of a very poor gold-digger though I expect the design and quality of the workmanship make them almost as expensive as the real thing.'

'I'm glad they're not real. I hate diamonds. That ring, there, it's like the one my ex-fiancé gave me. I can't stand the sight of it.'

'It's quite understandable,' he said gently, guiding me away from the case. 'By the way, what did you do with the ring if you don't mind my asking?'

'I sent it back.' That was true. Honey had. What would I have done I wondered? Hocked it probably.

'It was the only honourable thing to do,' he said. I dropped my eyes guiltily in a way which he misread for sorrow. 'In fact you deserve a reward. Look at this spray.' He pointed to a beautiful brooch and made them take it out for us. He held it up to my shoulder. 'Pin it on. Here – look at yourself in the glass.' He stood back studying me. 'Remarkable,' he said. 'Extraordinary, most extraordinary,' he said enthusiastically. 'It quite transforms you. What is it? That clean cut, austere, almost prim American armour seems to have a chink in it. The spray brings it out. Brings out the "other you" as the women's magazines have it. Gives you an air of naughtiness somehow. Yes. Gives you – oh dear, what is the phrase I want? The air of a rich man's darling.'

I wheeled around at his words to look at myself in the mirror and to my unutterable relief found it was my grown self confronting me and not, as I had feared, a tear-stained child (the impression was so swift it melted even as it formed); and then I snapped out of it entirely and began admiring myself, fingering the spray shimmering on my lapel, playing with its little leaves quivering each on tiny separate springs. I noticed with pleasure how my eyes reflected its soft brilliance and seemed to make them dazzle and glow and for the second time that day I felt the pangs of acquisitiveness.

'I'd like to give it to you,' said C. D. right out of the blue. 'Please. Would you like it? Do let me buy it for you.'

I caught myself. I must remember I was a nice young girl, I was honourable. I was not a gold-digger.

78

'Don't be silly,' I said lightly taking the pin off and putting it down on the case. 'I couldn't accept it.'

'No, of course not. I say, I didn't mean to embarrass you.'

On the other hand there was nothing to be gained by coming on like a prig, either. 'Some other time, perhaps.' I murmured silkily. And as he stood there baffled I turned to leave, reflecting that though one played many roles to attract a man one must be careful not to play them all at once.

Back down the billowing staircase we floated, the Archduke and I, and '*Goodnight lad-ies!*' the ghostly violins sawed away, resolutely propelling us into the night.

'Which would you choose – a brooch of Georgian paste or an early Meissen coffee-set?' asked C. D.

I considered. 'It would depend what I was up to – what part of my life I'm at; if I was at a certain point, well, like now for instance, I'd choose the brooch. As an eye-catcher, to let it kind of speak up for me. But if I were in love . . .'

'If you were in love? Go on.'

'Well, I can see myself having breakfast on some sunny terrace and I can see that coffee-set harmonising eloquently into the surroundings. And I can see myself pouring . . .'

'And who can you see sitting opposite you?'

'No one.'

But suddenly I saw C. D. standing behind me, touching my hair as I bent over, admiring the picture I made. 'I think I'd choose the coffee-set anyway,' I surprised myself by saying.

We were walking through a mews full of parked cars en route to Dody's flat. 'Which would you choose: Made in America or Made in England?' C. D. paused pointedly between a sleek, shiny Jaguar and a poor old beat-up Chevrolet that looked as if it had made the long hot journey on foot, its excess of fintails, bumpers and chrome splattered and dented and limp with exhaustion '— come away from that filthy Da Sota or whatever it is, this minute! You'll be covered in dirt. What are you doing with your nose buried in it?'

'That is the limit!' I exploded. 'Talk about hospitality. Someone's been scrawling obscenities with their fingers all over the windshield. What's it say? Probably "Yankee Go Home," or some such gracious invitation. I can't make it out. What's it say?'

'I am not an archaeologist. I don't read dust,' said C. D. with dignity, taking out his handkerchief and fastidiously brushing himself clean from its contaminating contact. 'Ah you're smiling again, that's better. I say, you mustn't pick one up so, I was only having my little joke about the wretched vehicle, you know.'

Night had fallen. The ill-lit mews seemed full of sinister shapes lurking behind implacable facades of parked automobiles; the air was poisoned with fumes of oil, rubber and gasoline. Dark patches on the ground, probably from leaking tanks, looked as if they might be blood. I began walking faster. The brick pavement underfoot was bumpy. I tripped and stumbled along, longing to break into a run. Curtains were drawn tightly across the windows of the mews cottages. Suddenly it was the gas-lit London of Victorian England and I was all alone in a dark alley with a demoniacal stranger. My scream would not be heard until too late. My body-heat accelerated by fear reached its boiling point, melted into a sweat and trickled in rivulets down the insides of my arms and between my breasts. I was panting by the time we reached Dody's. I leaned against a shop window to catch my breath.

'You're deathly pale, child,' said C. D. in alarm. 'See here, I've worn you out traipsing you around town like this. You'll want a nice cup of tea to bring you round. We'll have young Mrs. What's-her-name make you one the minute we get there. Can you manage? Lean on my arm. We've only a few more yards to go.'

'Dody's her name. Dody Schooner. I'm all right, really. I don't know what came over me.'

'Ah yes, Schooner. Why do I never see her with that clever husband of hers? Amusing chap. Always on the boil. One feels the lid's just about to pop off.'

'It did. And he popped off with it.'

'Oh? Where to?'

'India.'

'How sad for her.'

'Not really. Good riddance.'

'Steady, now,' he cautioned me. 'That facile cynicism's sneaking up again.'

'But wasn't that what you said to me at lunch today? You know, about he that made you bitter making you wise?'

'But that's quite different from letting he that made you wise make you *bitter*.'

'Is it? Well rah-rah.' I sighed. 'I guess *I* don't know anything.'

'I do,' he announced in a calm completely out of context voice, giving my arm a squeeze – or was it a caress?

'What's the scoop?'

'I know that my head is spinning from trying to make you out. Do you believe in the battle of the sexes? That is, do you believe it exists?'

'I don't know. Why?'

'Because I have the definite impression that we are at war with each other.'

'But I like you very much,' I protested.

C. D. smiled wistfully. 'That seldom has anything to do with it,' he said.

All the way up the stairs we could hear Dody's gramophone blasting away full force. We had to press the bell hard several times before she answered.

'It's *West Side Story*,' she said excitedly as she opened the door, raising her voice to be heard over the music. 'I went and bought it this afternoon. Isn't it marvellous? Scotty hated American musicals. Listen to that brilliant orchestration with all those wild repetitions. It's like a symphony. Don't you adore it?'

'The needle is stuck,' said C. D.

She looked at us while the gramophone blasted five more da-*da*! da-*da*! da-a da-*da*'s at us. 'You're right,' she cried and left us standing there while she ran to turn the thing off.

'How did you know?' she asked him, upon returning. 'I mean it sounded so on purpose.'

'It's always happening to my gramophone,' he told her kindly, while Dody gazed upon him with awe. Suddenly she shook herself.

'Come in, come in. Goodness, how rude of me. I'm all topsy-turvy these days.'

'I'll only stay a minute. Miss Flood is utterly fagged from our day's outing. Entirely my fault. Might she have a cup of tea?'

'But of course. Where are my manners?' She sprang into action. 'It's been so long since I've entertained. Oh damn and blast!' She stopped suddenly mid-flight and sank into the nearest chair. 'I – I don't think we've got any more,' she said in a small voice. 'Scotty decided a couple of months ago that he hated tea. He said it was a filthy English habit.'

'What is he drinking in India then?'

'I don't— Oh. So you know.'

'It's my fault – I told him,' I put in quickly. 'I didn't realize it was a secret.'

'No, it's only . . . I'm only . . . I don't know where I'm at.' And she waved her hand impatiently as if she would like to fling herself away from her. 'But what will he drink there?' she pursued. 'Isn't there some local brew?'

'Yes,' said C. D. 'Tea.'

'Oh of course. Indian tea. I'll run out and buy some now.'

'No, don't bother. Alcohol will do as well, won't it, Honey? What would you like?'

'Gosh, I don't care. Sherry, I guess.'

'Oh dear, I haven't any sherry either,' cried Dody in distress.

'Did he hate Spain too?' inquired C. D. politely.

'No. He hated gentility. He said drinking sherry was genteel.'

'How did he feel about gin?'

'We've got bottles of it,' she said brightening. 'Would you like a gin and something, Honey?'

'Don't bother about me please,' I said. 'I don't care much about drinking, anyway.'

'But you must have something,' insisted C. D. 'It'll do you good. I am worried about you. You still look peaky.'

'O.K. I'll have a martini then.'

Dody went over to the drink cabinet and stared at the bottles for a while. 'It's no good,' she moaned hopelessly, unable to bring herself to face us. 'No vermouth. I'm afraid Scotty—'

'Hated cocktails,' supplied C. D., going over and pouring me out a gin and tonic and placing it in my hand and standing over me to make sure I drank it all.

'Feeling better now?'

'Oh yes, much.'

'Won't you have one too, Mr. McKee?' asked Dody timidly.

'No, I must be off.' He smiled winningly. 'Do ask me back soon, won't you? I hate to leave but I'm already hours late for my next engagement.'

Liar, I thought, travelling to the door with him. And where was this mythical engagement when you were imploring Lady Mary to see you this evening? Nevertheless, I thanked him lavishly for the pleasure of his company, flattering myself as I stood waving him out that my own smile, if not as winning as his, was – at least – bravely showing.

'But he's so nice,' exclaimed Dody in wonderment as soon as the door closed. 'Why he's not a bit the ogre they make him out to be. He hardly frightened me at all. He's so kind and considerate and gentle. And the way he kept hovering over you, you are lucky. I can't imagine Scotty even noticing that I was tired much less offering to do something about it, I'd probably have to faint dead away before it even registered. How do you do it? It must be your magic touch, I wish you'd teach me. Not that it'd be any use,' she gloomed. 'It's the way I am. I bring out the worst in everybody. I'll bet Scotty's different with that Indian girl. I'll bet he throws his coat across the street every time she takes a step so she won't get her bloody sari muddy. Do they have streets in India?'

'Paved with gold.'

'Don't joke. I sort of imagine cowpaths or something. I suppose I should know more about the place. I could get some books and read up on it. Actually I've got a map of it somewhere but I daren't look at it. I know I'd go twice as crazy if I were able to picture them together in their accurate setting. It's bad enough as it is.'

'You're right, Dody. You must try to forget about him.'

'But I do try. I try all the time. Why do you think I bought that record of *West Side Story*? And then I didn't even realize the needle was stuck. Do you think that means that Scotty was right about it all along? Maybe the musical isn't any good. Is it?'

'Of course it is. It's divine.'

'You see what I mean? How would I know? I took his word for everything.'

'What else did you do today?' I asked, attempting to change the subject.

'I don't know. Fed the fish. Watered the plants. And I stopped the milk – except for a quart a day.'

'Dody, have you had anything to eat today?'

'Yes . . . No . . . I forget.'

'Come on, get your coat.'

'But where could we eat alone, just us two girls?' she protested.

'Any old Espresso bar.'

'There's a little Italian restaurant right around here. In Curzon Street,' she said.

After dinner I dragged her off to the Curzon cinema thinking if I didn't get a few hours respite from her incessant Scotty-used-to-say-do-you-think-he-was-right chatter I was going to go crazy. Peace at last, I said to myself, sinking into the dark springy luxury of my seat. Peace in the audience at any rate. On the screen all hell was breaking loose: a Brigitte Bardot film, crackling with carnality. As I relaxed into its comforting amorality I felt my Honey clothes becoming unstuck and myself slipping into Bardot's panties. I felt myself becoming immersed in Bardot's doings with an absorption not so much vicarious as actual, propelled by a need rather than a thrill. To lure C. D. I was going to need all the help I could get. Where else could I get it except from books and movies? Where else, come to think of it, had I ever gotten it? I was remembering the scrapbooks of my favourite movie stars I used to keep as a child: all female, all 'sex-symbols,' all immensely imitable: the hair-do, the eyes, the walk, the attitude. The most imitable thing about Bardot, I guess, is her strippingness.

I was with her on the screen that night. I was right up there with her – raising my skirts high above my thighs, pulling on sweaters and peeling them off, prancing about nude and dripping from the bathtub. Game for anything.

'Well, I'm glad we went,' said Dody, 'I didn't want to at first but I learned a lot.'

'You too? Funny. That's what I was thinking.'

'It didn't come over me until almost the end. I kept wondering: what's she done to make him behave in such a beastly way towards her? I mean, what's she done wrong originally? Why should she always get the dirty end of the stick?'

'I don't think I'm following you.'

'And do you know what I decided? It's because she kept forgiving him all the time. So then, of course, he thinks he really hasn't done anything wrong so he can go right on doing it. It's a lesson for us all, isn't it? You keep on being tolerant and looking the other way and patching things up and suddenly you get to be her age and there you are out on a limb and you've lost him anyway.'

'Dody, what are you talking about? Bardot must be all of twenty-two.'

'Bardot? Who said anything about Bardot?'

'I'm beginning to wonder if we saw the same movie. Who do you mean?'

'His wife, of course, you know, Jean Gabin's wife who kept on being so tolerant of him all the while he was making such an ass of himself over what's-her-name.'

Would it never end?

'Now, Dody, we've been through all that,' I murmured for maybe the hundredth time. I leant forward yawning. I bent down to pick up my shoes. The slightest effort was making me dizzy. It was one o'clock in the morning and I was exhausted. I rose and stretched and loosened the belt and zipper of my dress and rubbed my waist with relief. My clothes were itching and binding me, my skirt pasted to my body in lumpy bunches from having been sat in for so long.

'To bed . . . to bed . . .' A great roar of a yawn overtook my words and almost dislocated my jaw. 'We'll figure it all out in the morning. I'm finished, you hear? Beat. Bushed. Fatigued out of my skull.'

Dody was sitting bolt upright, taut and alert, crisis written all over her face. 'It's now or never,' she insisted in a trembly voice, shaking her head stubbornly. 'What am I going to do? *What am I going to do?*'

I knew that pain was making her selfish but at that moment I really hated her. I was so bored. I was so bored with being bored. I sank back into the damp, crumpled sofa and tried again, hoping that the loosening of my clothes might send the blood circulating through my system sufficiently to force my mind down new channels. How many women, I wondered, are sitting up this way at this very moment, all over the world, and asking each other this very question?

A new thought: What did my friends back home do when they got divorced? Not many of them had been married long enough to get divorced. However, first things first: *What did they do?* O.K. One of them had gotten a job, and one of them had joined an exercise class. The third went back to school.

'You could get a job.'

No she couldn't, she assured me, recoiling at the thought. A job: how could she in her present state? She'd fall to pieces all over the place. And besides, what did she know? What could she do? She was completely unskilled, completely untrained. The more she thought about it the more it confirmed her worst fears. She was fit for nothing. Absolutely nothing but running a house for her erratic husband and trotting along after him. And now, evidently, she wasn't even fit for that. She might as well kill herself.

'Or you could go to exercise classes,' I broke in quickly before we slid back into the mire.

This struck her as even more senseless. Whatever for? she wanted to know. What would that do?

'Well then, what about some kind of school?' I played my last card without much hope and started to unhook my garter belt under my shirt and strip off my stockings preparatory to flight. I had done all I could; I could do no more.

Dody rushed joyfully to my side hugging me and skipping about. I was a genius, she knew it. She knew I'd come through. School! To think she'd never thought of it herself. That was exactly what she'd been doing when she'd first met Scotty. She'd been in the middle of her third term at Art School and having a marvellous time too, when he came along. She should never have quit. None of this would have happened if she had. But never mind, she was going to be philosophical. It wasn't too late – thanks to me. She'd enroll again. Start life all over again. And she wouldn't feel silly doing it, either. That was the best part because all kinds of people went to that Art School, all kinds, and all ages, and oh, heavens! Look what time it was! And she must rush off to bed now so as to get up bright and early and go down there and register first thing in the morning.

And goodnight, goodnight. And pleasant dreams. And sleep tight.

CHAPTER SEVEN

I went to my room and stripped off the rest of my clothes, flung on my pyjamas and got into bed. The night began in earnest. I lay staring at the wall. Where once had crouched the toy animals of my childhood there danced kaleidoscopic images of the day. Suddenly the kaleidoscope gave a turn, a wrench, flipped over and there hidden under the bits of coloured-paper conversation was my pain: that moment at the Antique Fair when, brooch pinned to my shoulder, I had wheeled around to confront myself in the mirror. Something C. D. had said. A rich man's darling.

He had been right about me. I had been a rich man's darling, all right. A very rich man's very darling. And very cherished. And indulged. And cosseted. And adored. But only until I was twelve.

'Because you can't love her and love me too!' I screamed at my father. I, Betsy Lou Saegessor . . . Saegessor. Yes. None other than the step-daughter of Pauly who had married my father and then, when he died, went on to marry C. D. McKee. Surprised you didn't I? Or had you guessed already? I know. What a way to tell a story! But it can't be helped. It has to be told the way it happened. And it didn't happen 'at the beginning' (and Christ, if I had begun at the beginning I'd still be there, wallowing in self-pity, poor motherless child), it happened when I met C. D. And at first it didn't look as if I ever would, and then finally I did, and then this, and that, and the other, and here I was now lying in bed wide awake and remembering all that terrible time of long ago when I'd stood at the window crying bitterly, tears streaking down my face, looking down from the great height of our brand-new apartment, all the way down the length of Park Avenue, looking down while the lights of the cars flashed and flickered past and stuck pins into my throbbing head and aching eyes, and I was screaming at Poppie, 'Because you can't love her and love me too!'

Because he was going to marry her, he said.

I looked back into the window seeing nothing any more, blinded by my fright. To have reached the end of my life so young. To have successfully snatched Poppie from the husband-hunting, fortune-chasing matrons of Scarsdale, uprooted everything, hearth, home, worldly goods, single-handed with one gigantic tornado-like effort. To have successfully deposited him, in safety, in New York, only to lose him there.

'You can't marry her. You can't. I won't let you. I'll run away for ever and you'll never see me again and you'll see. You'll be sorry. It isn't fair, *it isn't fair*.' The rhythmic crescendo upon crescendo, over and over again. Facing him now. Showing him what he was doing to me, guts, gizzards, innards, everything, the red raw soreness of my pain. And what was he doing, my Poppie, to answer all this? What was he doing to console or to explain? There is no memory of it. Only his closed face and myself betrayed. And that whole year in New York – a whole year of betrayal.

I leaned my head against the icy window-pane (did he even say, Come away from that window, did he even care?). To have foreseen it for a whole year. To have died every day, each minute with its knowledge and still know that the ultimate death would be worse. To use every weapon known to ingenuity and to have them break one by one in my hands while my enemy looked on and smiled. In my mind I saw my dead body floating in the river and heard her laughter floating above, on top of the water, in the air, everywhere triumphant.

To have seen it coming before they did. To have watched it. To have inadvertently caused it to happen. Now to have to live with it every second of the time.

To be thrown aside. Shut out. He knew I had no friends like others. No one to turn to. No sisters, brothers, no mother who died when I was seven. No family, only him. Alone and shut out. Always, from now on.

To have walked into his office from the first day there in New York and seen her, the new secretary, not young but small, *petite* (that horrid word). A redhead. Bright red hair, whitish around the edges, white eyelashes and pale eyebrows pencilled in brown. A redhead's skin, dead white. A hateful perky look. Hard blue eyes and an efficient mouth. A hard pert little pointed nose. Even her clothes – a trim wool dress with a perky little bow, neat and shrewd. Experienced. 'I've worked for X and for X and for X.' All references excellent. Candid: 'My last salary was such-and-such but I left because I felt I was worth more.' She knew she was worth more. She'd worked all her life for what she'd got. Industrious. A little girl from the wrong side of some Middle-Western tracks. 'I have my mother to support back home.' Appealing? Hardly. Ruled by economics. All figured out. Not ambitious so much as efficient. Neat stacks of safe investments, small steady dividends. At least thirty, but that little-girl look in spite of it. (Why, I seemed to tower over her and I was only twelve.) Smallness, perkiness, unworldliness. Naïve. Her gauche, un-Society ways. All of which was supposed to blind us to the fact that the minute she set foot in his office she was out to catch Poppie, catch him and trap him. But no, it was me – irony of all – poor little motherless me, so lost, so all alone in the world, so always hanging around the office after school for want of anything else to do, she pretended, that first caught her sympathy, made it 'not just a job', interested her in 'us'.

If only I'd *not* been there all the time on guard – would she have taken longer to discover he was a widower and available, longer to figure out he had no one else in mind? But I had to be there whenever I could. I had to watch. And yet I couldn't stop her. For she was capable of going after what she wanted – and capable of getting it. And finally, in the end, nature told her exactly how she would triumph over me: she had age on her side. Age against my need, age against my love, age against the past, against everything. It was bitter, irrevocable. It had happened.

And I had seen from the beginning that dealing with Pauly was going to be different from dealing with the others. It was a whole different thing. How could I make Poppie see how awful she was when she didn't actually do anything awful? How shallow and limited and hum-drum she was when these were the very qualities that so admirably fitted her for the job of being his secretary? How could I make him see how her presence was going to spoil everything for US, now that the fun was beginning, now that Poppie was rich, getting richer all the time, spoil all our plans for the thrills and adventures that lay before us, my father and I, when her presence was so un-obtrusive?

With the others it had been easy, poor things, how easy it had been. All I had to do was make them criticize me. And since nothing is simpler for an adolescent, no matter how well-behaved, than to provoke the criticism of a Suburban Woman, it could be accomplished with the minimum effort. They came, these women, with their pre-formed patterns of behaviour, with their pre-formed social sets, very often with their pre-formed families, and with their pre-formed theories of bringing up children, and one by one they would fall into the trap. 'Should she be allowed—?' They invariably prefaced their fatal mistakes with these four words. 'Should she be allowed to stay up so late?' Or, 'do her homework with the radio on?' or, 'eat this food?' Or, 'read that book?' Or, 'play outdoors after dark?' It never failed. They couldn't keep their hands off me. They poked and poked until they found something; they were trying to be helpful. They might by-pass all the obvious 'Should she's' only to get caught up in some point of infinitesimal triviality ('Should she be allowed,' asked one, 'to wash her hair before going to bed?'). They rose to bait, and quick as a flash we would exchange amused glances, Poppie and I, and they were hooked, poor fish, they were cooked; their day was over. For what right had they to presume to criticize the upbringing of a child as healthy and happy as I; who was good in school, and liked by all, and who, moreover, was the apple of her father's eye? None, of course. They were nothing but bossy busy-bodies who would make our lives intolerable if allowed to intrude.

But Pauly, as I say, was different. Never having lived in a 'society' or a 'set,' never having been married, she couldn't presume; and therefore she was immune to the temptation. Besides, it wasn't in her nature. She was outside that. She was outside without being an outcast. She fitted in nowhere. She was a white-collar girl but she was not a career woman. She was in a state of flux.

What could I say against her? She was satisfactory.

Coming at the end of a long line of lazy, ill-tempered, slow-witted incompetents who couldn't grasp even the basic fundamentals of an expanding business, let alone one that was growing in leaps and bounds, Poppie was more than satisfied with her. She was a definite asset. At that time he was opening his chain of stores all over the country. She could be trusted with the details as if she was like a partner, but she was never like a partner, she never wanted to be. She simply executed his orders. She never thought for herself. That was what was so irritating about her. I mean she had a smallness of spirit, a lack of interest in things in general. As far as I could make out she never thought about anything – except the business. And him, of course. Oh yes, him. That was what she was *really* thinking about all the time but the business was the camouflage and it paid off. There was no doubt about it, she was very good for the business. Poppie was delighted. 'My secretary will handle that,' 'My secretary will see that it all goes smoothly,' he would say, each time with increasing satisfaction. My secretary. He never called her Miss Plant – and he never called her Pauly to my face. I saw that he didn't dare. And yet there she was, this ordinary, everyday little person, penetrating further and further into every corner of our lives just when Poppie and I, alone, should have been sailing to the height of our glory.

What could I say against her? 'She talks so funny, your secretary, Poppie (I, too, could never bring myself to call her by her name to him), she says *watter* for water and *awnge* for orange.'

'Why, Beetle, that's the way they say it out where she comes from. Kind of cute,' would be his amused reply, and what good was that? And so I would try harder: 'But she's so small. Do you think they stunted her growth? How old is she? Isn't she awfully old to be that small?' 'Now, Beetle, she's not all that small. It just seems so to you because you're getting to be such a great big girl. She's *petite*.' (There it was that horrid word.) 'Poppie, she has the strangest table manners. Did you notice last night how she cut up all her meat into tiny pieces first before she ate it?' 'All right, Beetle, that's enough. That will do.' And his tone would tell me I'd gone too far. It was hopeless; it was worse than that, it was harmful. It was putting me in the wrong position: it was putting him on the defensive, only it was she he was defending now, instead of me.

She took me to a matinée one afternoon: a Musical I'd wanted to go to. Afterwards I asked her to let me see where she lived. She objected at first, it was too far, all the way out in Queens, there was nothing to see. But I teased until she gave in. I *had* to find out what it was like.

She was right. There was nothing to see. She had a neat empty little flat in one of those huge developments. She lived alone, with her fitted furniture. All the furniture fitted against the walls, fitted into the corners, fitted like shelves one on top of the other. Everything turned into something else. The sofa turned into a day-bed, a board slid down the wall releasing two legs and turned into a dining-table. The bookcase collapsed into a writing-desk. The flat was utterly tasteless in the real sense, the food sense. It had no flavour; it was bland and unseasoned: one or two scrupulous stiff plants, a few books, a few magazines. There were glass ash-trays and glass-topped everything. There were no signatures, nothing betrayed its origin. I had to go to the bathroom when I got there and she led me to it through her tiny bedroom. I took my time after I came out, looking carefully at everything for some clue. (There was nothing to pick up, nothing to look at, nothing to play with.) It was exactly like the other room except for a silver-framed photograph of a middle-aged man by her bedside table. Not my father. I went right for it.

'Who's that a picture of in your bedroom?' I asked.

'Nobody.' I saw that she was embarrassed.

'It can't be nobody.'

'Oh, it's somebody I used to know. I don't know why I still keep it.'

'Is he dead?'

'Of course not.'

'How did you know him?' I persisted.

And because she was only factual, never lied: 'I used to work for him.'

'Your last job?'

'Yes.' She was unable to wiggle out. Her honesty had refused her an imagination.

So far so good. My perceptions sharpened by my success, I redoubled my attack on her living-room and now I noticed what I hadn't before: an enormous television set, almost the size of our own, fitted into something or other against the wall. The reason I hadn't taken it in at first was significant. Television sets were what Poppie mainly sold, they were the particular line his stores featured in those early days of television: the rock upon which his fortune was being built. Therefore, since television sets were ordinary fixtures in our own home, it hadn't struck me as odd. It did now.

'What a big television set you have. Wasn't it awfully expensive?'

'Why, yes, I guess so.'

'It must have cost a fortune. How were you able to afford it?'

She reddened but again she was stuck. 'It was a present.'

'From my father?'

'Yes.'

I went cold. So it had come to that. I made her take me home soon after. There was not a moment to lose.

'Did you have a nice time at the show today?' asked Poppie that evening.

'Yop. Great. Oh and your secretary took me out to where she lives and guess what I saw, a picture of her boy-friend. She's got it right by her bed-table.'

I dropped this last remark casually as if it would have no significance for us. Nevertheless I saw that I had hit home. We continued dinner in virtual silence and Poppie retired shortly after. Goody, I thought; that's done it.

Poppie was very quiet and thoughtful for the rest of the week. Then on the Friday smilingly he announced he wouldn't be home for supper that night. He and Pauly (finally he had come out and named her) would be going out to a show and then a night-club afterwards. 'And so, Beetle, no sleeping in the guest room tonight' – it was one of our games occasionally to pretend I was a distinguished guest, visiting him for the weekend – 'because I've invited her to stay over here so she won't have to go all the way back to Queens so late.'

'Won't her boy-friend be jealous?' I said, very quickly.

'There isn't any boy-friend any more,' he answered happily.

'Oh, but I saw—'

'Yes, but that's all been over for a long time. I'll let you in on a secret, Beetle, don't mention it to her, but he was really the main reason she left that job. Imagine the wickedness of some men. I'll never understand it. A married man with a wife and children carrying on like that, deliberately lying to the poor girl, telling her they were separated and that divorce proceedings had already been started. She left the minute she found out what he was. I don't know what makes some people behave like that.' Thinking about it made him very angry, I'd never seen him so angry. I held my tongue then, appalled at how badly my scheme had boomeranged.

But now in tears, my head against the icy window pane and with the awful finality of his announced intention of marrying Pauly ringing in my ears, I could hold my tongue no longer.

'That bitch. I know what's she's up to. She's going to try to kick me out of here, you see if she isn't. Well she's got another thought coming. Let her try. I'll beat her to it. I'm not living under the same roof as her for a second I promise you that.' And more, much more, it all came out. And what was Poppie doing, saying through all this? It's blank. Was he trying to make me listen to reason? Was I refusing? But what could he

97

say? They were guilty. They had done this thing, connived behind my back, reached conclusion without consulting me. Guilty.

'We are going out to dinner now.' I remember Poppie saying that. Saying it in his normal voice, bringing the inevitable closer to its close. He had spoken clearly, into a silence. It was strange and quiet around his words and I remember them very distinctly. They were clear and final and there was a hush all around the room. The screams and cries had been closed off and in the silence I saw Pauly's frightened face appear for a moment in the corner of the doorway and then disappear again. And then the noise began up again, long shrieks of pain chasing each other round the room, batting themselves against the walls and the window, trying to get out. A haze of screams through which drowning hands strained, and drowning arms strained, pleading. Then the block of haze dissolved and became all runny and ran down my throat. I started to retch. Nothing came up. I choked, coughed, had another coughing fit, and subsided. I sank into a chair; I had to catch my breath. And when I looked again, there was Poppie still standing in the same place he had been standing before, no nearer, still with his face closed against me. He spoke again. Severely. Something about the maid getting my supper. Something about not coming back until late. Something about Pauly staying overnight. Something about behaving myself. Then the doors closed, first mine and then, after a moment, the sickening click of the front door latch.

After a while I went to the window again – the same window, I suddenly remembered, from which I had thrown his diamond ring. I flung it open with the idea of searching for the ring now after three months – perhaps it was still there where it had landed, perhaps no one had picked it up and I would be able to retrieve it, and hock it, and with the money run away for ever. I leaned out straining my eyes fourteen flights below but my eyes blurred no matter how often I wiped them and all I saw was two people I was sure were Pauly and Poppie getting into a limousine. Suppose I threw myself out the window and landed right on top of them. I'd kill myself of course but I might kill them too. And how surprised they would be. But contemplating the act made me dizzy and I reeled back and closed the window standing as far away from it as possible.

There must be something I could do. I lay on my bed and thought. Then almost automatically I wandered over to my desk and got out my diary to record this final disaster. It was a beautiful diary bound in morocco, a present from Poppie into which I had poured all my private thoughts during that year. I opened it to the right date but I couldn't even pick up my fountain pen. I flipped through the pages. It was all there, the whole agonizing year with its account of my struggle against Pauly. One entry particularly captured my attention. On a day when I had been feeling especially miserable about her I had simply listed her failings. Her nervous cough; her nervous sniff; her pencilled eyebrows; her flat voice with its irritating Mid-Western colloquialisms, 'Anymore, I don't think they'd be interested now' (for 'anyway'); her confusion when confronted with a finger-bowl; her clothes when she got Dressed Up; the way she sat bolt upright on the edge of a chair patting her hair; the way she sometimes stood with one foot crossed awkwardly in front of the other as if she might topple over; the way her eyes darted about among a group of people anxiously from face to face unable to settle down; the way she wasn't able to inhale when she tried to smoke a cigarette, and on and on in endless detail. I studied the list for some time. It comforted me having it all there before me. If only she could see it too! And then I had my idea. The Guest Room. It was Friday; suppose I went to bed in it tonight anyway, as though it had slipped my mind that she was going to stay over. Then, when they woke me up, I would apologize nicely and tootle off into my own room. But – I would have left my diary by the bedside table opened at the exact page for good measure.

I went calmly in to eat my supper feeling nothing but pleasure at the brilliance of my plan.

The whole thing went off without a hitch. The diary was left, was seen, was read. It was a complete success. Except that they got married anyway and my father never forgave me.

Strangely enough Pauly did – to a certain extent. And often I would hear her trying to intercede on my behalf: 'She's only a child—.' Was it because of her essential humility, or that as the victor she could afford to be generous? 'She's only a child,' I would hear her saying from time to time to my father but he was adamant. I was sent off to a boarding school, even more select, more snobbish than the New York one. But this time I got on. No diamond rings. I was pretty. I was bright. I was popular. I was even nice. That's true. I never got into fights, never lost my temper. I never indulged in cattiness or stooped to bullying. I was known for my calm and my serenity. And life took over. I all but forgot those other two. Except for the casual, wholly factual letter I was required to send off every ten days, I hardly gave them a thought. I made my own way, made my own friends, made my own life. I went home less and less often during vacations. I began staying a lot with Honey's family. I think everyone thought Poppie and Pauly were my step-parents and I didn't bother to disillusion them.

And suddenly my father died. I hadn't seen him for ages. I missed the deathbed: I'd thought Pauly was exaggerating. She'd written me that my father was not feeling well, was very run down, and was going to the hospital for a check-up. Would I be coming home for Easter? I declined politely. We had grown so far apart we three, I simply couldn't face going back to them, trying to make conversations rise out of the silences. Besides, plans had been made for Honey and me to go to Bermuda. So I declined: was so sorry to hear, unfortunately other arrangements already completed, hoped they would understand, knew he'd get better, would fly back a day or two sooner. Well, he died. I felt – I felt nothing, really. Did I miss him? I don't think so. The child missed him. But it was as if I had already said goodbye to him five years before. I was cut out of his will. Oh, yes. That is, my college education was to be provided for plus a substantial allowance during that time to be donated by Pauly as she saw fit – and after that I was on my own. Drastic measures and yet I saw the fairness of it. For I had been cut out of his heart five years before. I saw his point. I felt no rancour. Fair was fair. He was dead for me; I for him. I might have contested the will I suppose but I never bothered. Come to think of it I was really most curiously detached about it all.

And, there were always my friends. As I said, the school was select, the girls were rich, and I was popular. So nothing changed for me. I continued living well, high off the hoof. Better actually, with the death of my father the added impetus to their sympathy and generosity. I had a ball that summer. Invitations flowed and flowered into other invitations. I whirled like a dervish and loved every minute of it.

Not so with Pauly. Our lines of communication broke down after the funeral but apparently she went to pieces. Not so surprising, she'd never been a Social Animal, her marriage hadn't changed that, and I guess she had nothing to fall back on. What *was* surprising though was that after she'd fallen apart *and* pulled herself together she took off for Europe, where, the next thing I knew, she'd become the wife of that distinguished Englishman: C. D. McKee.

And now Pauly too was dead and I was here in this strange

land, sleeping in this strange bed, hot on the trail of . . . how would you say it? My stepfather? My late ex-stepmother's last husband? Pauly's widower? No. I'll say it: The Heir.

The heir to Poppie's millions, transferred from Poppie to that bitch to him, to be his, to do with them what he wished, said the lawyer in New York apropos of Pauly's will, until he died: at which time such sums would revert to the nearest of kin of the former husband of the deceased: Me.

Me by all that's holy. Mine. And I wanted it right now, not then. More than anything in the world. What's more I needed it. I must plan . . .

Toss and turn. My arms were giving me terrible trouble. Under the pillow, over the pillow, straight down by my sides, dangling over the edge of the bed, everywhere I placed them they stuck out, got in my way. Oh to be able to unhook them. What did I usually do with them? Toss and turn. Money. What simple problems Dody had. Love. As if that had anything to do with anything. It must have been nearly dawn before I dropped off.

The sound of a distant bell calling me faintly, chillingly . . . ah, I think I know . . . Test it rhythmically. Yes, there it went again. Brng brng . . . brng brng . . . The telephone.

Waking from the innocent sleep into the corrupting day; bereft of mother, father, lovers, all gone; dead. What was the dream – teeth pulled or an arm broken? Loss . . . irretrievably with the tide running out, stranded on dry land. And now it begins: the corruption of the sands. First, the gay innocent-seeming umbrellas for the gay innocent-seeming betrayals. Then the beach chairs: the beginning of age is it? Or the beginning of *dis*-crimination. Have you enough money to rent one? Yes? Careful then, *here* not here. A better part of the beach here in this special section it's – well – more choice. There's *this* part – and the other. Y'know? The pace quickens: suntan oil, bodies, hotels, shops, restaurants, snack bars, the railway tracks. Smoke, filth; the City.

The telephone bell kept ringing. The apartment felt empty. Barefoot I ran down the hall towards it, towards wakefulness. As I ran there were torn from me the last shreds of innocence, of purity of images, purity of the last shreds of belief, of hope for the restoration of all the separate parts of a loved one into one pure Whole; torn from me all hope of a pure pearly dawn on a beach.

'Yes?' I said into the telephone, vague and anxious. 'Yes, hello, yes?'

'Hello.'

'Who is it?'

'I'm disappointed. I recognized your voice.'

'Oh yes, of course.' And my heart began pounding. 'But I'm easier to recognize than you,' I said collecting myself. 'I mean who else could I be except Dody?'

'And who else but me?' he countered.

'There you have me.'

'Well then, how are you today?'

'I'm fine.'

We were both fine and there was a pause.

'What are you doing?' he wanted to know.

I was getting the telephone wire untangled and I told him so and there was another pause so I asked him the same question.

'I'm staring at the ceiling.'

'How does it look?'

'Neat.'

There was another pause. I decided not to help it out. Let him carry the ball.

'I'm spending this weekend with some dear friends of mine in Shropshire—' he began (twinge of disappointment on my part), 'Sir Rupert and Lady Daggoner, and I wondered if you'd care to join me' (followed by twinge of excitement), 'I thought perhaps if it was agreeable we'd go down by train. Much the best way to see the English countryside. We'd leave on the Friday arriving in time for tea. Country clothes. But they dress for dinner. And the women wear their jewels,' he added with what seemed to me undue emphasis, conscious as I was of not having any. It jittered me half awake as I was and I almost snapped back, Hell, do I have to be told *everything*?, but sanity reigned and I realized he was only trying to be helpful.

'Thanks for the hint,' I laughed. 'And thanks for the invitation too. Only I don't know if I can make it—' I stalled automatically, marvelling at the strength of my reflex – the never-appear-too-eager one, for of course nothing would have stopped me. 'I'm hardly awake,' I explained, 'I'll have to look at my diary first.'

'Your engagement book,' he corrected me.

'Oh?' said I interestedly. 'So what's a diary then? Scribble scribble about my big thoughts of the day?'

'No. That's a journal.'

'I see. Well, look, I haven't got my *thing* with me now. I'll let you know as soon as I can. I've got to get dressed and stuff first. Suppose I call in an hour?'

'You're coming over here?'

'What for?'

'Ah, *telephone*, you mean. If you're calling, it means you're coming to see me.'

'Help,' I groaned. 'I'm too sleepy for all this.'

'And grouchy too,' he reprimanded me. 'What were you doing to keep you up so late last night?'

'Ummm – this and that, this and that,' I murmured noncommittally.

'Well my dear, mind you *call* as soon as you can. And then I'll *call* Lady Daggoner because she wants to *call* and invite you personally.'

'Yes, sir. Yes, sir.' I was very crisp and military.

'Crosspatch.' Then he softened. 'I did so enjoy yesterday,' he breathed, 'I do so much look forward to seeing you again.'

So then I in turn softened myself. 'Oh so do I.' And we said goodbye and hung up.

CHAPTER EIGHT

I saw C. D. at Paddington Station before he saw me and paused to admire the sight. What a fine figure he cut in his rich country plumage: soft woven tweeds, suede shoes, dark green woollen shirt and a bundle of weeklies rich in reading matter and informed opinion tucked under his arm. Radiating joy, confidence and anticipation he shone like a beacon in contrast to the milling crowd: the careful ones checking and rechecking their tickets, luggage and timetables; the frantic ones overburdened and rushing in all directions; the grim, the sorrowful, the dull, the anxious, the bored. In the midst of them all, there he stood. At ease and at leisure and at home.

We greeted each other and he steered me expertly down the ramp alongside the train and into the exact compartment desired, where he skilfully arranged our bags and cosily settled into his seat with an air of putting on his slippers and pulling out his pipe. We were travelling First Class. There was no doubt about that. It said so on the window pane next to me and on the door to the compartment. It said so on the two glass panels on either side of the door and on the window on the other side of our corridor. Altogether it said so not less than five times.

'What are you thinking?' asked C. D.

I shifted, trying to arrange myself so that the scratchy uphol-stery wouldn't prickle my back too much. 'Kind of old-fashioned,' I said.

'These carriages are twenty years old, I believe,' he explained placidly.

'Is First Class very much more expensive?' I asked, for looking into the various carriages as we had gone along I hadn't been able to perceive any difference.

'Oh yes, quite a bit.'

First Class. What an insane waste of money. And his clothes. Damn his clothes. You didn't need a trained eye to see that they were pretty expensive too. There was a moment, I am here to tell you! I remember it as clearly as if it were passing in front of me right now. Every single thing about it. Every single thing in that compartment. The blue and yellow pattern of the scratchy upholstery. The carpet under foot with BR woven into it. The seat opposite with one, two, three, antimacassars for one, two, three heads. The luggage rack above them. The posters saying Clacton-on-Sea and St. Ives, Cornwall. The train gave a lurch and a start and so did my brain, for a milestone had been passed. Henceforth I was to take strictly a proprietary interest in the way he spent his – the way he spent my money; I was never again able to indulge in any objective curiosity about how he amused him-self with it. I begrudged him even his weeklies.

I turned and stared moodily out of the window. The English countryside. Nothing but railway banks for miles and miles with a lot of weeds, Queen Anne's lace, buttercups and daisies. So what? Then backyards. It was a nation of backyards, with a Roman viaduct thrown in here and there for incongruity. And the colour of sullen suburban brick did nothing for the angry skies. Rain, stop, rain, stop, went the weather. It almost depended which window you were looking out of. We passed the town of Shifnal and the town of Wednesbury and I thought they were pretty funny names to an American but decided they were really not funny enough to comment on so I let it go. But then we stopped for ever at a couple of stations with people standing right out in the open on the opposite platform waiting for the other-way trains, some sitting on wheelbarrows because there weren't any benches, and I thought I ought to point that out to C. D. How much trouble could it be to put a couple of benches there for the poor rain-soaked wretches? – even if you didn't build them a shelter? But when I turned to say as much I saw that his glasses had slipped forward on his nose and his head was sunk in his chest and he was fast asleep.

By the time we had reached our destination I had written off the English countryside – or rather the English railwayside – as one big mess but I must admit I could not do the same with the liveried chauffeur or the magnificent car awaiting us; nor with the acres and acres and acres of ground we travelled across from the Gatehouse to the Manor.

There was a lot of uniformed staff activity in the entrance upon our arrival and in the midst of it a plump jolly-looking woman wearing a wild print blouse that was wreaking havoc with a rough herringbone tweed skirt. She greeted us heartily and immediately began giving orders for the disposal of our luggage. In the confusion I assumed she was the housekeeper, and by the time C. D. had corrected this misconception with a shy, embarrassed off-hand introduction, it was too late to make much of meeting my hostess, Lady Daggoner. In fact I was already halfway up the stairs in pursuit of my luggage.

'We're putting you in your old room, Cos, and Miss Flood goes in the Blue,' she carolled upwards. 'Come right down after you've had a wash. You're in time for tea.'

When I reached the room my bag was there, the maid was not – though it was her black uniform that had led me to it. It was a kind of magic. During my entire stay I was to catch only three brief glimpses of her and yet her handiwork was everywhere. The room was beautiful. Large and light and airy and, of course, blue, with exquisitely delicate mouldings picked out in white running along the ceiling. Out of the windows I could see the vast expanse of rolling green lawns and giant trees. I pondered: should I unpack? 'Come right down after you've had a wash,' had said the lady of the house. Better obey the command to the letter. So I didn't unpack because she hadn't told me to. And I did have a wash because she had. In an old-fashioned washstand in a corner of the room which pleased me no end for the quick flicker of superiority it gave me. Really, these old English houses, they certainly had their jolly little inconveniences, did they not? I supposed there was some communal bathroom way at the end of the corridor – too, too boarding-house. And then, to my chagrin, I discovered through a half-open door that I had my own bathroom as well. Hell.

C. D. was waiting for me at the foot of the stairs and we went into the drawing-room together. Introductions again. This time by the hostess but in the same off-hand embarrassed manner as C. D.'s and acknowledged, I noticed, with equal off-hand embarrassment. I began to wonder if the reason for this might not be just that: embarrassment at having to introduce anyone to anyone else in these particular charmed circles where of course Everyone was supposed to know Everyone already. Whatever the reason, I must confess they showed a remarkable lack of interest in meeting me and for my part I was able to stifle my own. There was a Mr. and Mrs. Something, a Colonel Something, a Miss Something, three growing children, an elderly Mrs. Something-Something and a couple of dogs who bounced all over me and were the friendliest souls there. Except suddenly for old Mrs. Something-Something, who had presented me with a very limp hand earlier in the proceedings, but who, upon realizing that I was the American invited, went completely out of her skull. She swooped down, carrying me off to a chair almost inside the huge roaring fireplace, explained that she was Pamela's – Lady Daggoner's – mother and began showering me with attentions. What about tea? She knew Americans didn't always care for it. Would I prefer a whisky? Or a cocktail? And was I comfortable? Not freezing? She knew how unsuited Americans were to this climate; the English would keep their houses so cold. No, I didn't want a drink, thank you, and yes I loved tea, and no I wasn't freezing, not at all, and yes, yes, I was comfortable, *really* (I was boiling). Was I interested in the Dance, she wanted to know. She meant of course the Modern Dance, so much stronger and more meaningful than that wishy-washy ballet. She had a delightful young American friend, Clara Hatch, a Modern Dancer, I must have heard of her – who used to come here for visits and poor girl at the end of the first weekend broke down and confessed she positively loathed the outdoors. I was not to allow anyone to bully me into showing me the grounds unless I was absolutely sure I wanted to go out. 'Pam,' she was calling out to our hostess, 'do get this child a jersey, she must be numb with cold.' In vain I protested, I was soon wrapped in a thick cardigan praying I wasn't perspiring visibly. Tea went round. I heard a lot more about Clara Hatch though I have no idea what because I had absolutely switched off until something in Mrs. Something-Something's anxious face made me realize she'd asked me a question she wanted answered.

'Yes,' I replied, and this pleased her because it made yet another bond between her and Clara and myself. *They* read them all the time and she'd put two perfectly corking spine-chillers by my bed-table. Clara's favourites. Poor Clara, when she came to visit them in the country utterly exhausted from these fatiguing and often thankless tours of England and Europe, she would lock herself up in her room and read and rest, read and rest. I was to try the John Dickson Carr first. Had I checked out again so soon?

But no, it was merely a conversational sweep. She was talking about those murder-mysteries and this one, she said, was Clara's absolute favourite.

Tea was over. People were drifting out of the drawing-room by the french windows. It looked beautiful outside: the sun had broken through and was blazing steadily towards its setting. I longed to join them. I was even asked to by my hostess who wondered if I'd care to accompany her around the grounds with C. D. I would have liked nothing better but 'Now, Pam—' began the mother warningly, so I declined, not feeling up to upsetting the old lady by sprinting outdoors after the trouble she'd gone to to save me from it.

'See you seven-thirtyish then,' said Lady Daggoner indifferently and left.

Now we were alone. 'You go up and get some rest,' the mother told me rising. She lived in a little cottage in the grounds. She would love me to visit it but something had gone wrong with the electricity that week. It was in a primitive state, she wouldn't dream of inflicting it on me. But before she went, she wanted to tell me about the Abbey. The Abbey was in the grounds, not too far away, I could see it from the corner of my window. The Abbey, or rather its ruins, was a 12th century one that had been razed to the ground during the reign of Henry the Eighth and all the monks slaughtered and I was in the Blue Room, Clara's – she'd insisted on that because from there, if one was lucky, one could sometimes hear the ghostly voices of the friars at their matins. Clara hadn't. It was one of their big disappointments. She devoutly hoped I might. And then she was off too. And now I was totally alone.

After a few false starts I found my way back to my room and looked for my suitcase to begin unpacking. Gone. Wrong room? Nope, it was undeniably blue. What had happened was that invisible fairy hands had pressed, folded, and hung up every

stitch of my clothing, polished my shoes, laid out my toilet articles on the washstand and my make-up on the dressing-table,
drawn my bath, made off with my suitcase and disappeared without a trace. I looked out of the window at the afternoon
splendour, located the Abbey ruins pink in the sun's reflection
and lay down on the fourposter bed. A neat little fire had been lit
in the fireplace. The peace, the quiet, the perfection – it was all
rather exhausting. I relaxed with a sigh of defeat: the English did
this sort of thing better than we did, they made us look like a
bunch of apes. But as I curled up to doze off my eyes happened to
fall upon my wrist watch. I got up and let the water out of the
tub. Could be that maybe they *overdid* this sort of thing? Or –
could be that this was my hot water for the day? Hurriedly I
turned on the hot water tap. Hot water came out of it. I wandered around the room trying to find fault with it. The furniture
was beautiful. I sat down at the dressing-table and noticed a small
but complete sewing kit and a pin-cushion as well. Ah, these
happy, happy thoughts. A candle, a gorgeous green jade-coloured
candle in the shape of a fat Buddha, was sitting there too. He
looked not unlike C. D. I thought, he really was too beautiful to
use. But there were other candles, equally lovely, one on the
desk, one on the chest of drawers, and one on the bedside table.
Hah! Electricity failures, disguise them as they may. Wasn't the
old lady having just such trouble in her cottage? I rushed to the
main switch and on went the lights without a moment's hesita-
tion.

I gave up. I went back to the bed, found the John Dickson
Carr book – it all took place in a country house too – and soon
became absorbed in it. Suddenly it was time to bathe and dress.
I ran the bath again hoping the water would warm up the bathroom for now a chill had fallen upon it. Then I noticed three
things: an electric heater clamped to the wall high over my head
with a long chain dangling down which you pulled to turn it on,

a hot water bottle on a hook behind the door, and the separate hot towel-rail for the large bath-towel. What infinite pains the English took to avoid heating their homes centrally!

I dressed in a pale grey chiffon clinging in Grecian folds, bound my hair in a matching grey ribbon, spent a lot of time on my make-up, and emerged on the dot of 7.30 entirely satisfied that my stark, jewel-less simplicity looked on purpose. I descended the stairs and entered the drawing-room feeling equal to anything. What were the other people like? I had hardly met them, couldn't even recall their faces. No matter, in my present mood I felt my charm and wit easily up to breaking through their stony reserve.

I was the second. Besides the dogs, I mean. A Rossetti-looking girl with long thickly waving hair, a thick chain with a heavy pendant hanging from her neck, pendant earrings hanging from her ears and heavy bracelets hanging from her wrists was sitting in a corner of a sofa in long trailing skirts sewing away at what looked like a piece of tapestry. Very picturesque she was with only the slightest suggestion of horsiness – a touch around the teeth.

I smiled at her. She looked up vaguely and went back to her fine seam.

We sat in silence until I decided I'd had enough of that. 'I'm Honey Flood,' I said in a clear voice that boomed into the silence. 'I didn't catch your name this afternoon.'

Another silence. A rustle. 'Ann,' she murmured just audibly. But the sewing stopped and she offered 'What a lovely day it's been.'

'Has it? I wouldn't know; I wish I did. I didn't get a chance to go out.'

'What a pity. We've had such a sky! I think the real drama of the English countryside is the drama of the sky, don't you? Have you noticed how splendidly it contrasts with the calmness of the gently swelling land? Take today. What wild variety in the masses and shapes and colours of the clouds – bright silver white to soft silvery grey, some stretched like thin strands of hair blown across the sky, some in great thick puffs like smoke from a steam-engine. We crossed a glistening wet road and I looked up: the little cotton cloud-coloured moon with its ridiculous paper cut-out shape looked so absurdly prim and proper, so somehow *touching* amidst the pagan splendour. It was all so very moving I had to sit down for a moment. It quite took my breath away.'

'Gee, I'll bet it was,' I said with soft enthusiasm, hoping my tone matched hers in gentle fervour. 'I could kill myself for missing it.'

'Do by all means see Pamela's Folly. I've just come in from it.'

'Her what?' I asked wondering if I was going to spend the whole evening flunking my vocabulary test.

'Her Folly. Oh sorry. I fancy that's a specially English thing. Though actually I believe it's from the French, you know, *folie*. It's what you'd imagine the word means; we build mad little summer-houses, or personal idiosyncratic gardens without rhyme or reason, arbours, bowers, hiding places. That sort of thing.'

'What's Lady Daggoner's Folly like?'

'A cypress alley.' She clouded her eyes and sighed, letting the mood sink in. 'An alley of cypress,' she mourned. 'I passed through it at dusk and, as the evening deepened and I wandered amongst the trees lined up in rows, suddenly I understood: They were men. Yes: suddenly I was at a ball and these trees had become men. Tall men, short men, eager, aloof, sardonic, gaily, bending and stretching towards me, seeking my favours, imploring me to dance with them. I became as if caught in a dream. I found I was no longer walking. I was whirling, flirting, teasing, testing – then choosing; accepting – then refusing. And all the time their desire for me grew and their insistence increased and they became realer and realer until I feared for my sanity.' This pretty extraordinary speech, delivered in her mellifluous voice, was produced without a trace of self-consciousness.

By now I was genuinely impressed. 'How poetically you express yourself! You should be a writer.' No sooner had the words left my mouth than I realized that that was exactly what she was.

'Actually I have done one or two little books,' she murmured deprecatingly.

'I'd love to read them. What are their names?'

Wordlessly she rose and left the room. Had I offended her? Probably I should have known their names. But how could I? I didn't even know *her* name. I was beginning to fear for my own sanity when she reappeared as suddenly as she left and dropped two books in my lap. 'I can't sign them for you,' she said, still with that supreme lack of self-consciousness. 'I can't find my pen.'

'Perhaps there's one around here,' I suggested getting up and starting to look around.

'Oh, no.' And now she was genuinely offended. 'I couldn't possibly use any pen but my own.'

'Well, thanks – uh, thank you very much,' I said staring down at them. I felt self-conscious as hell. Was I supposed to start reading them now or what? 'I'll go and put them in my room.' I gathered them up and excused myself. I was damned if I was going to cart them around with me all evening.

By the time I came back, rather breathless by now – it was no hop, skip and jump in that house from home base to the drawing-room – we were richer by one more. A gentleman had joined the ladies: the Colonel, an impeccably attired person with smooth thin hair and a long sharp nose. He rose and said something unintelligible to me. He had a way of clenching his jaw when he spoke that made it impossible for his words to exit. And then afterwards his face cracked into a ghastly grimace that made me wonder if he had not recently had a stroke.

I nodded and subsided into a chair. '. . . but then Greece has been terribly important to me,' the mellifluous Ann was continuing the monologue my arrival had interrupted. 'I must have mountains *and* the sea. And I must have complete seclusion. Once I start working in earnest I eat all my meals alone. And interesting walks; that's another necessity. One works, of course, equally hard when walking as when actually writing,' she explained to us pleasantly. And on she went allowing her placid egotism full reign; in constant communication with her own importance. It was literally impossible to tear her away from herself for a moment. 'No, thank you I won't: I don't smoke *or* drink as a matter of fact. I find it dulls the senses. Every so often I go on a strict regime – a great deal of what we eat is just . . .'

Thank God, the hostess. Poured into a long velvet evening dress that exposed her superb shoulders, and glittering with jewels, I saw she warranted a second thought besides the first 'frump' one I'd dismissed her with. The room filled up. It was fuller than at tea I noticed without being able to pinpoint exactly how it had happened. Then the host Sir Rupert who Did Something in the City made his entrance; stern and handsome and very much the head of the family. The growing children flocked around him. The dogs bounced. Drinks were served. Subdued hilarity. C. D. winked at me.

Dinner in the vast Dining Hall. Footmen behind our chairs. I was accorded the signal honour of being seated next to the host – my elation dwindling away a little as I watched how pointedly (she had taken both by the hands with an exalted look as if joining them in Holy Wedlock) the hostess was seating Ann and C. D. next to each other and as far away from me as possible. And that was very far indeed. Children and all, we were about fifteen.

A youngish man, a somewhat calmer version of the Colonel, was on my right. I decided I had not seen him before – nor the roguish, ravishing Lady Bessemer, who was next the host opposite me. They must have arrived with Sir Rupert. I looked at him. He looked at me. First the Unfolding of the Napkins and then, like a good host, he took me on. 'I'm worried about my eldest daughter,' he began, diving right in. 'As you're fairly close to her in age perhaps you can help me. It's two years till she comes out and I can't decide what to do with her.'

'How old is she?'

'Sixteen.'

'I'm way past that.'

'Oh, give or take a few years, that's not what I mean,' he exclaimed impatiently. 'You're roughly what I'd call her generation, don't you agree?'

For the sake of harmony, I agreed.

'Well then,' he complained, 'I wish you'd explain this generation to me. I wish someone would. They're going to rebel of course. Always have. I know all about that. That's nothing new. It's the shocking flabby form that rebellion takes nowadays that I can't stomach. I'm not having her run off with some frightful rock-and-roll singer, or some delinquent film star, or some damn photographer. It's all your fault over there, y'know. You started the whole thing. Gave those chaps too much money, too much publicity. Turned 'em into bloody heroes, worshipped 'em, that's what you did. And then we had to set up our own tin-plated imitations and now look what we've got. In my day the worst that could happen was one of those writer or painter chaps. Starving in a garret and so forth. Always the chance that eventually you'd starve 'em out. Fat chance of that nowadays. Those holy rollers or whatever they are probably make more in a week than I get in a year. No, it's all your fault, really. You must take the blame. You invented them.'

'I'm sorry.'

'Never mind. There it is. No use weeping about it. The Age we Live in, eh? I've been pretty fly though,' he went on craftily, lowering his voice. 'I believe I've subtly instilled in my daughter the desirability of marrying a rich older man.'

'How?' I wanted to know.

'By being a model parent. Firm but sympathetic. Devoting lots of time to her. Always making certain I remained foremost in her affections. When she eventually settles down, I'm sure she'll choose someone like me. Has to, don't you see? Potty about me. Damn clever, what?'

'Fiendishly,' I smiled.

'D'you know, it occurred to me – might be a jolly good thing to send her off to America for a bit. Let her have her fill of all that nonsense and vulgarity. Get it out of her system. She's bound to get fed to the teeth. What do you think she should do?'

'Join the Communist Party.'

'Ha, ha. That's a good one! I say, I must remember that. But seriously, it might not be a bad idea. Did young Darlington a world of good, his two years with them. Discipline and so forth. He was a perfect jelly-fish before.'

These English. Didn't they ever get *anything* right? The sole purpose of my remark had been to enrage him. It most certainly would have his American equivalent from whom I could have expected anything from a dead faint to ordering me out of the house. I felt like pouring my soup over his head. But that was out of the question. The soup was too good.

So. Over to my partner on the right: the young Colonel-substitute. He was a noisy boisterous soul, full of his new yacht, ship-shape and all set for a glorious Mediterranean cruise. If only he could lure old stick-in-the-mud Rupert aboard, what? Tiresome old Rupert. Lost cause, that one. Couldn't move him off these grounds with a steam shovel. Wasn't his *grounds*, gruffed

Rupert, was his table, he said piling into his next course. Anyone know of a better one? Agreed, agreed, best in the land, clamoured the yachtsman. But he had a French chef, first class, on board. Would old Rupert care for a dry run?

The food on my plate and the wine in my glass began concentrating on me. Yum-yum. Sorry folks. No recipes, no vintages. You'll have to take my word for it: it was the best I'd ever eaten. Lady Bessemer had been reading a book on extrasensory perception, she was all hung up on the subject. The yachtsman, whose ear and eye were permanently cocked in her direction, picked it up and we were off: hypnotism and table-tapping . . . the sort of thing you can listen to with one third of your mind and still come in with appropriate noises at appropriate times. It was the Changing of the Plates and I fell into my old habit of trying to guess who was the richest person in the room. First I raked the table carefully up and down to see if I could detect anyone as poor as or poorer than me. I was very sensitive to the outward symptoms: too much good taste, too much Spartan simplicity disguised as a Pose – my game, in fact. My other way of ferreting them out was much more extra-sensory and largely unsuccessful. I would look at each person separately until they looked back at me and then wait for their sudden recognition of our conspiracy. Most of the time people thought I was flirting with them. Anyway, I was the poorest of this gang – that was clear. Now, who was the richest? Start with Mr. and Mrs. Something. They were utterly colourless but they were sunburned and to be sunburned at that time of year always meant being fairly rich. But there was about them a complacency and mildness of manner I couldn't equate with the very *very* rich. Also they had a rather pimply son, a dead ringer for Dad, sitting next to the youngest Daggoner child and, God knows why, but that made them not so rich too. Ann Authoress was not poor. I'd glanced at her books on my way up to my room and they were privately printed. And Greece, all that jazz – that was not exactly poor either. And all that self-indulgence; I sensed two rich, loving parents backing that up. But was she an out and out Heiress? I doubted it. The man to the left of Lady Daggoner was in clerical garb. The local vicar. So much for him. The Colonel was a house pet. I'd seen Lady Daggoner ordering him around.

And so we came to the young man with a yacht. A yacht, that was something to conjure with. You don't run a yacht with a first-class French chef using coloured buttons for money. But maybe there was only a yacht. Yo-ho the Life-of-the-Sea and a one-room apartment on a chic little street. And then too, *he* was younger than *she* – (she being Lady Bessemer), and with a kind of dependency upon her and deference to her that might be based on money. Lady Bessemer. Bessemer. Steel. Maybe she owned all the steel in the world. If so I'd award her the Golden Calf Stakes hands down. But did she, or did her husband, wherever he was? By process of elimination, I saw that he was not there. And Young Yachter was. Lady Bessemer a divorcée? If I ever saw one. And wait a minute – 'My ex' she'd said during some part of the Occult conversation. Her 'ex' had forbidden her to take part in a seance. Too bad. Alimony is something but it is not All.

My host had a hunk, did he not, did he not, by Gad. What it must cost to run this show. But in cold cash? I wondered. Maybe it was all ploughed back in the land. So that left dear C. D. Or rather Me/C. D. That was still all cash, as far as I knew, good old available cash – minus whatever splurges in food, drink, clothing and general living it up he went in for. I was going to have to find out specifically about all those things at the earliest possible date. A good look at his bank-book for instance would help for a start. Wouldn't it be funny if after all he was the richest person in the room, I mean if *I* was?

'A penny for your thoughts,' said my host.

'I was thinking about money,' I answered frankly.

'Ah – you're in need of it?' It was a probe, not an offer.

'I was,' I smiled. 'But I'm not any more.'

CHAPTER NINE

'She doesn't like my being here. She's trying to fix you up with old horse-face,' I said to C. D. We had gone for an after-dinner stroll and were sitting on a bench in Lady Daggoner's Folly. It was mild and pleasant there sheltered by a high hedge. I looked up at the cypress trees trying to convert them into the suitors of Ann's heated imagination but for me they stubbornly remained trees while an enormous fountain in the centre (mysteriously omitted from her account), gorgeously flood-lit and softly splashing away, dominated the surroundings. I wondered how she'd avoided whirling, flirting and teasing smack into it.

C. D. laughed. 'If there's one thing I'm immune to it's Lady Novelists. Think of being constantly forced into daily contact with all her imaginary characters: "I had such *fun* with Jonathan this morning: I believe I *found* him," and so forth.'

'Still, I'm glad you recognized her from my description. Have you read any of her books?'

'One.'

'What's it like?'

'Chloroform.'

'She was telling me she's at work on what the French call a "roman à fleuve".'

'She reads as if she's been writing under water.'

He smiled at me benevolently.

'Why is Lady Daggoner so eager to marry you off?'

'Oh, you know what one's friends are. And it's much safer if it's someone they know – simplifies the seating arrangements. They know who's going to get along with whom. It's a while since my wife died.' He sighed. 'I suppose Pam's decided my usefulness as one kind of an extra man has ended. She has two categories: the fill-ins and the eligibles.'

'You are an eligible.'

He took my hand. 'You don't consider me eligible? You perhaps prefer the Colonel? Or Rozelia Bessemer's latest?'

'No, I prefer you. I can't speak for the others but to me you are easily the most eligible man here.'

He looked at me thoughtfully. 'That is the first nice thing you've said to me since we met—'

'It's the first chance I've had—'

'—and it was meant as a joke,' he finished.

'I—' we both started off together.

'You,' he conceded.

'No, you,' I urged.

'Why I was about to mention how fond I am of this part of the country,' he disappointed me by saying. 'I am thinking of spending my declining years somewhere around here. I was brought up in the country, though very different from this sort of thing. Wild, savage, rockbound. My earliest memories are of seaweed and sheep.'

'Seaweed and sheep . . .' I echoed dreamily, trying to picture it.

'More sheep than people,' he assured me.

'Isn't it funny, I can imagine you quite easily as a baby – but I can't imagine you growing up' – (I'd almost said 'grown-up') – 'what was it like?'

'Come now, you don't want me to bore you with all that.'

'Yes I do.'

'No you don't.'

'Yes I do.'

'Well then,' he cried with a sudden spurt of energy and settling into the stone seat as if it were an easy chair he began: 'Once upon a time on a sparsely inhabited isle in the Outer Hebrides – that's off the coast of Scotland – there lived a dashing young ne'er-do-well and his brave little wife. Not long after the brave little wife gave birth to their only son, the dashing young ne'er-do-well dashed off the isle, and from there – who shall ever know? By the time I was ten, we were penniless and deserted and the seaweed so rampant we could hardly get into the front door. Whereupon my brave little mother, keeping her wits about her, threw us upon her nearest relation, a sister who, as it happened, had married the Laird of the Isle. We went to live in the castle – people in those days having a rather stronger sense of responsibility towards their kin than now – where I was brought up along with the other children. The years go by and then, quite suddenly – well no, perhaps not all that suddenly, it took two tidal waves to do it – my uncle announced his intentions of abandoning the isle. It seems he'd found a sheep ranch tucked into the wilds of Canada and had decided to emigrate there with his family. The sheep turned the trick, I imagine, made him feel it was a home from home, or a sheep from sheep. I was not seventeen. My mother had died six months previously. To emigrate or not. The decision was left to me. I decided not. We had been educated at home, as was the custom in those remote feudal outposts, and, with all due modesty, I had turned out to be something of a prodigy in the schoolroom. I was eligible for a scholarship to Oxford. Curious how little the New World, even at that early age, attracted me. Never has . . . Where were we? Oh yes – I entered Oxford the following year, did well, as they say, eventually became a Student of the House.'

'What?'

'That's very special, means you're allowed all sorts of privileges like walking on the grass and motoring into the college – and settled down more or less happily to the academic life. Then came the war—'

'And your brilliant military career—'

'A fluke,' he said dismissingly, 'but deeply unsettling. It was no good after that, I couldn't go back; the academic life had lost its appeal and so I went to London and got mixed up in—' He broke off frowning and I followed his thoughts back to the disastrous Clute scandal. This time I knew better than to say anything. I kept my mouth shut and we both looked at the fountain for a while. I found myself thinking of Pauly . . . How had those unlikely two ever gotten together? I tried to remember the short note she'd written me at the time, of which only the fact of her marriage to an Englishman had remained. But there was something about a yacht, I dimly recalled; something about their meeting on a yacht. Somehow she'd taken a cruise on a yacht and he'd been there. I tried to picture Lady Bessemer's Yachtsman and Pauly together. Impossible. The Daggoners and Pauly. Equally impossible. And for the first time in my life I thought in a connected way – a way connected with myself: Poor Pauly.

'Don't waste your time on me,' he said suddenly, 'I assure you, I'm the least eligible man on earth.'

'Not to me.' I moved closer to him so that my face was almost touching his.

He kissed me.

And then, to my chagrin, I giggled.

'What's so funny?'

'I'm sorry,' I gasped, '"They kissed in the conservatory", I couldn't stop that phrase running through my mind. It must be all those sheep and seaweed and remote savage Isles and Gothic

Castles and this Folly. It's getting too much for me.' I kept giggling helplessly. 'I feel as if I should be wearing a crinoline and hiding behind a fan.'

'You're impossible,' he said stiffly and drew away from me.

'Oh please, I don't want to be! Please kiss me again. Please.'

This time we really kissed. I mean I took a great step forward and walked across an ocean of time and space and the fan dropped out of my hand and I stepped out of my crinoline and it was C. D. I was meeting head on. C. D.'s mouth joining with my mouth. And it was all right, it was fine, it was O.K. And when we parted from that kiss we were already lovers. The question had been answered. It was merely a matter of when. And where. Not, however, there. A heavy mist had rolled up drenching us through.

When we came back into the drawing-room there was Lady Daggoner, daggers drawn beneath the façade, almost springing out of the french window curtains to receive and separate us: C. D. to a bridge game, me to Mr. and Mrs. Slug. And very soon thereafter, Mr. and Mrs. Slug and I having discovered not exactly to our surprise that we had nothing in common, I began thinking of bed. Clara Hatch had the right idea about this house, I decided. Bed was the place to be. As much as possible.

'Cos and I are going to look over some land I think he might be interested in tomorrow morning,' Lady Daggoner said, tearing herself away from the bridge game for a moment. 'Hope you don't mind.'

'As a matter of fact I do.' What a joy it would have been to say it but instead I managed a cool, 'Not at all.'

'D'you ride?' she asked me indifferently.

'No.'

'Well then, sleep as late as you like. I know you Americans like to stay in bed till noon.' She tried a smile which was not a success and promptly abandoned it. 'Write your breakfast order on the pad over there and ring for it tomorrow whenever you're ready.' She was at the cards arranging her bridge hand snap snap. 'Oh,' she said as an afterthought, 'we're having some rather amusing young people in for luncheon.' That, I suppose, to discourage any notion I had of sleeping all through the day.

CHAPTER TEN

No doubt because of my being an American (though possibly the strain of all the mixed emotions I'd been feeling that day might have had something to do with it as well) I was out cold the moment I hit the sack that night and it damn near was noon next day when I came to. I rang the bell and I must have slipped back into sleep, or the pussy-footing was super-perfect – at any rate, when I registered again the curtains were parted, the breakfast tray was on my bedside and, you guessed it, the bath had been drawn. And all I'd caught sight of was the tail end of the black uniform.

I dressed and went downstairs into what I was beginning to think of as the non-Assembly Hall. I mean it was truly remarkable the way they all had of getting in there and spreading themselves limply about the furniture and *not* assembling.

Through the french windows, invincible in tweeds, impregnable in brogues, burst Lady Daggoner, an English Rose turned hyacinth from the morning's exertions, closely followed by C. D. and – peek-a-boo – Ann too, whom she'd also taken along on the expedition, the rat.

We all more or less looked towards their general direction – though I certainly wouldn't wish to imply any *group activity* in this movement.

'What was it like? Is the house nice?' somebody not much wanted to know.

'Absolutely *dazzling*,' said Ann stretching her neck prettily and giving us her profile. I wish I could reproduce that awful English *azz*. It always went right through me. It had a 'y' in there after the 'd' so you got a 'dyazzling', which is pretty horrible for a beginning, but it was the way they started to say 'dyazz—' and ended up flattening it into 'dyezz—' that set me on edge.

C. D. came over and sat by my side. 'What did you think of it?' I asked him with, need I tell you, a more than academic interest in his answer.

'Cos was being his usual tiresome self,' said Lady Daggoner with an indulgent smile for him. 'All we do is look and look. And all he does is fuss and complain. He's made slaves of us all.' She let her hand trail along the back of his neck in an intimate manner I didn't care for as she went in answer to the butler's summons.

And here came the Amusing Young People.

'Melinda! Peter! Your guests.'

Thus Melinda! (Daggoner Child One) and Peter! (Daggoner Child Two) were mobilized into action in the foreground while there began with the Daggoners Senior and their group a kind of collective (though I hate to use so strong a word) withdrawing and disappearing action into the background. Mrs. Something-Something, the Dance-loving mother, popped in for a second showering me with Clara Hatch leaflets and reading me selections from the latest Hatch letter, and then disappeared. I was sorry to see her go for her departure – along with whatever else was mysteriously going on at the same time – had left me totally isolated.

C. D. was leaning over the back of my chair. 'What're you doing?'

'Being ignored.'

He laughed. 'And doing it beautifully. Incidentally you've got it wrong. You're not being overlooked – you're being looked over.'

'Really? What's the verdict?'

'Formidable.'

'How so?'

'Well, you're an American, they can see that all right and they know what to make of that. On the other hand you're calm and reposed and they don't quite know what to make of that.'

'What do they expect?'

'Arms like windmills. Gushing about how quaint everything is. Drunkish. Loud. That sort of thing.'

'How charming.'

'I exaggerate to make the point. What I mean is – you've passed the test. They'll come around. You watch. Good luck. I'm off.'

'Hey – not so fast! What's up?'

'Oh – didn't you know? This is the Kiddies' Luncheon. We oldsters take off for other parts.'

'What about Ann?'

'She goes with us.'

'I see,' I said. 'It's all a hideous plot. That girl's not an hour older than me. I've seen her teeth and I know.'

C. D. smiled weakly. 'I think she must be. Anyway you're bound to find this all very enlightening. Keep your ears open. I want a full report at tea-time.' And he gave a lock of my hair a little tug of endearment and was gone.

The first one to 'come around' was Michael Ward Bell. He said 'Michael—' Pause. 'Michael Ward Bell,' with a certain amount of loathing at the sound. I said 'Honey. Honey Fl—' and he said yes, he knew. He flopped down beside me. Floop. He was handsome with dark hair falling in his face, eyes that slanted slightly, high cheek-bones, and a rosy healthy complexion. The dark searching eyes held me. He looked full of purpose. How young he is, I thought. He wasn't young. He was probably a couple of years older than me, but I realized with a shock that ever since our meeting I had kept C. D. so completely, undividedly in my thoughts that I judged all people from where he stood. And from where he stood Michael Ward Bell was young.

He smouldered at me balefully. 'You like it here?'

'Yes.'

'You do?' He was surprised, almost offended. 'You don't find us dull, quaint, slow, dead?'

'I think it's beautiful,' I said looking about indicating that I was keeping the conversation general.

'Yes, I expect it is. I'd like to show you around. D'you ride?'

'Unfortunately not.'

'Never mind. I'll take you around the Point-to-Point in my car tomorrow.'

'What's that?'

'It's a bore. God, I'm hungry,' he said angrily. 'Aren't they ever going to feed us? What time is it?'

I looked at my watch. 'Only ten of one.'

'What's that?' he said quickly on the alert. 'Say that again.'

'Only ten of one.' I wondered if he'd gone mad.

'Marvellous. It sounds like a literal translation. From the German.'

I sighed inwardly. I was getting very used to this. 'What should I have said?' I asked patiently.

'Ten to one.'

'Ten to one,' I enunciated precisely.

'No *t*', *t*'; ten t' one,' he said, so savagely that when he heard himself back, as it were, he had to laugh.

'Come on, clod. Move. We're going in,' urged someone called Peter who was standing over us. Not Peter Daggoner. Peter Wimbish (or so it sounded through their typical name mumble). There was also another Michael: Mr. and Mrs. Something's pimply-faced son. Two Peters and two Michaels, and a man called John. The girls were more imaginatively named. There was Melinda Daggoner whom I began my study around the luncheon table with. She must be the apple of her father's eye for she was a plain girl with nothing in her face or figure to indicate she would not remain so. As for rebellion I couldn't detect the slightest twitch of it in her. Then there was Lysander MacClaren and she was something else. About eighteen years old and a knockout. All three of the men she'd arrived with – Peter, Michael and John – were madly in love with her. You got that at once not only from them but from her. She made it quite clear by her exuberant possessiveness. She was so proud of it you couldn't possibly begrudge her them; she was enjoying herself too much. They were all three in love with her, but as the lunch progressed I began to perceive that they were all three in love with her quite differently: Peter Wimbish, who was utterly nice, utterly correct, whose face even in its youth possessed a kind of fading beauty, a solid, sweet, decent young man, loved her willingly; the tortured Michael unwillingly; and John, older than the others and of scholarly aspect (why he's the poor one! my reflexes told me), hopelessly. Nobody seemed to mind except a girl called Clarissa, who was also pretty, though she didn't trust her looks, and snippy and beady-eyed and full of challenge. And finally there was Lady Rosalind: Rosie, a large, vague, placid girl, with complete aplomb.

For a while the conversation – mainly about Huntin', Shootin' and Social Climbin' – floated five feet above me. About the latter, I must say they were devastatingly outspoken.

'Don't you believe it. Mind, I'm not saying he doesn't put on a splendid show about not giving a damn, but Tony would love to be invited there.'

'He's in for a shock. When you go shooting with them you're expected to bring your own sandwiches and eat them round the table,' growled Michael into his food.

'—that absurd way she has of trying to scandalize,' the large cow-like Lady Rosalind was saying calmly. 'I told her "You can't shock me. He could have been a big, fat, stinking Jew and I wouldn't have been shocked".'

A small silence. 'I say, Rosie – Black Mark,' John commented finally, schoolmaster to pupil.

'Well, goodness don't misunderstand me, what I meant was I couldn't care less. It's too silly of her to think she's being daring.'

Lysander took out a long cigarette holder, put a cigarette in it and turned to John to light it for her.

'I say that is vulgar,' said John. 'Look, Michael, isn't it deliciously vulgar, Liz's cigarette holder?'

'Yes, isn't it?' Lysander exclaimed at Michael flirtatiously.

'No. It isn't long enough. This way it's just common. It wants to be an inch longer. That would make it properly vulgar.'

'Naughty,' said Lysander, delighted at having gotten his goat.

'Eau, Francis was *so* funny about Adrian. Did you hear about it? "D'you mind if I smoke?" he asked him in the middle of a meal. "Not at all," said Adrian and then turned his back and wouldn't talk to him for the rest of the evening.'

'Adrian, always trying to be grand. Coventry Irish. Bicycles.'

'Bicycles?'

'Where the family fortune came from.'

'What sort of a time did you have this summer with the Frogs, Peter?'

'Rotten,' replied the young Daggoner. 'The usual French boarding-house. Whispering amongst themselves all the time. Shooting stray cats at tea. Got to be pretty end-of-tethering.'

'Poor you,' sighed Lysander.

'Wasn't that C. D. McKee you were talking with before he slipped out?' Clarissa asked me suddenly.

I said it was.

'But he's looking so much better since I last saw him. It was most extraordinary how the death of his wife seemed to upset him. When you think that they never got along. She died in America, I believe. She'd gone off and left him. Did you know Pauline?' I shook my head. 'Dreary little creature,' Clarissa went on, 'though I must say he was vile to her. A most unlikely pair. Nobody could understand why he married her. Her money I suppose.'

'Really,' I murmured faintly. I was beginning to feel sick, I wanted more than anything to change the conversation but my wits had deserted me and I could only go on. 'Was she very rich?'

'Pots and pots. She was a funny little thing. Meant well; just wasn't up to it. And drank so much. Drank badly. She said *tuth* for tooth. I mean what sort of class is that?'

'Why it's the part of the country you're from.' (Pauly, poor, poor Pauly. How our sins come home to roost. Forgive me, Pauly, for having done the same thing to you long, long ago.) 'You know, we don't have that sort of class thing in America,' I continued with more spirit. 'The way you pronounce things simply depends on where you're from. It has no more significance than that. We're not snobbish about regional speech. We think it's charming.'

'Oh come now,' tinkled Clarissa, though at the same time seeming to purse her eyes, 'We can't let you have that entirely your own way. You may try to disguise your class system with a lot of talk about democracy and equality but it's there, now admit. Look at all those books on Status Seeking they keep turning out over there. Socking great bestsellers every one of them. Why there're as many different kinds and shades and classes of Americans as English and we're getting to know about them.'

'That's right,' put in old scholarly John. 'There was a time when we thought all Americans were gangsters.'

'And we thought all English were gentlemen,' I replied.

'Hah, hah. Fair enough,' guffawed John as yet another one of my deliberately offensive retorts missed its mark.

'No, but tell, that pronunciation of tooth, would it be middle class?' Clarissa went back to worrying over her bone.

'I dunno. I guess so,' I said giving up.

'*Lower* middle class?' she persisted.

I paused, as if actually considering the thing carefully. '*Middle* lower class,' I answered finally. 'Or rather, half way between middle lower class and *lower* lower class.' I wondered if I was going to get away with this. Out of the corner of my eye I could see Michael glaring viciously at me.

But Clarissa seemed satisfied. 'Eau rareli,' she said nodding and lunch plodded on.

They talked of country matters. The neighbouring peasantry was in pretty bad shape. The rate of idiocy was rising. 'It's that inbreeding, of course.'

'The new bus routes are helping a lot, though.'

'Why?' I'd pledged myself to silence after my last exchange but this seemed too fascinating a non sequitur to let go.

'Gets them away from their villages a bit more.'

'Gets them away from their families, he means.'

'You mean incest?'

'What else?' gloomed Michael.

Back to my food.

'The last time I was in Paris,' Clarissa was telling one of the Peters, 'I found it completely spoiled. I was walking around the Place des Vosges having a gorgeous time thinking thank God they've left something alone and of course – wouldn't you know it? – some American came up to me and said, "Say, Miss, where can I park my car?"'

'What should he have said?' Michael snarled at her.

'Why quite,' she replied quickly and turned to me. 'Zactly my point. That's what I so envy you Americans, your sense of the contemporary. It's the only way to be now. The *assurance* with which they cover the Continent looking for car-parks . . .'

'Yes?' threatened Michael.

Clarissa faltered. 'What I mean is, we're such sticks about these things. We're hopeless abroad. Always afraid one's going to offend someone or that there's a law against whatever one's about to do. It's too boring. I expect we are whatchecallit.'

'Anachronisms.'

'Well I couldn't care less,' the pansy-eyed Lysander cooed languidly. 'Had the most divine feeling sailing down the Beaulieu river the other day in an old-fashioned motor-launch collecting shoals of people who'd somehow got us muddled with the Royals. I waved back. My dear, I felt glorious.' The cigarette smoke from the absurd holder curled lazily upwards and her lashes swept her cheeks as she melted her men, one after the other.

I decided it would be more rewarding from a research point of view if I stopped listening to the conversation as sense and looked upon it instead as a word-game, noting which words turned up with the highest frequency so that I could report my findings back to C. D. Lunch finally drifted to a stop and we were back in the drawing-room, the prickly Michael sticking to me like a burr, jamming me into the corner of a sofa. 'We're awful, aren't we?' he flung at me. 'Go on, admit that's what you're thinking. It's written all over your face.'

'My face is a blank,' I said, astonished.

'Exactly,' he replied. 'Well?'

'Well what?'

'What do you think of us?' he persisted.

I think you should all be stuffed and put into a museum was what I thought. Jesus, I suddenly felt enough vituperation in me for a five-page Philippic but a certain kind of cheap pride prevented me from turning it loose on him. It would seem as if I were allowing them to get me down. Which they were. And then there was that other thought – the bad one: These people were only, after all, displaying the kind of snobbery that I'd used towards Pauly.

'Come on,' he was prodding me.

'Well, it's hard to say. I do get a kind of amidst the alien corn feeling with you all. But I suppose that's only natural. You're so . . . different. That's all.'

'What's America like?'

'Different,' I said stubbornly.

'It better be!' he said in tones of such overwrought despair that again listening to their echo he was forced to laugh. Though a second later he was more serious than ever. 'Listen, you've got to help me,' he pleaded. 'I've got to find myself. D'you think I could find myself in America? God, I wish I could go!'

'What's stopping you?' I asked sharply. I felt sorry for him and all that (and patriotically soothed that England had her own version of our Crazy-Mixed-Up etcetera) but he was a real flip, this cat, and as for me I was hardly in the position to tell people how to go about finding themselves. He didn't answer my question but following his black stare enabled me to answer it for myself: Lysander, collecting her men, had found one missing and was advancing in our direction.

'Michael darling dolt, if you can't tear yourself away from your dazzling American – for which I shan't in the least blame you,' she trained her beautiful smile on me for a moment, 'we're going to have to dish you. We've long over-stayed.'

Although Michael almost visibly vibrated to her presence he made a tremendous effort at nonchalance. 'Shall I go?' he asked me, making sure she heard him. 'I'd like to stay.'

'Well, gee it is late and I've got to go and – umm – I've got something to do.' I pointed in the general direction of the stair-case which would lead to my room and what I had to do, whatever the hell it might be. It was all rather un-thought-out but I did have this overwhelming desire to cool it somewhat off the scene awhile. I rose.

'Come along, Michael,' she teased him. 'Don't you know when you've been turned down?'

'Shut up, you goose!' he hurled at her.

'Angel!' She came forward, close, staring him straight in the face so that he could get the full impact of her beauty, and then turned and walked lightly away, her skirts grazing his trousers, and his eyes followed after her, utterly bemused.

'Well, goodbye,' he said to me rather sheepishly.

'Goodbye.'

'Oh, about the Point-to-Point—'

'I don't think so,' I said.

'No. No, I suppose not. You know, I'm going to get away from that bitch someday.'

'Good luck. I feel for you, Michael. It's a bit like that with me too.' I put out my hand.

'God,' he said shaking it fervently. 'Then good luck to you too.'

And at last they were all gone.

CHAPTER ELEVEN

C.D. and I met at tea-time. I was feeling – how you say? – splenetic. This he dug like a stoat for he was on his feet in a trice manoeuvring us into a corner.

'Well?' he demanded in greedy anticipation.

'Well,' I retorted peevishly throwing the word back into his lap. He accepted it with equanimity; seemed even encouraged by my mood. 'Well, my dear, and what have we seen today?' he pursued with gay archness.

'We have seen the Past,' I snapped, 'and it does not work. Actually, it's been rawthaw end-of-tethering.'

C. D. smiled. 'You've been listening at any rate. What else have you heard?'

'Lots and lots. Oh, such masses and *masses*, dear boy. The elative d, for instance – dazzling, delicious, devastating, divine: and the deflative b – beastly, bloody, boring, the *bottom*.'

'Go on.'

'Nothing could stop me. Everyone *minds* here. They mind so much, they mind all the time, they mind like anything. They mind the step and they mind the door, and they d'you mind if I just. And there they were, poor dears, *minding* like mad. Everyone minds; but no one understands. They cannot understand what could have possessed such an odd couple to behave so curiously; it's all too hopeless, clueless, fatal, futile. The opposite from us Americans. We understand everything. We're always understanding. It's the thing we do. We can immediately see why the poor kid flipped after the raw deal she got. And what's more, when you come right down to it, we understand *his* compulsions too.'

C. D. beamed in approval. 'Quite true,' he said, 'you've a proper recording machine in your ear, young lady. What more?'

'Proper,' I said and sighed. 'Proper. Only that and nothing more. That's it. That's the key to the whole thing. A proper road, a proper car, and the car parked properly on the proper side of the road. Why they use it to mean everything – even improper – "Yes, but were they having a proper affair?" And finally,' I ended, panting to the finish with an ardour that was entirely heartfelt, 'if they can be insulting, why can they not be insulted?'

C. D. shrugged with becoming modesty. 'Thick skins,' he confessed, 'our secret weapon. And so I take it you've been having a delicious time.'

'Devastating!'

'Beastly?'

'Bloody, boring, the bottom,' I sulked.

'My spies tell me you had a great success with young Ward Bell.'

'He thought I might save him from Lysander.'

'And shall you?'

'What marvellous names all the girls get to have. Lysander. I mean really.'

'Yes, the upper classes have a pretty habit of naming their children after the Greeks, only they're often so stupid – and Lysander's family has a particularly long tradition of lovely open faces and small closed minds – they fall into traps from which it is virtually impossible to extricate them. Imagine thinking Lysander a woman's name.'

'Isn't it?' I had to ask.

C. D. frowned. 'Lysander was a Spartan Naval Commander. I remember once having collected the MacClarens' wits long enough to point it out only to uncover the more devastating truth that what they actually meant to christen the child was Leander. You know, like Hero and Leander.'

'But wasn't Leander the man?' I said puzzled. 'I mean so Leander's a man's name too.'

'Precisely. One always counts on the MacClarens to be thorough in their bungling. So – shall you?'

'Shall I what?'

'Save him?'

'Oh, well, he's awfully handsome and *all that*.' I said this slowly and looked worlds at C. D. while I was talking to see if he was receiving what I'd put into 'all that' and if it was disconcerting him. He had and it was. "But,' I finished quoting him back at himself, 'I don't think my happiness lies in that direction.'

He looked at me in what I decided was gratitude. We locked looks for a moment.

He leaned forward. 'About tonight—'

'Yes—?'

But old men dare not allow themselves the chance of being turned down. Old men have to be very very sure. C. D. paused and when he spoke again I could tell it was not at all what he had originally intended saying. Or rather, he went another route. 'You're going to find it all very boring again. I do wish I could think of something exciting or amusing for you to do,' said the old fraud, furrowing his brow.

'Yes,' I agreed, stretching my body a little and bending a glance in his direction intended to be subtly wanton. 'I do wish you could.'

'What sort of thing would excite you and . . .' His eyes weren't on me any more. They were on some exquisite little piece of china his chubby hands had picked up from a nearby table and I had the sensation that he was going to pop it into his pocket (with a conspiratorial wink at the passing footman); '—and what sort of thing would amuse you?'

'Why, to be with you,' I replied as though willing to make my feelings clear though a second later: 'And to be taken away from all this,' I added mockingly, unable to resist making them unclear again. Old man or not, the proposition was going to have to come from him.

C. D. let his gaze drift towards the french windows. 'Begun to rain. Looks like a storm too.'

'Dismal in and dismal out,' was my contribution.

'No after-dinner stroll then.'

'So where else can we go?' I was looking at him again, thinking: O.K., this far I was prepared to go and no further.

'Perhaps instead I can show you around—'

'Around—?'

He giggled. '—my room.'

At last. 'That's an idea. How shall we arrange it?'

'It's a lovely room,' he said as though he hadn't heard me. 'Quite my favourite. It's the room they always give me. I keep a few of my books and things here the year round. I had a hand in the decoration, selected the drawings for the walls. A Leonardo. I'll be interested in your opinion of it. I'll retire directly the men join the ladies,' he continued without a change of pace or tone, 'to avoid getting caught up in a bridge game. Come up about three-quarters of an hour later. We're less likely to arouse suspicions in the sequence, I think.' Then, on the back of an envelope (careful first to extract the letter, grrr) he drew a map of how to get to his room, which happened to be at the other end of the house from mine, and handed it to me.

'Cool, man, cool,' I said smiling sweetly at him as I took it. And I left him, his face a study.

By the time I was reassembled (or rather re non-assembled) in the drawing-room again I was almost too late for the pre-dinner drink. I had been all this time getting ready. I had been over every inch of my body with loving care. I was bathed and scented and everything touching me was fresh and clean. I'd filed my fingernails and clipped my toenails, scrubbed my ears and elbows devotedly. I had given up mud-packs and hormone creams at the age of thirteen but that evening I carefully washed my face first with very hot and then with icy cold water and had gone to the trouble to make a trip down to the kitchen for a cucumber in order to rub slices of it over my cheeks and forehead. In the bath-tub I washed myself in some places three times and put in my diaphragm. All this, I kept telling myself, for *just in case* – for I had by no means made up my mind that *It* was to be tonight. In fact (as near as I could make out what I was up to), it seemed to me I was rather tending to favour delaying tactics. It was strange but true that the more time and the more trouble I took over my ablutions, the more convinced I became that the idea of going all the way with him tonight was a lousy one. After all. This old man. This old, old man. Revolting, wasn't it? No, my mind was not ready for him. But oh boy, was my body prepared.

C. D. appeared in the drawing-room even later than I so we had a chance for only one small exchange before going in to dinner. However, it did much to make a shambles of the meal for me.

'You're late,' I said and then I looked at him more closely, for although brushed and combed and freshly shaved there was about him an indefinable air of chaos, a curious rumpledness about his features. 'What *have you* been doing?' I asked.

'Using you for imagery,' he replied blandly. 'Are you shocked?'

I wasn't right away. I didn't even get it right away. And if he hadn't pointed up the first part of the remark by adding the second part I probably wouldn't have. I probably would have regarded it as merely cryptic, what-the-hell. But finally I got it all right. And when I did, I felt myself go bright pink. I stared hard at my drink. 'No ice,' I mumbled shakily. 'How quaint. Just like they're always telling you in those Come to Britain books.'

'Yes it's frightful, isn't it?' he mocked me. 'How *will* they keep all these people here overnight without ice?' And then he repeated, 'Are you shocked?'

I waited for my answer. 'Yes,' I admitted at last very low.

'Good, then I'm making contact.'

With that we went in to dinner.

The seating arrangements this time yielded me up the Colonel (a trial in any circumstances, a death sentence in this), his face ablaze with all its oral and muscular eccentricities. He beamed a grimace at me that flickered up one side of his jaw then turned and swooped over to the other side until the same thing happened. It changed sides several times before he spoke. Conversation went like this:

'I say, you haven't been following the Blake-Sommers controversy in *The Times*?' he misjudged me badly enough to inquire.

'No I haven't,' I replied.

'Don't bother. Awful rubbish. Disgraceful business, the whole thing. Information entirely incorrect and misleading. I myself spoke with General Blake the other day and he was letting himself go unusually strong for him on what he said was the most unfair position Breckenfield had put Sommers into by insisting that Dillingham should be sacked.'

'Gee, really?'

'Absolute fact.'

'Amazing.'

'Isn't it?' agreed the Colonel. 'One's sorely tempted to write in and clear matters up once and for all.'

'But you should, you must.' It was my turn to agree.

He sighed and it came out like the hiss of a steam engine. 'Out of the question, of course.'

'But *why?*'

Grimace to me again. 'Hmmm. I suppose one would if one was a Yank, wouldn't one?'

I supposed so too, though what I was supposed to be supposing I couldn't have guessed. Abruptly I ploughed into my food, letting the whole military matter drop. I really had more pressing things to think about. What was C. D. doing to me? What was he *doing*, the Great God Pan, so alternately repelling and compelling.

I glanced down the table to where C. D., lounged back in his chair idly toying with the stem of his glass, was holding his audience rapt. I noticed that his plate was already clean. He ate faster and more invisibly than anyone I'd ever seen. How did he get it all off the plate and into his maw in so short a time? It disappeared. In *there*. I could see the beginning of his tummy visible over the rim of the table. He caught my eye and twinkled. Pig, I thought violently. Smug pig. How dare you use me for imagery. And without my permission.

Conversation circled around me, a duplicate of the lunchtime one as the children were duplicates of the grown-ups.

'. . . and ran into Daphne Hyssop at Monte.'

'Still in hot pursuit of the Textile King?'

'The hottest. And talking with an Italian accent now. My dear. Most odd.'

'What a curious affectation. D'you think she really will get him away from the wife?'

'Certainly looked it. Pity. The wife's an absolute darling. Very bright. Very good at word games.'

'Daphne, I should imagine, somewhat less so.'

'Especially with an Italian accent.'

'Still, it makes one listen.'

'Very hard indeed.'

'So what about him? What's he like?'

'Nothing at all. Sly provincial; easily offended.'

'I simply *cannot* understand . . .'

Salad. Dessert. Cheese. And out.

I was drinking coffee in the drawing-room with the ladies. God, I prayed, will the gentlemen never join us? Finally they did. I watched in that dream-like knowing-in-advance-what-will-happen state, while C. D. went through the motions of slipping away pleading urgent unfinished correspondence. As he left I looked pointedly at my watch and then at him. Then I marked time. I refused a bridge game on grounds of ignorance. I played with the dogs, smiled at the children and agreed with everyone how shamefully the weather was behaving. I moved over to where Ann was sitting and listened to some more of her literary confessions: 'Only on *one* side of the page, *un*lined, and in *very* large letters.' It took up what was left of my three-quarters of an hour. Bravely I rose. I bade goodnight to my hostess mumbling something about the rain making me sleepy. It sounded very feeble. I don't care if she believes it or not, I told myself.

I started upstairs studying the back of the envelope. Then for the first time I turned it round and noticed with a shock that it had a Dublin postmark. I studied the handwriting closely. A woman's? Lady Mary's? Must be. I felt a sense of danger, a sense of urgency. Urgent unfinished correspondence. I mounted the steps two at a time.

I was standing outside C. D.'s room knocking at the door. Come in, he called to me and since he did not come to the door I had to open it myself and enter. Uneasily I took in nothing about the room except that he was in the bed. Or rather he was on the bed. He had taken off his dinner jacket and his tie and shoes. He appeared to be reading, several pillows propped comfortably behind his head. 'My dear,' he said closing the book, letting it fall to the floor. 'Sit down, do.' He indicated the bed.

Still ill at ease I sat on the edge of the bed facing him but as far away as possible, my back against the bed-post. I looked around me trying to think of something to say about the room. 'It's nice,' is the only comment I found myself making. C. D. began to smile at me. The smile came in two parts – first his angelic blue stare glacial and spiritual and then slowly, deliberately, he allowed it to catch fire and his eyes glow red and his mouth widen with lust. Instinctively I moved closer, close enough so that if he sat up he could have taken me in his arms, but he didn't budge he just kept on smiling hot and avaricious until I found myself stretched out on the bed lying alongside him dazed at my surrender. Not two seconds before pressed against the bed-post I had decided my only motive for being here was to escape from the house-party and have a nice quiet talk with him. Talk above all talk, I loved talking with him. Yet now as we lay together in silence I felt no shame at my sudden reversal (it could hardly be called a capitulation), only peace at having finally burnt my bridges. He slipped his arm under me and I waited for the Occasion to begin. Still smiling he reached across me with his free hand (*there* was an expensive smell) and switched off the bedside light. He kissed me. My arms curled around at once. (Thank goodness they were long, he was so very large.) He slipped down the straps of my evening dress and began kissing my shoulders. I clung to him.

There was a knock on the door. I started up as a reflex but no, I cannot say that I was really surprised.

'Cos—?'

He switched the light back on. 'One minute. Who is it?'

'It's me, Pam.' As if we didn't know.

'Tell her to go away,' I whispered.

'One minute, Pam. Hold on, will you?' He got off the bed, smoothing his hair and putting on his dinner jacket, tie and shoes, all the time giving me the look of fury and disgust that was meant for her. I scrambled quickly to my feet, grabbed my purse and dashed for the bathroom.

I could hear Lady Daggoner enter. Her voice was cool and musical and unnaturally clear – for my benefit no doubt. She wanted to know would Cos be an angel and make up the fourth for their bridge table. The doctor had to leave on a call. It's as well, he plays atrociously and Rupert was winning so much it was embarrassing. Now perhaps Cos will change his partner's luck. He can't say no, he must look upon it as an act of mercy the same as the doctor's call. My not-yet-lover attempted a feeble protest. Mutters about pressing unfinished correspondence. About his headache. About sleeping badly the night before and his desire to get a good night's rest. Lady Dag wasn't having any. He can finish off the rubber, it won't take half an hour, it's the least he can do to help them out. 'Come on, slow coach, hurry.' She was all bustle and efficiency. 'You've got your tie on crooked, silly, here let me.' Now I hear triumph and amusement and something else. Shared laughter. Sounds from the past. They've had their moments together, those two. Ready? Yes. Scuffle, scuffle. Out of the door.

I was sitting on the edge of the tub shaking with rage. Most of it at first was directed against myself for rushing off to hide like a serving wench – but quickly I switched to her. What business was it of hers what we were up to – or rather, why this insistence on making it her business – arriving in person, of all tactless things, instead of getting one of her million minions to deliver the message – that would have been the polite, the discreet and above all the ordinary thing to do. Of course he might have refused the maid where he could hardly have refused old Pamy-wam. But no. There was more to it than that. Her presence was an open declaration of war – nothing short.

I dashed cold water on my face and left the bathroom. I walked around the bedroom poking into everything but it was the desk that really interested me. Dare I open it? Those pussy-footing maids. 'Unfinished correspondence', he'd referred to it twice this evening, and, suddenly, I was sure that it actually existed. I opened a desk drawer and there – carefully hidden under a neat stack of blank writing paper – two pages of a letter: 'Dearest Mary . . .'

My heart stopped as if stuck and then picked up again and went furiously pounding on. This was his writing. This was his handwriting in action to her. Saturday, said the date. Quickly I skimmed the page. '. . . that now, incredibly, it should fall upon you to save me. Only save me, I implore you. Rome, Venice, Athens – anywhere you like; it doesn't matter. It must be soon, there is no time to lose . . .' The pounding of my heart seemed to have affected my eyesight. The words blurred into meaningless-ness. I sat down to catch my breath but when I started to read it again my hands were still trembling. '. . . there is no time to lose . . .' (and blurr went the print as another line disintegrated into chicken tracks before I could get my grip) '. . . must agree that after one American disaster another is out of the question. And this one would be truly dangerous, this one would finish me off; this one would be fatal . . .' (a really big blurr and then) '. . . not in the very least straightforward, though to what pur-pose her lies, God alone knows. She professes to be rich – dresses well enough in that American style – yet it is obvious from those two infallible giveaways, her shoes and her handbags, that she is not. She professes to have come here for psychiatric treatment yet the story she tells of her unhappy love affair which, she claims, led to a nervous breakdown and subsequently to this decision struck me, upon consideration, as false and totally incompatible with anything else in her personality – though I must say she tells it well. In fact, I find I am constantly falling under her spell, ready and eager to believe anything she says – for the moment. She really is a most frightening blend of cynicism, implacable (though mysterious) purpose, and above all passion; a curious passion that seems to spring from my reminding her (I imagine unconsciously, of course) of someone she has been wronged by, or deprived of, in the past. I know. Always the complicated psychological reason. Of course, she may be after my money, that would be simple enough, but why not a rich man closer her age? There was a good one here today for luncheon. No, laugh all you like, it is getting me down. She makes a gesture which, even in the short space I have known her, has come to fill me with dread: she leans forward as though agog, one arm perched on her elbow, and with the thumb of her right hand she presses her front tooth and automatically, like one of those pinball machines, her eyes register first suspicion and then hatred. I have seen those eyes look upon me with such contempt and loathing I have almost feared for my life, the more so because I suspect this display of hostility to be entirely unconscious on her part. *Consciously* she is trying to attract me, seduce me, enslave me (fancy! an old man like me) but unconsciously . . .' and off it went into another mist straightening out only at the last sentence still left in mid-air . . . 'help but feel that, in a life where we are allowed only a certain number of mistakes, I am already well past my quota and therefore I implore you, my dearest Mary—'

What did I feel? Appalled. Astonished. Bewildered. I thought I was doing so well. I thought I was charming the hell out of him. I thought I had him eating out of my hand. Well: I thought I was getting away with it. I might have known. There is always a catch. But suddenly I felt very very young, like a child. Suddenly I wanted to run to – God knows whom, maybe God Himself – why is there never a face I can put to whom I want to run? – and cry 'But I thought he *liked* me. All I want is to be liked.' And then, thank heaven, cold rage and fury. Carefully I wiped the desk where the tear splashed. Carefully I put the letter back exactly where I had found it and closed the drawer. Quietly I slipped out of the room.

Back in my own room I locked the door behind me. If he was entertaining any thought for later on—! I was shivering with cold and started across to the glowing fireplace. On my way something tripped me up and I was flung headlong on to the floor murderously barking my shins and tearing my stockings to shreds. What was it? Some stupid old bric-à-brac, some 18th-century piece of crap, a footstool or something, anyway, now it was good and broken and in my exasperation I hurled it into the fireplace where it immediately combusted into crackling flames. Good. I collapsed into the chair by the dressing-table and fell into a blue funk. Shoes and handbags? I'll kill him for that. What's wrong with them, I'd like to know. They were in perfect taste like everything else about my clothes. They weren't real alligator, I grant you, and I didn't change them with every costume. Couldn't afford to, that's why. And the reason I couldn't was because he happened to be sitting on a bundle of bread that happened to be mine. Athens, Rome and Venice? Oh no you don't, buddy boy, you're not going anywhere until I'm finished with you. I've still got one card left unplayed (but with an old man – who can tell?) and if that fails— With a start I saw that I had gotten a hold of the green Buddha-shaped candle and had been jabbing pins from the pincushion into it.

What's more I had developed a splitting headache. Maybe I was about to get the curse. Maybe that accounted for my loss of control, I'm never quite myself at the beginning of it. No. It was at least ten days off. I went to the medicine chest looking for aspirin, which they had (natch), and took two. O.K. So, cool it. Clear head, steady nerves, that's what's needed. Get undressed, get into bed. Unlock the door, don't be a baby. Read something, help you unwind. The John Dickson Carr mystery. Well, well. Turns out it was done with an electric fire plugged in and dropped into the bathtub while the victim was having a bath, short-circuiting him. I mean how frightfully English, what? Like, where would you even get a hold of an electric fire in this day and age except in jolly old—. Watch it. Don't get all worked up again. Sleep. It's three-thirty. Sleep, that's the thing. Out with the light and now deep breaths . . . C. D. is getting ready for his bath – no really deep breaths I said . . . no but wait, first I have managed to unscrew the electric fire from the wall above. (Stand on the bathtub to reach it.) Tools. Get tools from the tool shed. Breathe! And ah, good now, I've got it. Electric fire comes off the wall quite easily really, nice long wire attached to it luckily. Now, hiding it carefully behind me call out to C. D. 'Your bath is ready, darling. Can I stay and watch you? I'll scrub your back.' Lean against wall, he won't notice anything of course, preoccupied as he is with um with um testing the water. In he goes. And in . . . breathe in, breathe out, breathe dammit. Unrelated objects unexpected faces materialise from nowhere. Don't try to make sense of it, surrrrrrealiss—

Was I really awake? I think so. Anyway I recognized the bedroom, it's where I went to sleep, but what is this sweet singing that fills the air? It's like a Gregorian chant. The ghostly monks from the Abbey. I hear them, I hear them! I am not frightened. It's curious it's as if I have lost my resistance to be frightened. Something strange is happening to me in England, in the Old World, that I am giving in to. It's all right though, I told myself. When the cock crows the singing will stop and as the thought formulates itself the cock does crow, the singing vanishes, the atmosphere lightens. The spirits have passed but how did I know that about the cock? I am sure, I am positive I didn't know it before and yet at the moment I made it up the singing stopped. And I fell back into a dreamless sleep.

When I awoke it was Sunday sunshine. I leapt out of bed simultaneously throwing on my clothes and gulping my tea. I felt like my own American self again in the Sunday sun and pooh-poohed the events of the previous night. Singing monks. How impressionable can you get? And that footstool fantasy. Well there was no sign of a footstool in the fireplace. There was no sign of it in the room either, so probably I made the whole thing up, don't remember seeing it before. But combing my hair at the dressing table my eyes fell upon the Buddha candle and with a sinking heart I saw that the pin pricks were there. I held it in my hands until it got warm and tried to smooth them away.

And that is enough of *that*, I told myself sternly, no more morbid thoughts. No matter what.

C. D. had taken the children off to church, Lady Daggoner told me when I arrived downstairs. Wasn't it sweet of him, he was for ever doing dear things like that.

'Would you care to take a turn around the rose garden?' she asked me pleasantly. Was she going to be nice to me finally?

Lady Daggoner walked me slowly around her rose garden, her conversation full of expertise cleverly disguised as apology. The wet weather in June had completely waterlogged the garden, the soil had compacted and the idiot gardener, the son of the old one who died last year, turned out to know nothing, absolutely nothing, had to be watched every second of the time, had gone and used some worm-killing compound. Oh dear, the blunders would be comic if they weren't so tragic, the new trees almost drying up because he forgot to remove the foliage after the plants had been lifted from the ground. And over there, look, turned her back for a minute and when she'd turned round again it was to discover he'd put the Royalists next to the Rubaiyats, the Crimson Glories next to the Brilliants. Did you ever? Filthy pruning-shears spreading rust . . . black spot . . . compost heap . . . caught using DDT against green-fly . . . mildew . . . bushes cut back . . . soil acidity. Eventually she broke off to remark 'But I can't think why I go on boring you with all this. You're not very interested in gardening, are you? So few Americans are. I keep forgetting.'

'No, I love it. I just don't know much about it.'

Why aren't Americans very interested in gardening? Because we are barbarians, that's why. Why couldn't it be stag-hunting or pig-sticking or bringing back the cat-of-nine-tails that we aren't very interested in, something faintly reprehensible? But calm, pleasant, harmless, healthy, good-for-you, beauty-loving, cherished-alike-by-peer-and-peasant, British-to-the-backbone gardening – *that's* what we aren't very interested in; *that's* what we don't know much about, I was thinking grimly.

Lady Daggoner was pursuing the same train of thought. 'Americans are so very different from the English I find, don't you? You know, in spite of our common language I sometimes think we have far more affinity with Europeans while you people strike me as being a lot closer in every way to the present-day Russians. Odd, when you're such sworn enemies, but I can't help feeling it all the same,' was the way she put it. 'What do you think?'

'You mean rosewise?'

Lady Dag, puzzled, showed no inclination to laugh.

'You know, gardenwise,' I explained, showing no inclination to laugh either. 'Like, we don't dig gardens. That was what you meant?'

'Well, no. I don't suppose I could know much about that,' she said helplessly, and then, stepping on firmer ground, 'actually I was thinking of Cos and his former wife.'

'Splitsville?' I queried sympathetically.

Lady Daggoner looked distinctly uncomfortable. 'She is dead, yes, if that's what you mean.'

'I meant divorced.'

'Oh, I see. I'm sorry, I didn't— No, what I was going to say was that it was such a madly unhappy business. I don't suppose they saw eye to eye on one single thing. Now I'm not saying they wouldn't have been a disaster in any circumstance but I can't help feeling that her being an American didn't help. I'm sure she was completely unprepared for what was expected of her as his wife. How she must have hated us all, poor thing, I don't wonder. I'm afraid people, oh I don't know, you know how it is, didn't take much *notice* of her after a while. We warned him. We were all against it. Cos is such a fool, I'm devoted to him, known him all my life, though of course I'm a good deal younger.' She had paused in our walk to take a rose between her fingers and frowned into its startled face. 'Where was I? Oh, about warning him. It was the greatest folly really, first of all marrying so late in life, let's see, he must have been about forty-eight then he's fifty-six now, goodness, old enough to be your father, *and* for the first time *and* to someone so entirely unsuitable. Well, of course, they had their own reasons. I doubt very much that even at the beginning it was what you'd call a love match, she was rich and a widow and I suppose they were both lonely, both looking for some kind of a change. Perhaps if she could have given him a child ... But the main thing is, dear Cos is a great snob, so absurdly ashamed of his origins. My theory is he's devoted most of his life to burying them as deep as he can, poor lamb, as if we cared.'

The bitchiness was something beautiful to behold, nevertheless I felt compelled to inject a bit of dissent at this point if only for its nuisance value. 'Wait a minute,' I said, 'I'm not with this at all. I must be thinking about two other guys. In the first place, he didn't seem at all embarrassed when he told *me* about his origins and in the second place I think it's dreamy. That remote island and the castle. Just because his father was a rat—' but her look of pitying amusement left the rest of my sentence unsaid.

'Oh dear, not still at it, is he? But don't you see, it's pure invention from start to finish. You'd think he'd have outgrown it by now. I must say I'd forgotten all about that little fairy-tale though now I think of it my eldest brother who was in the war with him did mention something about him circulating it at the time – how did it go, the whole family conveniently emigrating to Australia or Madagascar or some place like that.'

'Canada.'

'Exactly. No, my dear, I'm very much afraid that if anyone ever gets to the bottom of it they're going to come across something frightfully respectable. Take my word for it, they're going to turn up a father who was neither a coal-miner nor an aristocratic bounder but some decent little shop assistant or office clerk. That sort of thing is so much harder to live down, isn't it? You know, I'm convinced that's why he put off marrying for as long as he did. On the one hand that awful middle-class fear of marrying outside one's class and on the other the realization that one's wife would be quite likely to discover the truth. And so,' she went on triumphantly, 'don't you see, I am sure that's why he felt he had to marry an American, however much he disapproved of them in general – and he does deeply, I assure you, he's quite wild on the subject, nothing would induce him to set foot in the country – because an American being presumably classless would have no feelings about it. Well, it's all ancient history and no concern of ours, as I said, we all adore him and it couldn't matter less, but what was unfortunate was the choice of that poor wretched little woman. The real trouble with her – now I'm sure you won't be offended, I'm sure you'll take this in the spirit it's meant – but Pauline, well, you're much more advanced over there I know, you don't have these silly distinctions but, well, let's say temperamentally, yes, that's all I'm talking about really, *temperamentally*, and all her wealth apart, I shouldn't have been surprised if Pauline'd have been much happier as the wife of an office clerk.' Lady Daggoner had picked up a stick and was prodding the earth around a patch of Crimson Glories or whatever with it. 'No, now I am being unfair,' she decided. 'Actually she was an attractive little creature to look at, perfect little figure and marvellous red hair and a loyal devoted little character, utterly wrapped up in him, I think she might have been a perfect wife for, say, one of your Corporation Presidents. But oh, so utterly without conversation or interest. Sat around reading financial reports all day long I believe. Dinner there was agony. He bullied and broke her and then glared at her the rest of the time. Very off-putting for anyone. You can imagine what it did to her – not that she wasn't wildly irritating always limping along one step behind, poor soul, her remarks entirely composed of dreadfully dim questions. "What did he say she said?" and "Are you talking about the brother or the son?" that kind of thing. She wasn't stupid though. My husband used to have quite sensible talks with her about various business interests of his, said she was quite knowledgeable. Made packets playing the stock market, I understand. But that, as luck would have it, was the thing most calculated to alienate Cos. He'd had a terrible experience in the world of business and he never wanted to think of it again. So there he'd be trying to educate her in the arts and there she'd be talking about dollars. I suppose that is American, isn't it, for women to know so much about money, I mean I expect they have to, owning most of it, as they do, don't they? Anyway in the end he absolutely forbade her to mention it. In other words she wasn't allowed to talk about the one thing she could. I thought she ought to have been encouraged in it, I thought it would have been amusing, given her a certain cachet, well, it would have given her *something*, but poor old bourgeois Cos, he'd decided it was unspeakably vulgar. I suppose it is too humiliating, "What's your wife interested in?" "Money." It was true enough. Then she began the sulking *and* the drinking and towards the end my dear she was *insortable* . . .'

I was getting a bit fidgety. Fidgety? I was beside myself with hatred. How I hate you, I'd been saying to her in my mind all this time. How I hate you all, so smugly so daintily going about your dirty work growing flowers and withering people. If I could only shut her up. But how? My thumb flew up to my front tooth (and flew right back down again the instant I became aware of it). I looked her straight in the face. 'Why,' I asked slowly and distinctly, 'are you telling me all this?'

To my surprise she began to smile. 'How silly of me, you'll have heard most of this already. I am sorry to be such a bore. It's that I do find Cos so fascinating and complicated I assume everyone must be as interested in him as I, especially now that he's so madly rich and eligible, though what most people *don't* know—' and now her smile was pure mischief, 'what most people don't know is that when he dies the money goes right *back to America* every bit of it and not to his next wife. There's a small matter of a child, you see, of Pauly's first husband. She's off somewhere in school I believe. She's only about fifteen. But viewed from *that* angle he really isn't much of a catch for a young girl at all, is he?' And she looked at me quite coldly. She had finished her say. She had been as rude as she could and get away with it. And now she was going to get away from it. 'I think the children have returned from church,' she said and hurried off without a backward glance in my direction.

I strolled back slowly and by the time I reached the house I had made up my mind.

'I'm leaving,' I told C. D., 'right now. How do I get out of here?'

'What's been happening? You look like Rachel in *Phèdre*.'

'If I'd been a man I would have punched our dear hostess in the snoot.'

'Oh dear. I was afraid of this somehow. She's rather possessive about me and terribly used to getting her own way. Was she very rude?'

'Very rude about you, very rude about your wife, very rude about America and, finally, very rude about me.'

'How you?'

'She accused me of trying to marry you for your money. Warned me against it. Really. Rather an impertinence, don't you think, since I only met you two weeks ago and never set eyes on her until the day before yesterday?'

We were standing in the library where I had marched off to upon my return. C. D. sank into one of the chairs and covered his head in his hands. 'Yes, she can be like that,' he said. 'We can all be like that.' Then he rose and sighed. 'Come on. I shall do what's necessary.'

'. . . not feeling very well so I think it would be better if she returned to London as soon as possible,' I heard C. D. saying to Lady Daggoner while I stood some five feet away.

'You mean right now this minute?'

'Preferably.'

'I see. Well, have you told her maid? Have you told Cranshaw? Don't tell *me*, tell the staff, they're the ones who run this place. Oh, never mind. I'll do it.' She reached for the phone and stopped. 'I can never remember if the 1.15 runs on Sunday.'

'I was going to ask if we couldn't take the Daimler.'

'*We?*'

'But of course I'm going with her.'

'Cos, you're insane. Not before luncheon. We're having your special chocolate soufflé. Do be sensible.'

'About the Daimler,' he said implacably. 'It's all right if we take it, isn't it? I expect Rupert will be needing it in town tomorrow anyway.'

'No he won't,' she looked stubborn.

'Then we'll send the chauffeur back with it. Nothing drearier than a Sunday train ride, is there?'

'Then why are you going?' she snapped, suddenly showing her anger.

'Miss Flood is ill,' he reminded her gently. 'I do think she ought to be allowed to get back as comfortably as possible.'

'That was beautiful,' I whispered to him as we went upstairs to pack.

He looked at me sadly. 'Yes, but it was long overdue,' he said.

CHAPTER TWELVE

'Goodbye,' said Lady Daggoner punctiliously, appearing at the edge of the Daimler as we jumped in. Then her mouth went on moving silently until C. D. rolled down the window.

'—ly furious with you both for leaving,' she was saying emphatically. 'You must forgive me, Miss Flood, for having been so tiresome about the motor. To be quite honest I'd hoped to lure you both back into staying. Perhaps Cos has told you – I'm a perfect terror when I don't get my own way,' she added with utter simplicity.

'I understand,' I replied with even utterer. 'I am like that myself.' Then we drove off leaving her standing in the driveway.

'So: Act One,' I said heaving a hefty sigh of relief, looking out upon a car-scape a good deal prettier than the railroad-scape had been.

'Except that now we'll never know if she's really having chocolate soufflé for lunch.'

'You mean she's capable of just saying it?'

'She is capable of anything.'

'So am I,' I declared defiantly but in another moment, defiance evaporated, I slumped back into my corner depressed. The unpleasantness of the last two hours had left its mark.

'Dearest Honey . . .' He took my hand. *Dearest Mary* . . . dearest God! I sat up with a start. I hadn't thought about that Dearest Mary letter once all day, hadn't given one minute's thought as to what steps must be taken to counteract his suspicions about my character and desirability.

'Look,' I said, 'if you'd like to find out about the soufflé we can turn around and go back. I don't mind.' As if to prove my sincerity I leaned forward towards the driver.

'No – don't do that,' C. D. cried out, tugging at my hand so sharply that I almost toppled over, and I found myself looking into a face as naked as a plea. For an instant my astonishment was echoed in his own expression and then his consciousness overcoming his reflexes, he smiled ruefully to himself and gathered me into his arms, Lady Dag's chauffeur and all. But of course, I thought, what luck. First my martyrdom by Lady D. and then my rescue by Old McKee had automatically turned me into a heroine, installing me neatly on the side of the angels. It was no longer necessary to take any steps. I relaxed against him. Fate was playing my hand for me and for once in my life I knew better than not to go ahead and let it.

Eventually we stopped at a pub. 'Now don't fuss about a proper lunch. Take what you get and be glad for it.' As if I would let anything detract me from the joy of the moment. Not sad Sunday nor the paling sky nor the lack of a proper lunch. Inside: frosted-glass pub lighting and the wet metallic silver-polish smell of beer. Cold fat sausages, cheese sandwiches, a large gin-and-tonic. 'Ice, madame?' the barmaid, catching my American accent, had obligingly plopped some in, and I made a great point of crunching it loudly between my teeth for the horror and amusement of C. D.

'What time is it now?'

'About one o'clock. Two more hours and we'll be home.'

Once a young man, a nice ordinary young man, had asked me to go for a spin in the country. 'We'll screw,' he added jokingly, 'in every motel along the way.' He was a nice young man, he drove us carefully there and back, his eyes on the road, both hands on the wheel the whole time. But somehow those words had the strangest effect on me. I couldn't shake them, I kept looking at the motels all along the way. And when I asked him the time and he replied (but how weird – in the same words as C. D.) 'About one o'clock. Two more hours and we'll be home,' and I was reduced to the same jelly of excitement as I was now (later on in the young man's apartment I thought – if he only knew exactly what had accomplished his seduction!) Only here was the difference: the young man in that car had become more and more my ideal Young Man as we drove along – his profile handsomer, his hands stronger, his hair blonder, pushing me back into some romantic dream of him, while C. D., ever himself, merely became more so, thrusting me forward into reality.

And so we drove, and so we arrived at his house. And there he led me unresisting up the stairs into his bedchamber where, upon his lily-white bed, in the fullness of time he did lay me.

There is a time for asterisks and a time for speaking out. I don't know – will all this morbid introspection into my terrible itch for that randy old man reveal itself merely as an exercise in self-indulgence, a senseless waste of time? Or will it be that, having put down clearly and to my own satisfaction once and for all precisely what it was like sleeping with foxy grampa, I may finally come to understand what was going on in me? And what was making me go on like that? Maybe not. We must hope for the best. But it's so hard. I write three words and at the fourth memory seizes me. I waste hours mooning over a situation that play it as I may could only have been resolved by disaster.

Waking Monday morning at Dody's I sat straight up in bed, my heart pounding. He was old. He was my stepfather. I hated him. And I'd enjoyed myself. Promptly I slid back down again stuffing the pillow over my face. Any combination of two would have been enough to send me under – all four was too much. Besides, I hated him but I loved him too. Yes. I know all about that sort of thing. Christ, I should, I'd heard nothing else my last two years in New York. 'They have this terrific love-hate thing going', everybody said about everybody else. 'You watch, it's going to destroy them—'. But never about *me*. When I took to someone I took to them, and when I took against them ditto. Mostly I felt indifference. Hmm. If you don't mind I believe I will take this opportunity to apologize for my former fatuousness.

But about C. D. and me. We were oddly matched. We were mis-matched, such different ages, shapes and sizes; such different worlds. What I could not have foreseen was how I would *love that difference*. How the very effort of bridging the chasm seemed to make me come alive as if for the first time. How getting physically close to C. D. was a kind of triumph, as if my contact with the unlikelihood of Us became my contact with the world, became my only reality. As if before I'd only been a shadow. He made me opaque by constantly bumping up against me, by my constantly bumping up against him. Solid met solid. Boom!

And compared to C. D. all the other men I'd known – all the young men I'd played around with were just that: playmates. My brothers. And they were essentially alike. Not to yawn with boredom, it was all very pleasant, they were fine, they were divine truly, but they were alike. They talked alike, they felt alike, they touched and tasted and smelled alike. They even breathed alike, panting sadly to a standstill. It was always there mixed in with the bliss, this subsiding into melancholy. But I'd wanted to feel happy. 'Why are we so sad?' I once asked. 'Why do we always feel so sad afterwards?' 'Because we both belong to the same generation,' I was told sadly, 'and all our same worries come back to us at the same time.' But C. D. was jolly and obscene.

With C. D. I felt happy, amused, outraged. C. D. made me feel that I'd been violated and I had survived. C. D. went over the hill with a huge yelp of delight and then, every trace of greed and lust and all those appetites that kept him constantly on the boil finally withdrawn, he fell into an unrousable slumber. And I felt like laughing. And I felt good and I felt tough.

Compared with the slim hard-bodied young men his figure was a joke – round, tubby, pillow-paunchy, it had the consistency of foam rubber; rolling around with him was like rolling around with some big beach toy. But he flung himself into it with a devotion that was disarming. A tyrant on his feet, he turned out to be a real woman-worshipper in the sack. And subtle too. And full of tricks. He knew a trick or two, that one. And then it turned out I knew a trick or two I didn't even know I knew. He could play a whole jazz concert on me. When we were finished we were covered, absolutely covered with each other. And yet I was never surprised at finding myself, six or seven hours later and in my own bed, in real trouble, seized with a shuddery revulsion of shame and disgust. How could I have? All those things. And with that fat old monster? And on top of everything – who was using whom? The original idea had been to enslave him for ever with my womanly wiles but rather the opposite seemed to be happening. For in spite of those sixth- and seventh-hour shudderings at the ghastly unnaturalness of the liaison, in spite of the painfully sharp recollections of my slender, delicate, gloriously young body stretched out alongside his vast old bulk – I am still at a loss to explain it – but in spite of all this – not once was I able to resist him in the flesh.

Enough of fruitless excavations. That afternoon, that first time, there was a bowl of fruit by his bed-table. When he awoke he selected two peaches, offering me one and biting into his as he might into my own flesh. 'Well,' he said, 'take you home now, shall I?', patting me patronisingly on my butt, heaving himself heavily out of bed and into his clothes as if my surrender was an everyday occurrence to him, the most natural thing in the world.

'Hey – not so fast! I haven't had a square meal all day. Remember?'

'My dear. Of course. How unfortunate. I told my couple they could have the weekend off so I don't suppose there's a thing in the house. Still, if you'd like to forage.'

'No I would not,' I said firmly. 'I mean I know English Sundays are hell and all that but there must be some place open for dinner.'

He looked doubtful. 'Let's see . . . Air terminals . . . Railway stations.'

'I don't want to be difficult but I feel I must tell you that I am very hungry and I do want to eat and I have no intention of doing so either in your kitchen or an air terminal or a railway station so let's not be silly. Take me to the Ritz. You do have a Ritz here, I've seen it several times.'

'Well, yes, but—'

'Well yes but look – what is it? You all pooped out? Sorry it's been so exhausting. I had no idea. I'm ready to dine and I have the feeling some of my friends would be only too glad to oblige, cheri—' I'd had my back to him combing my hair – the post-lay sight of myself in the mirror soft-eyed and full-cheeked was pleasantly reassuring. I turned around now and faced him, '—so can I use your telephone for one little minute?' I added spiritedly. 'And would you mind clearing out while I do?'

I stood with one hand on my hip, the other with the comb in it indicating the door.

The Buddha smiled and then he sighed. 'How expensive you look when you're angry! Like some gangster's moll. It's that rich man's darling all over again.' He heaved himself out of his chair. 'Righto. To the Ritz then,' he conceded.

His measured tread was slow and heavy behind me on the staircase. I didn't care. I didn't care whether his reluctance was made up of boredom, exhaustion, the desire to be rid of me, or all three. The only thing I cared about – and now at last I confessed it openly to myself – was that whenever there was a clash of wills between us I *win*. But through my grim determination had come my first chill indication that one Lay was not going to make a Lawn (no, *you* ungarble that). The second one came at my doorstep.

'I may be very busy this week. I'll telephone you first chance I get,' he had the interesting idea of saying to me, kissing me good-night on the cheek.

'Gosh – hope I'm still here,' I had the presence of mind to reply.

'You're not thinking of leaving?' He gave me a sort of unstrung look that seemed to indicate those appetites of his might be stirring again.

'Some of my friends want me to go to Paris with them,' I threw off idly.

'Don't dream of it.'

'Well, but if you're going to be so busy.'

'I'll be around for you tomorrow evening.'

'Okie dokes. See you then.'

Kiss.

Kiss.

G'night.

CHAPTER THIRTEEN

A nd so back again to waking on Monday morning at Dody's. Finally I pulled aside the curtains. The English sun all shy and dewy-eyed softly illuminated the street below. How sweet was my little London street sitting in the sun. How English everyone striding to and fro upon it. How bowler hat, little toy brown felt hat balancing on the tip of their noses. Those sharp noses. Those scrubbed pink skins. Those white collars. Those Savile Row clothes. Those Rolls, those Jags, those black square taxis. To the east: Berkeley Square. To the north: Grosvenor Square. Next door: Farm Street Square. London: City of Squares.

I knocked on Dody's door. Oh, but of course – she was off to Art School by now. I went into the kitchen and made myself a pot of coffee and began to feel quite wonderful. I wandered about the flat. Hadn't I the right to crow? I stared awhile at the solitary killer goldfish in his threadbare golden armour. This flat, mellowing in the sun, was full of delights. The round polished black table in the living-room. The wooden bowl of fruit set in its centre – oranges and grapefruit glowing rich and golden against the shiny black. And the books and the pictures and the gramophone records. And how nearly it had all come to not happening: two weeks ago I was desperate in a dark little hotel room full of ugly shin-barking furniture. And now a pink carpet covered my bedroom floor and voluptuous roses bloomed upon my wallpaper.

And all for free.

I sipped my coffee, contentedly thinking about C. D. It would be a fight to the finish but I would win. The telephone was ringing. Lazily I lifted the receiver. It would be my lover calling to pass the time of day. It was. Only he was calling to say, in the chilling tones of a man with other things on his mind, that as he had feared he was going to be too busy to see me until Wednesday. Was Wednesday all right for me? And do you know I was scared, literally scared to death to say no?

Droopingly I trailed back to my room. I decided against a bath, listlessly registering that it was probably the first time in my life I'd ever voluntarily skipped it. Because I wasn't going to see him? Or was it the English climate? It was said to be debilitating if you weren't used to it. I looked out of the window again at the damp dulcet sun and suddenly I longed for the raw healthy blaze of my own native one. I went over to the chest of drawers to get out some fresh underwear when my eyes fell upon the two bottles of pills I'd stolen from C. D.'s medicine chest the first time I'd been there. I picked them up and turned them round in my hand. *One capsule when necessary*, said the first one unhelpfully. *Two tablets as directed*, said the second. And the date. And the prescription number. And the name and address of the chemist.

'Could you please tell me what's in these,' I asked the man at the prescription counter. 'I know it's stupid of me but I haven't used them for so long I've clean forgotten what they are.'

'Pleasure, Miss. Bit chancy leaving unidentified medicines about, eh?'

'One thing we know,' he said returning. 'They're certainly not for you, are they?'

'What? Oh – aren't they? Oh. Wait a minute. They're my husband's. Yes, of course.'

'He still much overweight?'

'I'm afraid he is. But tell me again exactly what they are.'

'This one's preludin and these are thyroid tablets.'

'I know I'm awfully stupid, but would you tell me again exactly what they do? It's been so long.'

'Appetite depressers. But see here, he wasn't taking the two of them together?'

'Oh no. I mean I can't remember. Why, would that be bad?'

'It would indeed. Most dangerous. Strain on the heart. Strain on the nervous system. One or the other is quite sufficient.'

'Yes – it's coming back to me now,' I said putting the pill bottles back into my bag. 'Well, lucky I checked. Cleaning out the cabinet and stuff. Thank you very much.' And I was off.

So all I had to do was to keep dropping one of each together in his coffee whenever I could and hope for the best. I began walking fast. I'd gone all the way to Chelsea to the chemists yet almost before I knew it I found myself back in Grosvenor Square. I sat down under the statue of Roosevelt and stared at one of the fish ponds, trying to collect myself. A shrugging fountain flung out its watery shroud in a crazy ghost dance, spraying me with every third bump. I consulted myself seriously, pleading with myself to let me in on what I was really up to. I threatened myself I couldn't be nutty enough actually to be thinking of doing him in because he had broken a date with me. I tried frightening myself with the consequence of such an act. Getting caught. The trial. The sentence. The death. They hanged you over here. And all this time other thoughts were racing along. The sublime thing about these pills was that even if an autopsy should be performed and they showed up, they just weren't the sort of pills you ever associated with murder – they were strictly in the self-administered accident category.

But what about the man behind the prescription counter? Would he suddenly read about it in the paper, remember me and come forward? Well, but I'd be safely in America by then and under my rightful name collecting my rightful loot. Still, it was a risk. In fact, face it – that man remembering our exchange over the counter was just the sort of unlikely but dead sure thing to lead slowly and inevitably to criminal charges against me. The wheels of fate could make mincemeat out of me. On the other hand, suppose I didn't kill him outright with these pills but just used them to contribute to the general disorder. Yeah – and then weaken him in ways like – No. Stop! This was impossible. I suddenly found myself laughing out loud. Pills in his coffee! Young American girls still in their college skirts and sweaters and polo coats didn't sit under the statue of Franklin Delano Roosevelt in Grosvenor Square in the middle of a sunny day plotting the murder of middle-aged Englishmen. It was some crazy game I was playing to pass the time of day. I shrugged the whole thing off like the fountain's shrugging dance.

'Something to drink? A cup of coffee? I've made a fresh pot,' I asked C. D. when he arrived for me on Wednesday.

'At six in the evening? Whatever for? Are you trying to poison me?' he replied indignantly.

'I'm having some. What's the time got to do with it anyway? It's so dreary out I felt like something hot.'

'Then guzzle it out of my sight then. And please be considerate enough at drink time to offer me a drink.' He softened this a little by leaning over to kiss me. 'Where is your girlfriend?'

'Dody? She's become an art student. She's off with the Chelsea Sex Set or whatever they call themselves on the King's Road.'

'Sounds interesting.'

'Not really. I went along with her last night. I don't know what it is – them or me. I'm either ahead of it or behind it but I'm not with it. I get the feeling that the essence of everything for them is to be thrown fully clothed into the fountain at Trafalgar Square at three in the morning.'

'Were you there? I've been reading about it in the papers. Sounded madly gay.'

'It wasn't. Such organized high jinks. Such a determined bunch of cut-ups. And why this addiction to fancy dress? The last masquerade party I really enjoyed was when I was about eight.'

'Blasé.'

'Maybe. But it seems to me they're not really happy unless they're at the same time on public display and at their worst. That's what one of the girls actually said to me last night. "Was I rude to that little man in the Underground? Goodness, I hope so!"'

'It's the traditional Bright Young Thing attitude.'

'Well I'm giving it the traditional So What.'

'I wonder if England really is the place for an American,' he said ruminatively.

I let it slide. 'I'll get you a drink.'

'And then what would you like to do?'

'What would *you*?'

He grinned. 'I suppose it's too early for that.'

I was standing way over on the other side of the room by the drink things but I felt quite breathless.

'So I thought we might go to a cinema,' he went on, making the *c* hard, no doubt like in the original Greek pronunciation. Why didn't he go the whole hog and call it the Cinematograph or the Magic Lantern or whatever they said before the flood?

'What's on?'

'What do you feel like – murder, outer space or sex among the working classes?'

'Murder,' I said.

'Good. So do I. That Hitchcock thing, *Psycho*, is back again. I'm told it's an absolute blood bath. I'll look through the paper to find out where it is.'

Before we left I went along the passageway to the kitchen and put away the unused coffee things I'd carefully arranged on a tray. Silly precaution maybe, but in my mind's eye they had seemed to be staring at me accusingly, warning me to cover my tracks. Then I checked to see that his pills were still in my handbag.

'Oh-oh. It's queuing up time in kine-land,' I remarked as our taxi drew up in front of a large Phantasmagoric Palace.

'I say, do you mind?'

'Not at all. Give me the chance to observe the highways and byways of your happy folk at play.' I looked down the grim unbroken line of mackintoshes.

However, when we came to rest, directly in front of us as fate would have it (and fate was having it pretty much all my way in those days, if you remember) stood a striking couple with the hard bright glitter of New York so sharp about them I felt a tidal wave of homesickness surge up inside me. The girl had that extravagant lacquered flash: black hair, thick lashes, bright lips and smooth white face. Her body was built on generous, even gracious lines and you could feel all the abandon of her sensuality in the slow rhythmic rise and fall of her bosom as she breathed, her shining mouth permanently parted. The man's elegant dark Negro face with its broad mouth and high cheekbones, its thin delicate bridge of a nose between flaring eyebrows, was the contemporary mask of Comedy or Tragedy depending on which way he turned the corners of his mouth and eyebrows. Clothed from head to toe in Italian silk, he looked more New York American than anyone I'd ever seen.

'Behave yourself,' whispered C. D.

'What do you mean?'

'Such undisguised lust. If I were him I'd call for the police.'

'Oh shut up. There's something familiar about them both, that's all.'

'My, we *are* getting chippy on the shoulder.'

At this point the man turned and caught my stare and smiled vaguely back at me. The girl too swung around, almost automatically, and did the same. They were impersonal acknowledgement-of-recognition-type smiles: professional. But who were they? After a moment the girl turned back to the man and opened her mouth as if to speak. I strained forward for a clue.

'I forgot to pick up the pie,' she said.

'Oh, *baby*, not again,' said the man, his voice hoarse, caressing, coaxing, full of southern winds and midnight-blue New York nights.

'And I was thinking about it all afternoon,' the girl went on softly. 'I don't know how it . . . I must have been real . . . real . . .' She shook her head ruefully and let her voice trail off, her lips parted, breath coming voluptuously. God, they were relaxed those two. There was an eternity between them.

'What about the roast? Sure you turned down the oven?' Twitch of the mouth and eyebrows. Mask of Comedy. 'That could be a bad scene if you didn't.'

'Oh, baby, I'm not that . . . y'know . . . that . . .'

Mask of Tragedy. 'You're fine.'

Then there was a mass move and we all went in.

The idea of going to a murder movie in the first place was to watch it closely in the hopes of picking up some valuable pointers. I have since had people tell me that this particular one was the most grisly, fiendish and gruesome they have ever seen. Whether or not this is true I cannot say, as my body, assuming various knotted positions reminiscent of the Laocoön, was entirely bent on *not* seeing it. If this was what killing someone entailed – and presumably this was precisely what it did . . . my handbag had slid to the ground. I'd bent over to pick it up but found it impossible to straighten out. Better stay there for a while.

'You all right?' C. D. leaned over.

'Of course.' Steel bands clamped down on my forehead, pressing at my temples. 'Only I think I'm fainting.' I rose and stumbled out to the lobby, C. D. following with my bag.

I was all right after that. We had a good meal at some polished walnut of a restaurant and lots and lots to drink and then he took me back to his place where he – well, we've been through all that already, haven't we?

But what seems to have escaped me until just now was that it was the first time in my life I'd ever gotten drunk.

CHAPTER FOURTEEN

C.D. McKee . . . Cosmos? Darwin? Don't you believe it – C Charlie D Dog McKee. You were a fraud and a fool and a fat flabby fifty-six-year-old rake fake, C. D. *Seedy* McKee. Lying around every room of your house, my feet upon your chairs and sofas, 'Oh *teach* me how to sneer,' I would say, remembering some disparaging remark of yours earlier on that day, let us say about a snuff box hopefully brought round for your approval by one of your worshipful friends: 'Yes, it is an eighteenth-century snuff box' (pause for closer inspection – timing was everything in this game) 'but it's a poor man's one.' (Seedy, I shall always think of you as a poor man's snuff box. How merrily our eyes met, dancing over the defeated head of the downcast Collector.) But later on, I would start feeling sorry for her – it generally was a woman – for her carelessly spoiled pleasure, and I would remember (still earlier that same day) you to the proud owner of the newly decorated house in Brompton Square (and decorated only for your dismay it would seem, would it not, Sir Seed?): '*Never* put a Buhl clock on top of a Bahut Bretonne desk – not even a bogus one.' Oh good stuff, good stuff. And what was the other? 'Well, if you're going to collect Staffordshire you're going to have an awful lot of awful things.' And so, 'Teach me how to sneer,' I would say.

And you, your shoes off, curling your toes in your rich thick woollen socks, answering mildly enough, 'At what? At things a Yank like you ought not to have the right to walk amongst, much less criticize?' Steel blue met steel blue with a blast of blow-torches and then I would reply: 'Youse is slippin', mah boy. You'll have to do better than that.'

And then, of course, you would giggle.

'*The American girl syndrome, by which I mean the entire course of a relationship with one, has speeded up a lot during the past twenty-five years. Initial stimulation is now followed almost immediately by disinfatuation. Cuteness turns to banality overnight. The pert wise-crack degenerates into a maddening quack. Mental cruelty sets in about the third day . . .*' An Englishman reviewing some book or other about an American girl. Pointed out to me by C. D., natch. The American girl syndrome. I kept saying it to myself over and over again. *Syndrome.* It's such a lovely word with its undertones of cymbals and drums, of sin dooms and sun downs, only finally, I wasn't exactly sure what it meant. So I looked it up. Syndrome: a concurrence of symptoms forming a clinical picture. Charming, I thought, to describe a relationship with an American girl as if it were a disease; as if knowing an American girl would make you catch something. Like death.

C. D. was taking me around London. Luncheons, dinner par-ties, concerts and Art Galleries. I definitely got the feeling he enjoyed being seen with me. Hell, he liked us being talked about, the old goat. He loved the stately commotion we were causing among his friends and cronies, the heads we set in motion, the tongues we started wagging, and, though I say it, the sighs of envy we occasioned. He was focusing on me all right, concentrating, but I still couldn't help feeling, with his constant corrections of my English, my education, my posture even, that it was the schoolmaster rather than the lover in the ascendant. And this angered and frustrated me as did, even more, the nagging feeling that anyone else, given my age, sex, looks and incentive, might have had the whole thing sewn up by now.

The days slipped by. The pills lay in my bag unused, a constant reproach to my cowardice. My ineffectualness increased my impatience which in turn increased my ineffectualness, and as they both increased my temper caused my Anglophobia to grow in leaps and bounds. Not that I would have considered his little groupie a bargain over any counter and the fact that most of them shared Lady Daggoner's view that another American liaison would be disastrous for our fat friend did nothing to improve my goodwill towards them. And so, like letting the cat out of the bag, I let the catty side of my nature slip out, shocked at how readily it jumped. But whereas before my lapses into bitchiness would have provoked a mild reprimand from C. D. now they actually seemed to amuse him. In fact, the more vindictive I became, the more he was delighted. And this too added to my annoyance, this corroding of my soul for his enjoyment, for after a while I couldn't stop it, did it automatically like a reflex.

'But don't you find So-and-So spirited and gay?' he might inquire.

'About as gay as an undertaker gone berserk,' would be my snappy rejoinder.

'At any rate her luncheon parties are the most sought after in London.'

'Yeah – where people come not so much to eat as be eaten,' I would flip back quick as a flash.

Or: 'I thought little Miss X quite an exotic bloom – a Gauguin really.'

'I see what you mean. Those purple cheeks. Those blue lips.'

Suppressed giggle from C. D.

After a while I didn't confine myself to the people but spread myself out so I could take in their homes and furnishings as well.

'You'd think in that hideous brown drawing-room of hers the women would have had enough sense not *all* to show up in black,' I might complain.

And then, moving out of doors and into the Art Galleries: C. D. lost in admiration in front of a Bellini. 'There really is so much to be said for him, isn't there?' he would ask.

'Yes, all those terrible actors, he paints.'

I had begun by imitating him, went on to compete and ended by outdistancing him – like waiting until he'd finished a loving description of some old Regency hand-cooler or whatever and then saying quietly to all present, 'It isn't nearly as pretty as he says it is.' Gone too far? Apparently not – for there he was hissing with laughter.

And then, suddenly from nowhere, a major crisis. Dody barrelling into my room early one morning with a letter in hand that she'd just received from her husband Scotty. My God, I thought, I'd forgotten all about him. She began reading from it hysterically, breaking up sentences and injecting comments in a way that made it almost impossible to make sense of. It seemed that now Scotty thought it was all a big mistake. The Indian girl didn't seem to be so Indian any more in India. Turned out to be rather Western, in fact. And a bit of a bore. In fact, he d had to face it that one can be Indian and still be a bore. He was completely disillusioned on that score. Dody was far more exotic, really. Dear little Dody with her vague ways, far more mysterious and interesting. How he missed her. What a fool he'd been. What should he do? What should *he* do – what should *she* do, Dody kept breaking off to ask me and then going straight on without waiting. He was in despair. He wanted to return. If Dody would say so he'd take the next plane back. What should she do?

What should she do indeed. What should *I* do was more to the point. With Scotty back I'd be out on the street. There was no question of shacking up with C. D.; he was very proper, he never once even asked me to spend the whole night with him. I needed this place. That month of hotel living had taught me how much I needed this place. I needed it not just for the roof over my head or the smooth sheets on my bed or the closet space for my clothes or the iron for my blouses. I needed it to make coffee in, have a glass of milk and a snack during the day. I needed it to stay in when I wasn't going out and to come back to when I had been. I needed it to listen to its records, read its books. I needed to be able to go from one room to another when I felt like it; not to have to go through a lobby of strangers, myself a stranger, every time I came indoors or out. I needed it so that when I got up in the morning eventually I didn't feel as bad as I did when I first woke up. And of course I needed it not to get that weekly bill payable immediately. In short I needed it desperately and there was no question of giving it up.

'I see what you mean,' I said to Dody, 'this needs careful thought. Let's review the situation.'

'He's awfully impulsive. He means no harm.' Dody kicked off with.

'Nuts to that,' I said, catching the ball and running in the opposite direction. 'And nuts to he's really a child at heart. Children don't leave their wives to go off to India with other women. You remember what you said the night we saw that Bardot film? About how the wife kept getting a raw deal because she kept forgiving her husband and that made him think he hadn't done anything wrong so he could go right on doing it?'

'Oh, that was just a film.'

'And this is just a letter. I mean, looking at it realistically, I suppose you are facing the fact that if you take him back he'll probably go ahead and do the same thing all over again.'

'That isn't the way he sounds,' she protested weakly.

'Oh come on now. Going by all you've told me of him it doesn't seem possible he could become a reformed character in two weeks. And going by what he himself said to me—'

'How do you mean?'

I paused. 'Oh nothing – it was something he said to me that night before he left. Of course he was drunk. Forget it.'

'No. Tell me. You've got to.'

I steadied my qualms. After all it was going to be the truth. And, back to the wall, I had my own castle to defend. Thank God for my excellent memory, I thought, as with scrupulous accuracy I reproduced for her the bit of our conversation about his wife not liking his Indian kick. 'She thinks there's something sexual about it. She's damn right there's something sexual about it. There's something sexual about you too,' up to his asking me to come along to India with him. 'And he'd only known me for about three minutes,' I added.

Dody looked at me dazedly, poor little lost satellite skidding bewilderedly between orbits, her head drooping to one side. 'Yes I know. He's like that,' she murmured. 'What shall I do? I can't seem to think properly any more. What shall I do?'

I received this with more irritation than satisfaction. If only she'd become angry, resentful, suspicious, put up some decent resistance, I would have been spared the false but persistent fear that I was taking advantage of her. After all, the thing to remember was how crummily Scotty had been treating her all this time. I was merely doing the right thing for the wrong reason.

'There's only one thing to do,' I said slowly with great weight from a great height, 'nothing.' It's always easier to make people do nothing than something. Also, I was not going to run the risk of having her sit down to write him one sort of letter and end up writing him the opposite.

'*Nothing?*'

'That's right. Don't answer his letter. Since you don't know how you really feel it's the only honest thing to do, isn't it? And quite frankly as long as there're women like you – blind, trusting and forgiving – there're going to be men like Scotty. Right? So that's the word. Nothing. Let him stew in his own juice a while.'

Dody was delighted. The idea struck her as brilliant. I should have known it would. She was a little lost satellite but she skidded from one orbit to the next with great passivity. And so she spun off to Art School leaving me to intercept every mail – in case.

The English postal service is one of the glories of its nation. You cannot go into a drugstore for some popular brand of toothpaste without being told they're sorry it's on order and will only take ten days. You have to face the fact that certain telephone exchanges are ungettable from certain other ones without begging the operator to intercede for you (KNIghtsbridge and MAYfair weren't on speaking terms when I was there). Laundry or cleaning might take anywhere from three weeks to three years. But mail is delivered regularly, sometimes four times a day. Londoners think nothing of posting their letters in the morning for their friends to read at tea-time. And their families in Manchester can contact them by the same method in the evening.

So there I was, sprinting back for every post. My morning sleep shot to hell. And all in the name of justice.

CHAPTER FIFTEEN

One evening before dinner at C. D.'s, while I was riffling through his mail in his bedroom and he was having a bath, I came across a letter that made me freeze in my tracks. It was from Lady Mary, containing more than a suspicion that she was in the process of getting herself unstuck from the Sean-must-be-back-in-Dublin-in-time character we'd seen her with at the Antique Fair (and who, I gathered, was a jockey) and might soon be pointing Londonwards. I put down the letter, reached for my bag, and took out a couple of preludin and thyroid tablets from their bottles and hid them in my corsage. Nor was I reassured by C. D.'s mood during dinner. He was irritable and fault-finding, flatly refusing all wines and spirits, moaning about his health and threatening to go on a regime.

After coffee was served in the drawing-room I turned to him and said very sweetly, 'Darling would you be an angel and go back to the dining-room for my purse? I don't seem to have left it there.' I had carefully arranged this so that while he was gone I could pop the preludin and thyroid tablets into his coffee.

'Blake will do it,' he said and rang for his man without stirring from his chair, the lazy bastard. Then after sipping his coffee he rose, stretched, announced 'I am going to go pot myself'; picked up a book and left.

Here at last was my chance. I dropped the pills into the dregs of his coffee cup, mashed them about and sent for some fresh hot coffee in about twenty minutes. No hurry. He was always a good half-hour on the can. What do men do in there so long?

When he came back I handed him his cup of coffee and sat on the arm of his chair. 'Drink it,' I said.

'Don't want it,' he pouted. 'It's probably cold.'

'No it isn't. But drink it anyway,' I said sternly, 'or you'll fall asleep.'

'Ugh—' he drained the cup. 'It's disgusting. Why shouldn't I fall asleep?' he grumped. 'I want to sleep.'

'Because I'm bored,' I said, pacing restlessly up and down. 'I'm so bored. Let's *do* something. How about a fast game of Cat's Cradle? I'll get some string. Or a nice long chat about whose second cousin Billy Saxenborough's third wife married?' I suggested, collapsing into a chair and throwing my legs over it. 'Let's do something. Don't you English ever do *anything*?'

'We sit still. Sit still. Can't you sit still?' I was pacing up and down again. 'That's a pretty dress,' he said in an attempt to pacify me.

'I'm tired of it,' I snapped. 'And I'm tired of what's in it. And I'm tired of everything. I wish we could find something nice to do.'

'You are ungrateful. Will you look at that face. At the very idea of being grateful you put on your American-girl sneer. I take you everywhere. We've been out at least three times this week. What more do you want?'

'I want to go to a night-club. You never take me to night-clubs.'

'Nor do I,' admitted C. D., surprised at the idea. 'They don't seem to have been part of one's life. I really wouldn't know how to go about it. Let me think. I know, I'll telephone Rupert, he's staying in town tonight. He's a great one for that sort of thing. But not too late. I'd like to get a good night's sleep for a change.'

Eventually we went round to Sir Rupert's, who gave us a batch of little pasteboard cards with his name on them, membership cards without which, he assured us, we would not be admitted to any of the really gay glamorous ones.

We went to three night-clubs in quick succession. They were sad and sleazy and awful in a way I'd never quite come across before. It was the sadness mainly. The what-went-wrong look on the waiters' faces as they stood staring bewilderedly at an empty room most certainly on the brink of bankruptcy. One thing that went wrong was the night-club comic with his hair too long and combed all funny singing 'There's no business like Shoe Business' to 'There's no business like etc.,' and doing impersonations of King Kong falling for a butterfly. Another wrong thing was the young man with a guitar who sang dirty Scottish ballads about goats sleeping with women (Trad.). Another was the girl in tights with a stocking cap pulled down over her eyes and ears who did a totally inexplicable dance with the lights out, mostly writhing on the floor. And lastly, the audience – a sprinkling of debs and their escorts who jeered and hurled pennies on the stage as the acts progressed – they were awfully wrong. It was discouraging. How was I going to get C. D. hooked on this dissolute way of life – let alone how was I myself going to bear it? How was I going to keep him out till dawn every night, exhausted and spent and running downhill until the final – what? – how about a heart attack? – would carry him off? What I had in mind was some divine little boîte that had good jazz and a sensational entertainer; one that was dark, smoky and unhealthy and served rot-gut strong enough to melt the mind, rip out the lining of the stomach, explode the liver and curdle the kidneys. Or, if that was too much to ask, at least a place interesting enough to keep him up late. He went to bed much too early. They all did in London. I never saw such people for leaving each other's houses at the stroke of midnight.

The fourth night-club was a strip-tease joint. I got us out of there even faster. I wasn't going to have him going around with erotic images other than my own on his mind if I could help it. The fifth – an enormous one – had not only tumblers but ice-skaters and a ventriloquist. We left during the juggling act.

We almost didn't get into the sixth. The man you had to pass before they let you in recognized C. D. as not being Sir Rupert and it took a telephone call and the intercession of the original card-owner and a year's membership dues in advance before we gained access. It was called 'Maretta's'. And it was more like it, I could tell immediately. It was dark and smoky and unhealthy and crowded. The decor was tufted plum satin on the walls that looked like the inside of an old coffin but it had glamour – or almost. And it had atmosphere – for a London night-club.

There was a good dance band and C. D. surprised me by asking me to dance and then surprised me even more by being an excellent dancer moving lightly to the music with obvious enjoyment. Only to make sure that no one mistook him for my uncle – or my father – I kissed him on the mouth as we danced. Were we not playing at Nymphs and Satyrs?

'Gosh, that was fun. I had no idea you danced so well.'

'It's ill-bred not to know how to dance,' he said rather old-fashionedly. 'Women like it. Is dancing a class thing in America too?'

'Here we go again. No.'

'No. I don't suppose it is here any more either. My mother taught me how to dance and countless other airs and graces.'

'How sweet, how quaint, how too too gracious!'

C. D. was silent for the moment, staring at me with the sightless eyes of an old man who had forgotten who he was or what he was doing. 'My mother was a lady's maid. She was the personal maid to her Ladyship at the Castle. I was allowed in the school-room with the other children because I was clever. That's the true story. Aren't you even surprised?' He was no longer looking at me but rather at the goods he'd delivered plop upon the table.

'Lady Daggoner mentioned something of the sort when she was being so surly to me amongst the roses. Not a lady's maid exactly but some dark mystery.'

C. D.'s face went ashen and his hand shook as he lit my cigarette. 'You're not playing the game,' he said grimly. 'English gossip isn't supposed to get back to the person it's about. Half a century of trying to cover one's tracks,' he sagged back into his seat. 'Stupid of me to imagine I was getting away with it because they didn't actually come right out and call me a liar to my face. I expect what's known as my denial factor must have been operating very strongly.' He smiled giddily. 'I feel so odd. What is it? My heart's pounding. Or is it the lack of drink? I feel drugged. I feel quite light-headed. As if I should enjoy confessing all manner of things.'

And he did. His father the footman and his mother the lady's maid. The new life beginning with the scholarship to Oxford, far, far away from the castle. The family emigrating to Canada taking with them the two trusted servants. His hatred and fear of women at first – his mother always correcting him, always catching him up. His bumbling attempts to become homosexual. His failure – not only because it was not his natural bent but because of his gradual realization that the Queer Set was the most snobbish and prying of them all. And so, aiming for solid accomplishment; studying hard: achievement. The double first. Fellow of Christ Church. The Professorship. The painful past receded. The present became almost comfortable. The surer he became the surer became his touch with women. Mistress succeeded mistress. Then the war. And precisely as he was trying to figure out how to bluff his way into a smart regiment without any credentials – irony of ironies, he was saved by his hobby – cryptography – the hobby stemming as did everything about him from his snobbishness and fear of discovery. His interest in cryptography dated back to all the notebooks he kept as a child and young man into which he meticulously wrote down the Done Thing – words, phrases, gestures, manners, reflexes (how his mother used to upbraid him for any slip) – all the minutiae that distinguished the Gentleman from the Not-quite – he wrote them all down in his own code in case the other children discovered them. And then, no longer trusting one code, he would invent another and another, until he became passionately interested in the subject – was finally considered an expert. Yes, wasn't it ironic that this expertise so ignobly born and shame-fully motivated should stand him in such good stead in the emergency of war, hurtling him into high places, carrying him right up to the rank of Brigadier General?

All this he told me as if in a dream, speaking of himself objectively as a third person. 'Portrait of an Englishman,' he finished, 'crippled by snobbery.'

'But if your friends knew all along and accepted you anyway, surely it means they didn't care.'

'They may not have cared, but I cared. Can't you understand that? You talk as if snobbery was a matter of logic. It's not. It's a matter of temperament. The pretence was necessary; I would not have wished to be accepted without it. The trouble is I don't care any more. All of a sudden after some fifty years, I don't care any more,' he said placidly, his face mellow, his hair shining silver in the phosphorescent light. 'It leaves a void.'

That I'm going to fill, I promised myself as we sat quietly together in the night-club, that distinguished old man and me. I was happy. I really love him, I thought. I really love this bad old man, though of course, I checked myself, remembering the money, I wish him dead as well. For there it was: C. D. stood in the way of my getting my money but – and here was the catch – my money stood eternally in the way of my getting C. D. For sooner or later he must find out who I was and then – And then what?

A girl began to sing. It was the same girl who'd been standing in front of us with her Negro boy-friend outside the Hitchcock film. Her voice was cool and pleasant and sexy. She was Jinkie Dallas I realized, that's who. I'd heard her half a dozen times in various clubs around New York. We were seated on a banquette one table away from the band. At the table next to us there suddenly materialized her boy-friend, alone and elegant in Italian silk. Now that too clicked. He was what's-his-name – the jazz musician. Blew a beautiful sax.

He looked at me and smiled. I smiled back. When the set was over he said as though merely continuing our conversation, 'So how did you like it?'

'Wonderful. I think she's wonderful.'

His grin broadened. 'I meant that movie.'

'Scared me to death. I had to leave.'

'Yeah, it was a gas.'

'Well, it knocked *me* out.'

'How about all that blood draining slowly out of the tub?'

I shuddered. 'I can't bear to watch the water running out of my bath any more.'

'Hell, I won't even go into the bathroom alone.'

'Thank God for somebody else,' I exclaimed gratefully. 'I thought it was only me being neurotic.'

Flash of white teeth. Mask of Comedy. 'When it comes to that, lady, you are looking at Exhibit A.'

'I'm Honey Flood,' I said. 'Exhibit Z.'

'Jimbo Jarvis,' he said and we shook hands.

'You going to be playing over here?'

'Nope. I'm taking a year off. Like about a month ago all of a sudden I stopped going to my analyst. I mean he was all right but he was getting too personal, you know?'

'Too personal?'

'Well, yeah. Like, he thought I should only take my break when he took his. You know? Like he's so involved in my life we can't make a move without each other. See what I mean?'

'Yes, I see what you mean,' said C. D. suddenly. 'I see exactly what you mean.'

'I mean that could be a bad hang-up – fixing my life to suit his. So I thought I'd cut out on my own and see how things looked. So I came over here.'

'Yes quite. I think you're absolutely right.' C. D.'s manner towards him was extraordinarily different from his usual starchy one. 'And what have you seen of our country since you've been here, Mr. Jarvis?'

'Not much. Guess I don't like to look at places I've already read about.' This last was delivered in a slow soul-searching tone without a trace of arrogance. 'You going to be here for another five minutes?' he asked, suddenly materializing on his feet. 'I'm going to hustle up Jinkie and maybe we can all have a drink together. O.K.?'

'Thank you very much,' said C. D. as he left. 'We'd like that.'

'Will you never stop surprising me?' I asked, rather annoyed. 'Why are you being so nice to him? Why aren't you prejudiced? After all he's coloured and you're supposed to be a snob.'

'Why? I can't think on what grounds to discriminate against him. His aspect is beautiful, his manners are his own and his bearing is that of a king. I'm a real snob. I only dislike people who are trying to be like me' – C. D. caught himself and gave the faintest hiss-hiss of his giggle – 'trying to be like I was trying to be. I only dislike in others what I dislike in myself,' he finished austerely.

Jimbo returned with Jinkie, a neat black contrast to her larger-than-life technicolor, and we had a drink together – except for C. D., still stubbornly sticking to mineral water.

'They're letting me off early tonight,' said Jinkie in her husky rusty voice, 'so let's split, huh, and make the . . . make the . . .'

'You want to come along make the scene with us?' asked Jimbo.

'Can it be done?' I asked. 'We've had six tries and this is the first decent place we've hit.'

'It ain't easy but it can be done.'

'Anyway, let's . . . let's . . .' said Jinkie.

'Finish your sentences, baby. Come on, now. Try. She won't finish her sentences. You know what the man said. Like it's an act of unconscious aggression.'

'Bullshit to that, baby,' said Jinkie.

'And so is that.'

'So what about you? You hate us aufays, don't you. Yes he hates us spooks. He puts down anything white so hard it's a joke. Awhile back they asked him on television what he thought of the Beat Generation and he said it was a lot of white shit. They went crazy in the control room.'

'Yeah, but at least I'm aware of it, baby. That's all I'm saying. I'm not kidding myself.'

'O.K., lamb. You got me coming and going.'

'So let's go.'

And out we went. They took us to a small jazz club with a very good quartet and I observed with pleasure that it was not only small and crowded but very hot which meant good pneumonia possibilities. I made a note of its name.

'I'm hungry,' said Jinkie finally. 'Let's go back to our pad and I'll . . . I'll . . . *cook* us something to eat,' she finished with a slow smile at Jimbo.

They lived off Notting Hill Gate. You went down a dark alley and up two narrow flights of stone stairs and along a dark passageway, pushed open a door and there it was – Fairyland: a large studio with a balcony running around inside it and leading off the balcony a bedroom whose windows overlooked a lush and secret garden. I left my coat in the bedroom and by the time I'd fixed my face and come down a rich aroma of cooking was wafting through the Studio. We sat down to a dish called Dead Horse, a savoury stew of minced meat and onions and kidney beans and several million kinds of delicious secret ingredients over which greedy Seedy made a lip-smacking pig of himself. Then the telephone began jingling and slowly the room filled with musicians in from their work. Marijuana was produced, rolled into cigarettes and silently passed around. The floral pattern of the oriental carpet made pekinese faces back at me. There were no chairs, only a few low divans and lots of cushions. 'Throw me a pillow,' said the musicians to each other by way of greeting. The gramophone played steadily. Dizzy, Miles, Jimbo, Ornette, J. J. and K. Jinkie appeared proudly with the newest model Mixmaster, plugged it in and began mixmastering carrots into carrot juice. The carrot shreds flew all over the floor.

'You want a vacuum cleaner attachment to go along with that machine to suck it all back in again.'

'I can't understand. It never did . . . it never did . . .'

Somebody lying flat on his back was flipping an elastic band trying to hit the overhanging ceiling of the balcony.

'You makin' it, man?'

'I'm working on it. He-ay, it just went *through*. Won't Jinkie be surprised when she finds a rubber band in bed with her in the morning?'

'Where'd you last come from?'

Pause. 'Venus.'

The gramophone kept playing, the marijuana smoke filled the room with a smell of autumn leaves and bonfires. I looked over to see how C. D. was taking all this. Yes, he was taking it. He was Dad and Daddyo for a while and once even Gramps but he was never less than charming, patting his silver lock, bubbling with interest, drawing them out in exactly the right tone: Kafka, Gide, Camus, Mexico, mescalin. It was extraordinary – this squarish, middle-aged upper-classy Englishman in the middle of a bunch of jazz hipsters; a sitting pigeon amongst the cats. They could have torn him to shreds with their ridicule but if there was any danger of this there was nothing in his manner that betrayed his awareness of it. They subsided into admiration and easy friendship; they dug his jokes.

'What do you do, Dad?'

'Do? I do nothing. I'm far too distinguished to do anything.'

'That's cool man.'

'Cool? The English invented cool.'

I'd been having some difficulty talking. Everything I said sounded like a Thurber cartoon. 'But music is your *life*,' I heard myself earnestly entreating Jimbo.

Jinkie by now had gotten the mixmaster to work properly and was mixmastering celery. Everyone turned out to be some kind of a health nut and they all began putting forward their pet health theories. 'Brewer's yeast – but it's got to be straight from the brewers, gal, you send away for it. Kent.' 'Honey and vinegar . . .' 'Skimmed milk.' 'Kelp.' 'Throw some spinach in with that celery, Jinkie. It's the greatest.'

'I used to drink too much,' one of them was telling me. 'Got all hung up on the sauce. Stopped showing up for my recording dates and that can be a drag. So they've got this pill, see, it's called Antabuse, you take one and it lasts four days. You try out even one beer during that time and you are *out* but bad. First sip and you turn bright red and it's like your ears are exploding, then palpitations, vomiting and a blackout. They give you this card to carry around with you, see, it tells the hospital how to bring you round in case you're crazy enough to try to booze in that time. I always have some on me' – he produced a pill box – 'just in case I feel tempted. I'm smart, see. I don't think I'm God.'

193

I reached for the pill box and took one out. 'Can I keep it, please?' I asked. 'I've been hitting the bottle pretty hard myself. I could use four days to get straightened out. Please. You'd be saving a life.'

'Well okay, but you gotta follow the rules. Take it first thing tomorrow morning and then absolutely no booze nowhere nohow for four days. You promise?'

'My solemn oath.'

'Remember what I said, gal. It's for real.'

C. D. had wandered off to a corner and was lying on one of the low divans. I went over and sat by him.

'It's beginning to take its toll,' he said dreamily. 'I ate too much and this jazz music is far too exciting. My heart keeps pounding. Or is it you? What are you doing to an old man like me . . . Shall we go?'

I stretched out beside him in a marijuana haze. 'No. I'm enjoying myself for the first time in ages. After all, I stuck through all those dreary parties you took me to.'

'I'm falling asleep,' he said petulantly. 'I wish I could have some coffee.'

There. He'd said it. 'I'll make you some,' I replied, my mouth dry with excitement.

As in a dream I went into the kitchen and heated up the coffee and dissolved the Antabuse tablet I'd been given into it. Then, as in a nightmare, I watched C. D. drink it. Now the thing was to give him some booze so the stuff would work. I took a couple of puffs on a stick of pot that was going the rounds for courage and poured out a glass of wine. I started over to C. D.'s divan but found I'd finished drinking the wine by the time I got there. I went back and filled the glass again but the same thing happened – I'd finished it before I reached C. D. – and then suddenly I was bolt awake in my bedroom in Dody's flat and it was four a.m. in the morning. I got up and looked out of the window at the still, silent moon shining on the pavement some thirty, forty feet below. *And let go*, I thought. Let go. Let him go, let go of this dangerous and disgusting situation. Splash, splosh, splatter. Train wreck, as we used to call that stewed tomato and rice slop we had at school. I opened the window wide and climbed on to the window-sill and sat there dangling my feet over the ledge. I stared down into the darkness at the pavement. Head first . . . or should I jump? And if I jumped maybe I should put shoes on so it wouldn't hurt so much when I landed on my feet. Well, it didn't matter. I'd heard you usually died from fright in mid-air. I closed my eyes and leaned forward and in that split second my heart began roaring up into my ears and the whole feel of falling filled every corner of my body. It was so complete a sensation it was almost as good as the reality but I gripped the sill and clung with all my might and it passed. I climbed quietly back into the room and when I got in bed I was sweating hot and cold in turns. Supposing anyone had seen me – how to explain that I was only kidding?

I rang C. D. early the next morning. 'Listen, don't touch a drop but not a *drop* of alcohol for the next few days. Someone at the party told me it was death to drink on top of marijuana for at least four days.'

'I never heard that.'

'Well but apparently this was a special kind of marijuana. No, I mean it. The man there told me and it was his stuff. That's probably why I passed out.'

'You certainly become drunk very suddenly these days. Actually all that talk about health has started me thinking. I'm going to take a nature cure for about ten days. There's a health farm in Kent that I occasionally go to. I thought of leaving this afternoon. What with one thing and another I've been feeling a bit seedy of late.'

'I think that's a good idea,' I forced myself to say.

'I shall miss you, my dear. Look after yourself.' He gave me the telephone number of the place and I promised to ring him if I felt lonely and he hung up leaving me with that desperate (I first wrote 'disparate'), violent (and that 'vilent'), *awful* mixture of relief and chagrin I was becoming so familiar with.

CHAPTER SIXTEEN

Get away from the scene then. Break up my morbid pattern of death thinking. Straighten out. Jimbo and Jinkie were going to Paris – Jimbo had changed his mind about not playing for a year – he was doing a guest spot for a week at one of the boîtes and they said why didn't I come along. The plane fare wasn't much; I figured that if I economized on things like washing my hair myself for a while and getting all my shoes repaired instead of buying the new ones I'd planned to, my budget could stand it. We could all stay at the house of some friends of theirs. But of course, getting my passport out and staring into the unsmiling eyes of the girl in the photograph called Betsy Lou Saegessor, I suddenly realized I wasn't going to be able to travel with them! The secret was too loaded to share with anyone. So I said I had things to do and joined them a day later.

Straighten out. But it wasn't any good. Every time I had a little too much to drink – which was every night as I listened to Jimbo blowing his beautiful sax, or went back to the house on the rue de la Seine where we balled it until morning (and where, incidentally, I was first turned on to deximyls, those peerless hangover cures), bad, killing thoughts of C. D. would rise again gripping me in their vice of iron. Because he deserved to die. Because he'd killed Pauly. Poor naïve, straight-forward little

American – how that bloody Englishman had driven her to suicide just as if he himself had put her in that car and locked all the doors and closed all the windows in that rented garage of that rented house on Long Island to which she'd escaped that summer hoping to recover from the suffering he'd inflicted upon her with his fake superiority – and he himself had turned on the engine. Well just let him try – let him *once* try coming on superior with *me*. And it was odd too because only the weekend before Pauly had surprised me by ringing me up after all these years and inviting me out to stay with her – I couldn't make it – but now, here was this damn Englishman, all his sins rewarded; in full criminal possession of *American* money, American money made by a hard-working decent self-respecting American to be squandered on all his evil English greeds – it was not to be borne! Knife him, poison him, sandbag him, the gentle pressure of two fingers at the base of his throat while he's asleep . . .

'Hello from Paris, dear Maestro, it's me.'

'Yes I know,' I could hear C. D. breathing heavily on the other end of the line, 'I've been ringing and ringing you. I finally got on to Dody and she told me. What are you doing there?'

'Looking at the rain.'

'So am I.' More heavy breathing. 'When are you coming back?'

'Tomorrow afternoon.'

'Good. What airline?' His voice sounded strangled.

'It's the B.E.A. seven-something-or-other. Wait a sec. Seven-one-five.'

'I'll meet you at the airport.'

'That's awfully sweet of you but why bother?'

'Because I'm in a hurry.'

'In a hurry? Why, where are you—'

'My God,' he exploded, 'do you understand nothing of lechery? See that you're on that plane.' And abruptly he hung up.

Well, I thought. Well, *well*.

I only had time to register that the C. D. of the airport was certainly not the C. D. of that long ago day at Paddington Station before he stepped forward and planted a big moist kiss hard on my mouth.

'You all right?' I asked. He looked terrible, all drawn and haggard.

'Dreadful. Didn't complete the course. The idea is to starve, irrigate and sweat the poisons out of you first and then when you're all weak and pure and empty gradually build you up again. Only I bolted before that part. They're furious and my system is furious, raging with headache and indigestion.' He pulled me towards him unbuttoning the top button of my coat and squeezed one of my breasts right there in front of all Gate Five. He gave a great sigh and seemed to relax. 'Can't be helped,' he said. 'One was simply not in the mood.'

I was feeling agreeably power-mad by now and decided he could do with a bit of a tease. 'Don't forget to give the driver my address,' I said perkily as we stepped into the car. 'I must touch base chez Dody and unpack and such like.'

'No. You're coming straight home with me.'

'Why?' I made my face look surprised.

'Because I want to do you. Right now.'

'You're awfully sure of yourself,' I murmured. 'Suppose I say no?'

'Ah darling, darling . . . if you knew how my guts were crawling.'

And well, I thought again. Well, well.

To be flung upon a bed – clothes pulled up, clothes pulled down, clothes pulled off every which way – to be the uniquely needed

199

object of a passion so strong that early on it passes you to go soaring endlessly off into an undreamed-of blue infinity. Isn't that what every woman wants to experience at least once in her life? Not her own fulfilment, not her own orgasm, delicate or lusty, but to be the conducting rod, the spring board from which rises this awe-inspiring fanatical motion. There was no question of my joining him that particular afternoon or even joining in. I must say he presented an interesting if rather alarming sight as I watched him reaching reaching reaching, his hair all mad and awry, his face bright red, veins standing out with strain, his breath fast, his mouth open and aghast. I lay very still, very soft, very open while his heart pounded and his sweat poured over me and finally believed what I had never believed before. That it could kill you. And, lovingly, I wished that he had died like that. I wish he had died that way.

CHAPTER SEVENTEEN

L ater that night, sitting at Maretta's, we recognized to our thrilled astonishment at the table next to us, and in the company of a man who was extremely drunk, none other than The Legend himself, magnificently carved out of granite. The next thing we knew the drunk had got ahold of one of the violins from off the bandstand and was wandering around the room sobbing as he tried to play it. Gently The Legend led him back to the table. 'It is his Magyar blood,' said The Legend turning to us. 'It comes to boil whenever he gets near violins. His second wife has left him.' Then with unparalleled simplicity and grandeur he introduced himself. 'I am a Legend in my own time,' he said smiling shyly, his eyes moist with modesty. 'The last of the kind they don't make any more.'

'Yes,' I breathed, 'I know.' And I looked at him in wonder seeing him so tanned and tough and fit, thinking of all he'd been through – the wars and revolutions, the plane wrecks and train wrecks and shipwrecks; the floods and famines and droughts.

'What does the name Annabelle Hunt conjure up for you?' he asked me.

'Nothing,' I gasped, still breathless from this brush with the Hall of Fame.

'Exactly. It is, however, the name of Hank here's second wife.

A movie starlet. One of her delusions is that she is a household word. I've got it!' he roared, suddenly startling me by banging his fist on the table and chortling with glee. 'A delusion of Annabelle Hunt's, is to think that she's one of the Lunts. Got it at last. Been working on it all night.'

Hank winced and ordered a double vodka.

'My dear friend—' The Legend shook his head sadly at this. 'Excuse me, pretty girl,' he said to me in what I took to be courtly international Who-Who-ese at which it was impossible to take offence, 'excuse me for horning in on your evening like this but I would like to use you in the little moral I am about to point out to our melancholy friend. Look here,' he said to Hank. 'Here is a girl fresh and lovely and well-groomed. And that fine gentleman with you, is it your husband? Ah – she laughs. What a fine laugh she has. You see? With every turn of the earth we are delivered up of delightful maidens, good and cheerful and adaptable. Will you and the distinguished gentleman who is enjoying your company join us in cracking a cool, clean, sparkling bottle of the best?'

Legendary as he was I could not help noticing that he was also slightly loaded but we joined them in a flash, C. D. as goggle-eyed as I by the encounter.

The Legend then proceeded in his Legendary way to deliver himself of pronouncements whose style varied from the leisurely rhythmic – 'That girl who was singing is good. She has it and she knows what to do with it and how to look while she is doing it, what to do with her voice and hands' – to the terse informative – 'Irish loony bins are the best in the world,' and I was exposed for the first time to the Royal You: the Royal You being as royal as the Royal We but more inclusive as it doesn't mean Me but – Us (and what could be more flattering?). Thus I learned that You always have a good ripe piece of dead stag or old ewe handy in the hard weather when You set up Your cage trap for hoodie crows.

'C. D. McKee,' The Legend was eyeing him thoughtfully. 'It tolls a bell. There was a British General in the last war with a name something like that.'

'Yes, that was me, but how on earth—'

'I had some dealings with British Intelligence then.' The Legend raised his glass. 'To the man who broke the German diplomatic code,' he pronounced.

'Helped break,' murmured C. D.

'Right you are. I'll go along with British understatement then. And' – glass aloft again – '*helped* invent the virtually unbreakable British diplomatic code after that punk of a valet in Turkey stole the dip code book from the British Ambassador. I know all about you.' Another slug of champagne rolled around his tongue approvingly. 'A fine toast to a fine and clever man.' The Legend's eyes moistened again with emotion.

We all sat around looking happy and proud and even Hank got his nose out of his double vodka long enough to aim a vast if unco-ordinated look of admiration in C. D.'s direction.

The Legend, it turned out, was marking time between legends for a week or two before he was off to the Middle East and, his friends in England being either dead or out of town, he was doing all his hunting, fishing and shooting in the Trophy Room of a magnificent house in Belgravia which the Duke of Something had loaned him (the Duke having prudently taken to the hills until it blew over) whither we eventually repaired.

The Duke's Trophy room was an arrangement with one part of a recessed wall revealing a shooting gallery and the rest hung high and low with various stuffed animals so peculiar in aspect as to make me wonder whether they had ever been real. For instance, there was a sort of buffalo who wore his *hair* parted in the middle and his horns very low, and the animal next to him was a sort of – I don't know what – but he wore his horns high and his ears low. These ears were so enormous that the effect (or maybe the truth) was that of a donkey with horns glued on. And then there was this thing which was, no kidding, no bigger than a mouse. With horns. A dik-dik, said The Legend, one of the most difficult animals for You to hunt of them all. This was a specially rare specimen. A *female* dik-dik. Then there was, let's see, Your usual sports paraphernalia: skis and fishing rods and all that; Your usual boxing cups and rowing cups and silver-framed signed photographs of old deposed royalty, and Your usual pair of huge over-sexed dogs who salivate and snuffle all over You until they have to be told down, Prinny, down, in order to save You from being hurled against the wall by them and impaled on the horn of a dik-dik.

It was not long after we arrived – some four whiskies after – that The Legend, having put on the gloves and done some shadow boxing (and almost connected with Hank stumbling across his path on his way to the bar), and a bit of fly casting, ambled over to the shooting-gallery and expressed a desire to shoot a cigarette out of C. D.'s mouth.

'I don't smoke,' said C. D. faintly.

'Why don't you just shoot the tops off those flowers in the vase, ha-ha?' asked Hank even more faintly.

The Legend was not amused. 'What is the sport in that?' he asked, enunciating carefully, and Hank, grey as an ash, realizing that shooting flower tops was one of the things You didn't do, took himself off to bed dragging his disgrace behind him.

The telephone rang. The Legend left the room to answer it.

'Extraordinary the way he stimulates one's hero-worship,' said C. D. 'I suppose like all legends he is irresistible though I never actually went through that phase myself. Think it's too late for me to start playing Huckleberry Finn to his Nigger Jim?'

'Listen—' I noticed I was drunk again. 'Listen, why don't you only let him shoot one little old cigarette out of your mouth? I dare you. After all it's just a shooting-gallery gun. He can't be a Legend for nothing.'

The Legend came back. 'Pepe's fighting six bulls in Saragossa on Sunday,' he announced cryptically. 'I should be there with him.' He worked out with some Indian clubs for a while and then sat down. 'More whisky?'

It was all wearing thin for me. Although I yielded to no one in my admiration of his genius I was getting tired of hearing great empty sentences like 'Normality has infinitely more variations than perversion' or 'A soup made of raw fish and vinegar; You have it first thing every morning' uttered in tones of such terrible finality. And C. D. sitting in rapt attention was beginning to worry me. All I needed was for the old man to pick up and go trailing off with The Legend to the Middle East or Saragossa. Yes . . . I was drunk. And searching the room for death traps. Go on, Mister McKee, put on the gloves and step into the ring with Mister Legend . . . Or: what better way to polish him off than to give Fatty a pair of skis and a pair of sticks and shove him down the side of the mountain. I sipped some more whisky. It was getting harder to concentrate. Split his head open with an oar. My head was splitting wide open with a roar.

'Shoot the cigarette out of my mouth.' It was me talking.

They both looked at me. 'What?'

'I said shoot the cigarette out of my mouth. Come on.' I had risen and was making my way towards the shooting gallery.

The Legend shook his head slowly. 'It is not a game to play with the ladies. It is too hard on them,' he declared. 'And you've had a little too much to drink as well.'

'But I'm dying to see you do it. And I don't mind. I'm not afraid. I trust you. Please.'

'I say, try it with me.' At last C. D. had spoken up.

I watched while they put C. D. into the shooting gallery. And I watched while they put a cigarette in his mouth and turned him profile. I watched while The Legend loaded the gallery gun and took his stance. Then quietly I tip-toed over to a wall and counted three. And then I yelled 'Ouch!'

The next sound I heard was the sound of the shot a split second later. And the next sound I heard was that of The Legend's hand as he slapped me hard across the face.

When I came to there was C. D., the broken cigarette still numbly clutched in his mouth, and The Legend towering over me in an ice-cold rage. 'I'm sorry—' I gasped, 'that horn – it almost went through the back of my neck, I couldn't help—'

The Legend dragged me roughly to my feet and the look he gave me sobered me up at once. 'Yes, you could,' he said slowly. 'What you did was deliberate. And what I did was deliberate. One deliberate act deserves another. What's the matter with you? I might have blown off his face.'

'Oh come now,' said C. D. 'I'm sure Miss Flood didn't mean to.' he trailed off weakly and pulled out the remains of the cigarette which still stuck to his lips.

The Legend turned and looked at him quizzically and then back to me again. He took my face in his hands and I thought for a moment he was going to hit me again but instead he pulled down the lower lids of my eyes and stared at them professionally like a doctor. 'Get rid of her,' he said to C. D. finally. He took a step back and I saw to my amazement that he was trembling. 'Get rid of her fast. Can't you understand that she's crazy?'

CHAPTER EIGHTEEN

Now a certain vagueness creeps into the narrative – a certain confusion as to the sequence of subsequent events. For instance Scotty suddenly showed up three days – or was it three weeks – later? And was that before or after C. D. had gone to the Daggoners' that weekend with Lady Mary and she made off with that fierce young man I'd met there called Michael Ward Bell? And exactly when was that great moment when I stood C. D. up? That was a landmark. And when did I start getting my regular supplies from that friend of Jimbo, the pill purveyor? I really don't know. It all comes under the heading of After That.

The Legend had said 'Can't you understand that she's crazy?' and After That there was C. D. comforting my weeping form in the taxi on the way back to Dody's and After That: Scotty's return. Scotty and Dody and Jimbo and Jinkie . . . well, I can't remember much of that but then: Scotty and *Jinkie*. Dody and *Jimbo*. That was the switch. Did Scotty take one look at Jinkie and – finding at last his hipster of all time – flip out first? Or was it after (or because of) Dody and Jimbo falling quietly, deeply and contentedly in love (she would sit for hours sketching his beautiful face)? Anyway, clever Mother Nature. Taking care of everyone. But me.

We all used to go out a lot together, Seedy and me and the other four. All the time. All those nights.

But the night finally came, a night strung on to our long luminous necklace of bumpy baroque-pearl nights so apparently endless I never dreamt that this particular night would be – at last – the clasp. It was a night, I mean, beginning so usually, so insignificantly, so like all the rest, I wasn't even looking when it happened.

We were in pretty bad shape by then, both Seedy and I. I was smoking the roof off my mouth. I had lost fifteen pounds and any interest in food. I ate about every other day. On the other hand I was drinking a great deal. Drink had become important to me, it kept me going for long stretches at a time, although in the end, passing out around every three nights as I did, it tired me dreadfully so that I was sleeping well into most afternoons. Actually I kept myself going on a blend of nicotine, caffeine, alcohol, barbiturates, stimulants and a modest use of narcotics (only four or five puffs per evening on the communal marijuana stick; never more than one spoonful of hashish jam at a time). After a while I was able to balance one stimulant or sedative against another (rather like Alice nibbling on the two sides of the mushroom that made her grow or shrink) with such deftness that, by a dash of this, a few grains of that and a puff of the other, I could play the most indescribably delicate airs on my psyche. Heard melodies are sweet but those unheard . . .! I cry now at their memory, blurred though they be. Sometimes I would arrange my pills neatly on my bureau top: dexedrine, deximyl, drinimyl, benzedrine, librium, seconal, veganin, etc., etc., anything I could get my hands on, in neat rows, spansules to the front in their pretty two-tone capsule-jackets; deep-green and white, or plum and bright-blue, the tiny pill grains of contrasting colours sparkling through the transparent celluloid; then the 'shorties', those heart-shaped 'happy-pills' of soft musty mauve, pale blue, or apple-green, with that faint incision down their middles; a scattering of the stark white bennies, and, finally, the vitamin pills – Vitamin C *forte* (just for the hell of it) tailored in chic yellow-and-brown costumes, and looking at them I would feel within them (or rather with *them* within *me*) the possibilities of a whole symphony. First movement: (gulp) Dexedrine: Allegro. Second movement: (slurp) Gin-and-tonic: Andante. Spansule . . . (pouf!) Minuet. Third movement: Benzedrine: Scherzo. Rondo and collapse. Ah, that scherzoid rag. Or how about going along with those programme notes for Beethoven's 6th? 'Awakening of Serene Impressions on Arriving in the Country': A soupçon of hashish jam? 'Scene by the Brook': A touch of drinimyl? 'A Merry Gathering of Peasant Folk': A couple of scotches. 'Thunderstorm': A couple of hundred more. 'Glad and Thankful Feelings after the Storm': A miltown and a seconal. I don't know. Something like that.

It was curious how this heightened state of emotion affected my lachrymal gland so that quite often while witnessing some perfectly ordinary event I would find myself – for no reason at all – surprised by tears. I would notice, for instance, a young girl all dressed up for a party getting into a car with her mother and father, all of them going off together, and the familiar stinging behind my eyes would begin. Or that cheerful, pregnant waitress at the corner Espresso always so pleasant to me: 'Afternoon, love. Saved you a bun. Bit soggy now – shall I heat it up?' Only that, and the sun shining through the windows on that particular corner of the street and pow! I was off again. Or a jar of honey at Fortnum and Mason's, a pretty blue jar of honey. Imagine! My sense of direction too had become weak – would desert me – would even work in reverse sometimes. I didn't know left from right any longer; didn't know up from down. At least I would ponder it for bewildered minutes in Harrods. I would be on the fifth floor and want the elevator to come and take me down. Did you push the *up* button or the *down* one? I must have known once, it was a thing I had done all my life. But I didn't know it now. I was always getting lost and having to ask for directions. Second turning on your right, they would say, and I would arrive at the second turning only to wonder – right? left? staring hopefully down at my hands waiting for them to yield up the answer.

Not that I was losing control. That was the funny thing. I was very much in control. It was as if I had so much *determination* on my mind I couldn't concentrate on anything else. And my whole determination, of course, was centred around C. D. For again I was becoming aware of his attempts to slip away from me. I seemed to feel it even before he did. Lady Mary's grey eminent shadow reappearing; that weekend with her in the country – saved by her bolting off with Michael Ward Bell – but wow – *close*. And at the same time, starting up slowly but gaining momentum, any amount of vague activity all pointing to a closing down of the interests of one side of Seedy's life and an opening up of others. Oh, there was nothing so definite as *packing*. Most of my clues I gathered from straining outside the kitchen door trying to overhear his conferences with Blake, catching the odd 'blankets to the cleaners and the morning room curtains too, I think,' and 'for that month of course shan't be needing' and 'not absolutely necessary to forward', until finally there was no doubt. Preparations for a journey. He was spending a whole month at the Daggoners'. From my point of view it couldn't be worse – the Daggoners were his most ardent pimps and the air would be lush with aristocratic young English girls. All those sad young gels. Oh no you don't, C. D. Oh no you don't. And pit myself against those languid dreamy *real* heiress-kooks? I wasn't having any of that. The only thing to do was somehow to keep him in my power and under my eyes and weak. But how weak? That was the question constantly exciting my imagination. I had satisfied myself by now that the idea of actually trying to kill him was a purely puerile prank playing itself out strictly between myself and my fantasy even if sometimes it ran away with me, and there was that constant Deathbed scene which I spun over and over again, working myself from a kind of sick frenzy into an orgy of wild weeping.

You are probably wondering at this point why I didn't spirit him away completely from the temptations of the Island – from the English climate, the pretty leafy English squares and pretty leafy English girls, or Bread Sauce or Detachable collars, or the English railway dining-car smell, or the Arsenal-Manchester Cup Final or English sex scandals, or the Caste System, or whatever it is the Briton is supposed to hold so dear – and carry him off to some other country, some cannibal isle where I could eat him in peace, where at least I could have him and his money – dammit, *my* money – to myself. And in many ways this presented itself as the only logical solution. After all he did love travelling. At that time, however, I was hard at practising on myself the complicated perversity of worrying about why my true identity had *not* been discovered all this while; worrying why the faces on the streets *didn't* happen to be those of American schoolmates. I took this as a sign that Providence was giving me a break, at the same time warning me that the safer it had allowed our known route and rut to become, the unsafer it would be to step outside the magic circle. Added to that were all the technical difficulties that would be caused by my real name on my passport and the hotel registrations, and all the endless subterfuges against outside circumstances which I knew I was by then *too concentrated on him* to deal with effectively. And what other unknown dangers might not be lurking in foreign lands? He knew every place and he knew everyone everywhere; it was his business to know, as he had once put it to me. Except for America. I often wonder what would have happened if it had ever been possible – setting aside the gigantic risk it involved me in – for us to have gone to

America together. Of course the question can never be anything but academic. For even if I had taken my courage in both hands . . . and . . . and what else? Worn dark glasses solidly year round? Hidden in the Hills of Forest or the Heights of Brooklyn? Informed every friend and acquaintance and the mailman of my deception? Even if I had had genius enough to work out some system, the bottom of the trouble was still old McKee. I mean he never would have gone. The New World, as we all know by now, represented to him a denial of everything he held sacred. It was a personal slap in the face to him – smug snob, poor, square, demented Esquare, ugly old obsolete monster. No wonder it became so important for me to ki— to destroy him.

But what I find now, thinking it all over, is that the *real* and *final* reason The Rape of C. D. (good idea for a painting) never took place was that, for what for want of a better word I shall have to call our 'affair' to remain at its healthiest (by that I mean of course at its unhealthiest), it was absolutely necessary, as Jimbo would have put it, for us to make the scene in England and nowhere else, absolutely essential for C. D. to be constantly under the surveillance of his friends, always within hearing distance of their well-meant-never-listened-to advice and politely put objections. How he preened himself every time he heard 'Poor old McKee. Making the most frightful ass of himself over that young American. She's got him quite besotted.' And what about the young American? Wasn't *I* making the most frightful ass of myself over him? Spoiling the best years of my life – well, one of them, ruining my health, throwing away my 'chances'? All to devote myself to dragging the old satyr around from night-club to dreary night-club.

Then his attempts to get off the hook and wriggle away from me as fast as his tormented body could crawl: it was around five in the afternoon, C. D. in one of his critical moods, surveying the furniture and myself with something less than admiration. He rang suddenly for Blake and I thought oh-oh we're in for it.

'Don't you think it might be a good idea to bring the tea in now?' he inquired irritably. And in answer to Blake's look of surprise at a demand for a repast which now Seedy never partook of: 'Yes, tea. You do still know what the word means I suppose?'

A bad sign; an anti-myself sign whenever he was feeling 'traditionally English'. I sat and waited and watched while C. D. paced up and down irately pursuing the notion that our tealessness was due solely to a churlish staff 'sitting out there in the kitchen eating their heads off without a thought for anyone else.' I was reminded horrifically of the old loon's ungraciousness on my first visit to his house.

Presently he sat down and gave it to me straight: His high blood pressure. The highly excitable, exciting nature of the life he was leading with me wasn't good for it. Frankly, it kept his bowels in an uproar, it led to indigestion, it would lead, unless the utmost care was taken, to a recurrence of that awful amoebic dysentery of some five years past. Then: his wretched, wrenched knee-cap (when was *that*? – oh yes, that day we went to look at the Rolls and he fell out of the car). It was causing him to limp, which was throwing his spine out of line, and this was promoting – any minute now – a slipped disc. How beautifully organic his troubles grew, one out of the other! Executing a stunningly graceful arabesque he managed to connect his hacking morning cough with his split lip (pulling tobacco off it after cigarette shooting incident) and banged fingernail (forgotten how). Oh dear – how could one not feel sorry for him? It would be only doing the decent thing to leave him alone for a spell, to turn him out to pasture and let him graze there peacefully awhile before the big push. Passionately, plaintively, pathetically he continued, delving deeper and deeper into the sources of his illnesses, looking so romantically *awful* that particular day, enfolded in his skin rather like a sick turtle, that even though I was not always attending closely I was relenting; my heart was melting. Then with a jolt I caught something he said. For two weeks now he had felt his hands too unsteady to trust himself shaving – he had given himself some fearful gashes with the razor (a frisson went through me at the great opportunity missed: a slice through the jugular vein and wouldn't *that* have done it just!) and had therefore been forced to employ the *daily services* of Bunty Suffolk's special barber. So for two whole weeks he'd been throwing away my good money on luxurious kicks for his private pleasure. That was a spine-stiffener.

Then, a hiatus. For two whole days (I think) everything was still. I had the very definite feeling of coming to the end of a phase. I felt positively surrounded by an urgency to sit down and reorganize my whole approach. Every sign, every portent, every bone in my body warned me of danger and yet no sooner would I try to grapple with it, to plot and plan, than I would find myself slipping off into that day-dream I mentioned earlier: The Death-bed fantasy. Briefly: C. D. on a high white bed, his hands playing weakly with the coverlet. His friends anxiously around him. I am not there – but I am watching it all the same in the manner of dreams. He has been run over, fatally wounded, trying to cross the street to get to me on the other side. Or thrown from a horse trying to impress me with a jump. But I am never more intimately connected with his death than that. I mean he wasn't trying to save my life or anything (thus absolving me from the guilt of having in any way delivered the *coup de grâce*).

Gradually, as his hour approaches, C. D. begins talking (about me of course) and then, as the wings of the Angel of Death beat about his head in earnest, I arrive to hear his last words – always the same ones whatever else varied in the dream: 'To think that I have wasted years of my life,' he gasps, 'that I have longed for death, that the greatest love I have ever known has been for a woman who did not please me, who was not in my style.' And with that he expires. And these words would strike me as so unbearably sad and beautiful and true that I always ended in tears.

Suddenly, in the midst of my weeping one day, I took out the sentence and looked at it squarely. That it had a strong literary ring I had of course been aware. This in itself was not unusual, I was constantly dreaming me into the heroines of my favourite books. What was maddening that day was that so far I had been unable to identify the quotation. I tried again. Not Shakespeare at any rate, I couldn't jam it into the iambic pentameter for one thing. A Brontë? The elegiac mood was right but the word 'style' no good. Austen? 'Style' O.K. but mood wrong. A translation? Ah-ha, I felt – getting close. And then I got stuck at Chekhov. I gave up, wiped my eyes, and tried concentrating on the problems at hand when all at once, for no reason, I switched my literary inquiry to France and got it in one: Proust. My old friend Swann about Odette. I rose from the bed upon which I'd been lying and began walking around the flat in my excitement. In a flash I saw everything. As if I had read it yesterday I recalled that section in which Swann falls irrevocably in love with Odette at the precise moment that she does not show up where he expected her to be. My path became clear. I saw how I had been blundering. I had been pressing C. D. too hard. Pressuring him. No wonder he thought in terms of escape. Was it too late or could I, by simply following the text verbatim, still save the day? The more I thought of Swann and Odette the more it seemed right. 'To think that I have wasted years of my life . . .' How marvellous!

Now, let's see. We had no Verdurins but for a favourite trysting salon Maretta's would do. I rang up C. D. and suggested we meet there that night. Latish. (A more witching hour.) And in a voice full of deception I told him I had things to do before but if

I hoped it would arouse his jealousy I was wrong. He sounded faintly relieved, replied that he also had things to do and went me one better by adding it would have to be a quick drink if I didn't mind. Of course I didn't mind, I said, grinding my teeth. 9.00 then? Fine.

Would he fall for this preposterous scheme? Really, why should he? It was so arbitrary; so something I'd read in a book. He might conceivably – barely conceivably have been a Swann, but I was in no sense Odette. And that point cannot be stressed enough. To put it at its strongest: I might have participated in her every adventure, practised her every vice, and still I would not have been Odette. For one thing, I was no femme fatale, no trained courtesan; neither a Lorelei, nor an enchantress, nor a witch. I had no feeling for, and absolutely no belief in, the extra-mystical powers of my femininity. I was (yes, indeedy, I still am) a plain ordinary American girl. All-right-looking; all right – even good-looking, attractive when well groomed, but in an entirely *unreminiscent* way. Looking at me one didn't suddenly (or even at leisure) recall the Zipporah of Botticello 'which is to be seen in one of Sistine frescoes', nor yet a Tanagra figurine. If I reminded one of anything else it was merely of other American girls. I was, I repeat, nothing special. Only determined. I was that. Hey, am I a new type to history? Betsy Lou Saegessor, girl cad? And a far cry from the Green Hat, a farther and even fainter cry from the Verdurins and that glamorous Côté de chez Swann. But would C. D. seeing Maretta's bare of me feel his heart wrung by a sudden anguish? Would he shake with the sense that he was being deprived of a pleasure whose intensity he began then for the first time to estimate?

Would he, by all that was reasonable, behave like someone in a novel I had read?

I don't quite believe it myself but here's what happened. About an hour after I was supposed to show up at Maretta's the phone began ringing at Dody's – I was sitting there filing my nails – and continued ringing at about half-hour intervals through the night (I'd made Dody and Jimbo promise not to answer it). At ten the next morning, a wild-eyed Seedy staggered round, took my hand in his and said, 'Please let me hold on to you for a minute and catch my breath. It gives me the temporary hallucination that you're here.'

'I'm sorry I missed you last night,' I said nicely. 'Some friends of mine came in from New York and we didn't get around to Maretta's till about eleven and by then you'd gone.' (I checked his departure with Jinkie.)

'But where did you go? I looked for you everywhere.'

'You probably just missed me. We had a few drinks here and there and actually I got back quite early. I was dead beat.'

'But I rang and rang. I was frantic. I thought something had happened to you.'

'Guess I didn't hear. When I'm that tired nothing wakes me up.'

I could see he didn't believe me. And I was dimly perceiving through the layers of artificially created excitement drawing us both into its coils that it soothed him *not* to believe. It Made the Situation. There was no longer any need for him to draw on his own resources to endow us – to endow his desire for me – with truth. In that night's search for me his taste had indeed become 'exclusive'. And he was again feeling the 'insensate agonizing desire' to possess me.

He was looking at me, his eyes welling with affection, gently clasping me to him in the way I had seen him clasp certain of his favourite objects – so mildly – as though making his peace with his love for them, his face totally devoid of cynicism, assuming in its harmony of concentration an ineffable tenderness; a kind of ruined beauty. Never had his inability to deal with life seemed so touching.

I behaved solicitously towards him. I leaned forward. 'Would you like something to drink?' I asked.

'Would you – would you mind dreadfully—? It's been such a shock. I feel quite faint. I don't think I could stay here another moment. Won't you come back to my house with me? But anything you like.' His grip tightened on my hand and he spoke with a panting mixture of anxiety and anticipation. 'Everything you like.'

Pe-pp-pl-auck!

(That's the sound of the string breaking in the Cherry Orchard; a sound heard round the world.)

The morning after that I awakened to find myself in his guest room. It was the first time I had been permitted to stay overnight; stretching under the softest linen, being served a breakfast from the most delicate china with the tiniest roses, of the most aromatic coffee, golden strips of toast, the spiciest marmalade, the best butter; a tiny vase of field flowers; the phrase in clover, in clover, clovered.

I was in clover. 'In clover!' I said it out loud in my joy, snuggling into the fluffy goosequill pillows, elatedly contemplating the shining miracle of the love that *Proust's* magic so unbelievably had wrought. Proust – that's where the little stab of disappointment, the tiny twinge of shame even, came worming through the triumph and causing me to sigh 'Only I can't really take credit.' It was like following some childishly simple recipe and ending up with a perfect soufflé. And it wasn't only myself I was disappointed in. I was disappointed in C. D. as well. More, I was furious with him. Didn't he know a Literary Allusion when it hit him in the face? Served him right then. He'd have to take what he got. By the time I'd gotten dressed my confidence had wavered to the point where I found myself desperately wishing I was Odette. I more than wanted to – I *had* to be to keep the magic potent. To stay in power (as I combed my hair) meant to stay in Character. And I wouldn't have to look too closely at what I was doing. (Drop a deximyl into mouth.) How convenient to be someone who disappeared into the printed page. I know this is the printed page, but I'm talking about – dammit – you know. I looked at myself closely. Might I not have become 'reminiscent of a Botticelli' overnight? Nope. I combed my American hair and lipsticked my American mouth. I tried to remember what Betsy Ross looked like as I went downstairs (or what she'd done).

C. D. in the morning. Still under the spell (very powerful). 'Let's go shopping. I want to buy you a present. You come with me. I've thought and thought and I don't know what you'd like.' We bought me a beautiful Georgian pin like the one we'd seen at the Antique Fair. I always wear it.

Moving from Odette, to Lady Brett, to Scarlett. Who shall I be today? (Oh, surprise me, I said to myself.)

'*You* remind me of Rembrandt,' I said to C. D., 'I always tell you that. Don't I remind you of anyone? You know, paintings and so forth? Goya, Manet, Degas, Modigliani? The Coca Cola girl? You never say? I feel shapeless.'

He shook his head and laughed. 'You are the perfect shape for expressing yourself.'

Ah – how often I repeated that to myself. So it was me – the me-ness of me – he loved after all.

Shape. Where was I? Oh, yes. Shape. That's what I was saying at the beginning of all this. We were in pretty bad shape Seedy and I when that night came. We had been going it some, hadn't we? I had inoculated Seedy. I had finally given Seedy the disease of love. I was plenty aware he was stricken with love as a disease and the one thing I could not afford to do was to allow him to get well. It wasn't his 'well' state, this love for me. I knew his well state. It was robustly malicious at the Daggoners' or exchanging snobbisms with Lady Mary – or tormenting poor Pauly. Now it was he who was being tormented. The game had become for both players. And when they shook their heads at the club and said 'Poor old C. D.' they said it with alarm now and without a trace of indulgence. He had become Seedy. Everyone thought I was bad for him except C. D.

'I am in love with you as the earth revolves around the sun. If I don't see you every few hours I shall take to my bed and have one of those wasting diseases people died of in Victorian novels.'

He had a way of getting things upside-down. Brushing aside the pretty sentiment I was perfectly aware that the truth lay really in the opposite direction – that if he stopped seeing me he would be well in no time.

The thing that kept me going was momentum. The train was moving too fast for me to jump off. There would be no next stop. I'd have to wait for the crash. The only way I can explain it is to ask you to observe how often a child learning to ride a bike will ride it straight into a hedge or a tree to stop it rather than try to jump off or use the brakes.

CHAPTER NINETEEN

I have said about that night that it was a night like all the rest, a night beginning so usually I wasn't even looking when it happened. But going back over it now I can see in how many ways this was not in the slightest true. For one important exception, a heavy fog had folded us up into its cold grey blanket. For three days we'd groped and gasped our way through a London from which streets, pavements, cars, even buildings and people had been quietly erased. A London no longer a city but a great cold, glowing field where the refraction of the street lamps, unable to pierce the opaque fog, none the less lit up the vast loneliness with an eerie yellow glow.

That's it! That's what I've been missing unremembered until this very moment: a taste in my mouth. I want that taste in my mouth. A taste of fog. A taste of C. D. Music in my mouth. And smoke. Alcohol, dope and desire. A taste of dry breathlessness under my breath. A taste of lung, liver and rusty blood. But above all, the particular taste of London air.

Maybe it was the London air. I'm sure it's unhealthy. At least it had an unhealthy effect on me. Yes I'm sure it did. Or was it foreign air? Air foreign to my nostrils. If all the magic pills and potions I was pouring into my stomach could have such an effect on me – why not get sent through all the orifices? Man is not fed through the stomach alone. Was that what was releasing all my wildness? A whiff through the nose, a taste on the tongue? All right, I was wacky. I was cracking up, but I'll never be the same again as in that litmus-paper state where if you held my hand in yours for a minute your imprint was on me for ever, where my shadow permanently stained the wall, where the air was real and active, tactile, writhing all around me. And when I say London air I am not talking about the fog, which of course was the exaggeration, the stirring up, the pouring out, the laying it on thick. I'm talking about the ordinary everyday London air, lying low through September and October, pretending anonymity, only to rise in November, pungent and dangerous. Come to think of it, it was C. D. that pointed it out to me. He sniffed the air and said, 'Now it's beginning to smell like London again,' and when I asked him what he meant he said that for instance Paris smelled like apples and French cigarettes and Seville like rancid olive-oil and hair-oil and Barcelona like decaying bodies and bull sweat. London, he said, smelled of a well-bred mustiness of old newspapers boiled with vegetables. But I thought it had an evil smell. I know it did: The Sulphur Fumes of Hell; particularly apparent during fog.

And I must say that in my exaggerated state of Anglophobia I was quite happy to see London given a good mud-bath. It meant the gods were angry too. It meant I had Satan on my side, belching out great spills of sulphur fumes from his Underground. (What the authorities couldn't seem to grasp with all their nonsense about smokeless zones and put-out-the-coal-fires was that *these gases were shooting out of the ground* – not descending upon them from the sky.) Dear old London, my cosy old chimney-pot.

But back to that night. Satan was pumping fresh waves of smog steadily into the already besieged city. (If you don't think that fog is caused by supernatural powers then why is it able to penetrate *walls*, I'd like to know, a trick neither the wind nor the rain seems to have mastered.) We had gathered at C. D.'s house that night, Jimbo, Dody, C. D. and I, staring greyly at each other's grey outlines in the fog-filled drawing-room. Not a night to venture forth in, you would think. But I who had made my pact with the devil longed to be abroad in his weather. I always like to be out in emergency weather, blizzards and thunderstorms and heat waves and things; and that wandering around in a bad fog would do C. D.'s health no good barely influenced my decision. As a matter of fact we all wanted to go out. We'd been out every night before, that week. Been out and come back and stayed up and stayed overnight at C. D.'s. Always the four of us. It was like a kind of house-party in Limbo.

I see the tableau in the softly greying room: for the past hour no one had really spoken – that is, no one had said anything that required either comment or answer. Jimbo always sat, or rather stretched himself out, on a sofa, feet straight ahead, relaxed but not properly collapsed, so that there was a triangle of air between the straight line of his back and the angle of the sofa. I could stare for hours hypnotized by that triangle of space. My eyes might wander over the contours or rather the flat planes and surfaces of his body, but they would always return to that spot. The essence of the Jimbo silhouette was that it defined the things around him – as a bird defines space. That was Jim – on the wing. Jimbo would sit in a chair (he would sit the same way on anything, even a bench), and the chair was what you would see. With C. D. it was the opposite. He sat only in armchairs, and only the best ones at that. He had a way of placing himself in a straight-backed chair and looking so uncomfortable – not unhappy, too obvious, uncomfortable – that he was immediately offered the best chair in the room: a gift he would accept without any modesty, and the chair would snuggle up lovingly around him. It was on C. D.'s upholstered body that the eye rested, rather than on the chair's.

Jimbo on the sofa, C. D. in the chair and Dody curled at his feet looking lovingly at Jimbo. C. D. was stroking Dody's soft brown hair. I was bolt upright, very uncomfortable, near the fireplace, arms and legs akimbo. I was trying to teach myself yogi for I was beginning to feel I was heading straight for Nirvana by a short cut and that I ought to get in a few basic exercises for the sake of authenticity.

I watched C. D. stroking Dody's hair. He twirled a soft brown feathery curl idly over his thumb. It was so domestic. Father and Daughter. Family Portrait. A thought struck me for the first time: he would have made a wonderful father, miserable wretch. Now, I know at this point the brightest boy in the class is going to jump up – that is if he hasn't already – and yell Oedipus at me. But he wasn't anything like my father. My father was fair-minded, just, stern, and unforgiving; dignified and austere. Seedy was prejudiced, rollicking, monumentally greedy (and covetous and avaricious and eager and hungry).

Oh.

Or isn't that what they mean?

C. D. sighed, looking at us three, and said, 'Mes enfants. Mes enfants du Paradis. What shall we do tonight?'

Dody stretched and yawned. 'It feels like that play that *always* takes place in a cottage on the moors with a stranger coming in from the fog.' She yawned again.

'Let's go see if there's one on,' said Jimbo without moving.

I leapt to my feet. My legs were throbbing with pain. 'Shouldn't we phone them first?'

'My dear girl,' said C. D. 'You wouldn't have heard about it of course but our London theatres remained open during the entire last German attack. You don't think we'd allow anything as usual as fog to close them up, now do you?'

'I meant of course,' I replied sweetly, 'that maybe they won't have any seats.'

'That is not what you meant. Don't attempt irony. It doesn't become you.'

'What does?'

C. D. shifted his eyes from their vagueness and focused them on me for a long moment. 'Naïveté,' he said finally, deep out of his old man's wisdom. That is exactly what he said. I remember it now. Was he warning me? I remember making the mental note: Yah, you wait, C. D. old Seaweed. I won't seem so naïve when you finally find out what I— But I anticipate.

'If we are going to the theatre I want to see the one with all the Dames in it,' said Dody suddenly. 'At the Haymarket. What's its name again?'

But C. D. didn't know. And C. D. didn't care. For C. D., bless his proper heart, subscribed to the notion that the upper classes attend theatre only to see American musicals. And though, as an Intellectual as well, he might be allowed to 'send' himself off from time to time to the various Art Theatres to 'report back' on these events to his non-theatre-going friends, he never under any conditions referred to – or even knew – the actors by their actual names. He was, nevertheless, most generous in his praise of them: 'That awfully good chap plays the father. You know, the one we're always seeing in the cinema.'

So he sent for that inveterate theatre-goer, his man Blake. 'We want to go to the theatre, Blake. The play with all the Dames. What did you think of it?'

'Oh very good, sir. Excellent. Very well spoken, if I may say so, to my way of thinking. Of course it's a *British* play – begging your pardon, Miss – so it was a bit easier for me to follow than most of what we see nowadays. Of course it's not a musical.'

'We didn't expect it to be.'

'Ah, then you won't be disappointed, sir.'

'Well, go on.'

'I hardly know what else to say, sir. When the curtain rises Dame Edith Evans and Sir Ralph Richardson come down from town looking very discouraged—'

'Who the devil are they?'

'Those are the leading actors, sir.'

'I supposed they were but who are they as characters?'

'I don't rightly recall their names.'

'I mean what do they do?'

'Why they're the Duke and Duchess. They live in the country somewhere. Great Missenden, I believe – Yes,' said Blake brightening, 'there're several very good jokes about that. They've been complaining about taxes and having to sell' – he broke off laughing reminiscently – 'that's a very funny bit there. When—'

'I'm sure you don't want to spoil it for us,' said C. D.

'And then, sir, Dame Peggy Ashcroft – I beg your pardon, I'm afraid I've forgotten her name in the play too – she's Her Grace's sister been away for ten years in some sort of trouble, you see.'

'What did she do?'

'I'm not quite sure, sir. They talked about it but they kept going round in a circle, if I make my meaning clear. I mean, sir, they don't come right out and say what it actually was. They keep being interrupted by the housekeeper whose daughter – that's Dame Sybil Thorndike – (the housekeeper, I mean, not the daughter) – anyway, the daughter has become a film star. She returns in the nick of time – you know what film-stars' salaries are and – oh – there's a very sad part where she's supposed to marry Sir John Gielgud – he's the visiting diplomat and they've become engaged during the play – but nothing comes of it. She breaks it off.'

'Thank you, Blake,' said C. D. dismissing him. 'It all sounds very distinguished, I'm sure.'

And out we surged into the night.

I had expected from Blake's description to be positively dazzled by the display of osprey feathers and satins and tiaras. I was completely unprepared for a stage set of unparalleled dowd upon which a succession of actors and actresses dressed in muted monotones appeared to be vying with each other in bleakness. 'Where be your English love of pomp and circumstance now?' I whispered to C. D., who told me to shut up. And at that moment the fog rolled on to the stage obscuring them entirely.

'Very well spoken' had been Blake's verdict, and as the players dimmed I began to appreciate the judgment for I could still hear their tones, clear bells piercing the gloom, though I was not always sure from whose mouth they were coming; beautiful sounds, comforting sounds – sea-bells tolling us safely to shore. The fog rolled on into the audience. The fog bound them together. And I felt my foreignness all over again. The people in the audience – except that they were slightly better dressed – looked exactly like the people on stage. C. D. was sitting there rapt. It upset me.

'Really for me it was like seeing a Chinese play,' I said angrily later. 'Beautifully done, exquisitely done, but goodness, they're all so *stylized*. Don't tell me people are really like that.'

'Perhaps they are,' snapped C. D. 'Perhaps some people are what you'd call stylized. Civilized people.'

'C. D., you loved that silly play. You adored it. Admit it. You found it positively r-r-rrripping!'

'I thought the actors behaved quite accurately. I thought the observation was exact. Yes, I was impressed. Where do you suppose they learned it all? Don't they all go home to their bed-sits in Paddington and cook over gas-rings and that sort of thing? I hardly suppose the grand ones do nowadays but didn't they when they first began? Touring the provinces and living in digs.

'What did you think of it?' C. D. asked Jim.

Jimbo thought for a moment. 'Jejune,' he said suddenly. 'Jejune in January,' he sang. And then he thought it over some more. 'On the one hand Sir Ralph's toupee the frowsiest yet, on the *other* Dame Edith had more patches on her gardening jacket.'

'But Dame Sybil's was the baggiest—'

'And Sir John had the oldest tobacco pouch.'

'Where shall we go?' said C. D., giving us up. 'Not too far, I'd like to get some sleep for a change.' There was no doubt. The play had stirred the England, My England! in his bones.

But I had another worry. A big one. The fog to my horror was lifting. Why couldn't the four of us have stayed as we were alone in our crater of the moon?

'Want to fall by Ronnie Scott's?' said Jimbo.

'No,' said C. D.

'What was the name of the new one we heard about last night?'

'The Zazou.'

'How far is it?' asked C. D. yawning. 'Can we see our way to walking there?'

Then they all noticed it too.

'The fog is lifting,' I said. 'We can see our way everywhere.' And sadly I watched the Haymarket emerge, buildings solidify themselves by our side, pavements redefined. At Piccadilly Circus the traitor Eros reappeared. I saw the atmosphere thinning out, breaking up into long kites of smoke and rise rushing high into the sky, wantonly deserting me. Satan had other fish to fry.

'I think this is it,' said C. D. suddenly and stopped and I positively jumped. No, it's not hindsight – I really thought then that he was on to me. My nerviness I suppose that night was not solely caused by premonition, but by his increasing irritability. But he only meant the street that the club Zazou was in.

A new place. Not only to us but to itself, as I sensed instantly upon entering by its hopeful air: it still held its head high. It could still be excited by the idea of itself. Emptiness, cynicism, bounced cheques, the book accounts, the protection racket, run-ins with English licensing laws hadn't yet set in. A French proprietor. Downstairs in a cellar. Halfway down the stairs I paused and looked into the faces. Young people. I didn't know any of them or their faces or their type. They were neither bums nor poets nor beat-bunnies. 'Come along,' said C. D. crisply, pulling at my arm. 'They're French, that's all. A lost colony of French students.' So that's what all the noise was – French. And the behaviour too – French.

'The weather hasn't dampened their spirits,' Jimbo noted.

'Three hundred exhibitionists and not one voyeur,' said C. D. uninterestedly. 'It's damp,' he added complainingly. He was rallying all right. My ear perked up. This was the old C. D. clamour. This was not the docile fossil I'd been leading around by the nose, any more.

The place was damp, though. That was the main thing. And the dampness of the cellar produced a nice thick muggy throat-catching atmosphere almost as good as fog that made everything cling and clog and get stuck to everything else. The smoke we poured out of our mouths poured itself back into our hair and clothes; in our ears and up our nostrils. Our eyes stung so much that after five minutes tears rolled down our cheeks whenever we opened them. In addition, they'd given us a tiny table in the corner under the staircase where we sat jammed stuck together on a bench with about a quarter of an inch of seat apiece, dripping with sweat and drinking fast to make up for the liquid we were losing. C. D. for good measure was squashed directly into an airless hole formed by the overhanging staircase. It was a good strong crowd there that night, I noticed professionally, through my tears. These healthy French students had plenty of staying power. The ones that weren't going to bed together at their tables were going to bed together on the dance floor where they stood writhing and swaying to the not very good jazz combo; a tightly packed herd whose docility would have been the envy of any sinking submarine's commander (such was the claustrophobic thought gripping me as I noticed we were windowless, sinking fathoms deep into the sea). I took three quick swallows of my drink and rubbed my leg against C. D. for reassurance. He was not enjoying himself. Zazou, zazou, I said to myself until it clicked. Jazz. French for hip. The few that were really dancing were putting on a display of squaredom you don't often see nowadays – jitterbugging and jigging and flinging themselves violently against each other in the most outlandish way. 'Ils ne sont pas très zazou.' That's what I would say to C. D. I rehearsed it in my mind for a while for my French had been very good in school and he liked me to have these little accomplishments.

'Ils ne sont pas très zazou,' I finally said.

'Za-*zoo*, za-*zoo* – not za-zeuh!' he flung back at me in a rage. 'Where did you get that frightful pansy French accent?' It was the last thing he said before it happened. But there was that in the tone sufficient to make me think to myself that my Odette days were possibly numbered, n-u-m-b-e-r-e-d. And then the lights went out and a floor show began that simply wiped that and everything else from my mind. A man was hypnotizing a chicken. It's relative of course. It's a matter of degrees of un-reality. First there was the unreality of us four together in the unreal London fog in a French night-club. That would be painted on the canvas: C. D. and I crunched together down in the right-hand corner of the painting, Jimbo and Dody on the left, peering round people's heads at the floor show. Now, punch a hole in the middle of the canvas and behind that hole we have the real unreality: the man hypnotizing the chicken.

Always alarmed by the presence of unexpected animals in

unexpected places as, for example, a seal in the bathtub, I was literally hypnotized with fear by the man hypnotizing the chicken. The man was pale, more than middle-aged, and looked as if the act wasn't often in demand. I wondered how he'd gotten into it in the first place. And what had made them book it in there? And where they ate and slept, the man and the chicken? Together? Most certainly.

It is the only animal act of which I remember every searing second. First, the man hypnotized the chicken (I suppose we must take his word for it), then he made it walk around in a circle. Then a figure eight. Then he blindfolded it, turned it around several times, drew a straight chalk line and made it walk it. That was the worst – probably the hardest too. Then, as a climax, he lifted the stiff chicken on to a table and said he would hypnotize it into thinking it was dead. The chicken keeled over and lay flat on his back, feet in the air. At that very moment C. D. doubled up into his sweathole under the staircase, erupted with a strangled rasp and toppled over too, his heavy frame falling on top of the table, on top of the ashtrays and glasses, sending cigarette-butt sparks flying, rolling the drinks over plop into our laps.

My first thought – my thoughts pulling themselves reluctantly away from the chicken – my first thought was that it was C. D.'s idea of a joke to keel over when the chicken did. My second thought – how slow the mind works in emergency – was to discount the first because – get this – because, I told myself, that would have been too American a joke. The wetness of the drink in my lap at last forced me into contact with reality and I had my third thought: C. D.'s stroke.

It had finally happened.

I let out a scream splintering the air around me. I heard the scream dying far away into the hush and then saw, like waves, questioning faces surging up towards me. I screamed again. I couldn't find the words until 'Stroke!' I howled, 'stroke, stroke, he's dying. Move him, move him, MOVE HIM, get him out of here. He mustn't die in here. He mustn't die.' My voice screaming and screaming, calling for an ambulance over and over again.

And when they tried to get through to him they couldn't. For I was stuck in the way, rooted hysterically to the spot.

Then someone lifted me up and passed me over the heads of the crowd up the stairs and out into the street.

CHAPTER TWENTY

Clanging up Piccadilly towards the Emergency Ward of the St. George's Hospital, C. D. unconscious on a stretcher, me by his side relentlessly retelling the attendant 'He's had a stroke, he's had a stroke. Because of *me*. It was my fault, it wasn't a mistake, it was my fault.' Praying dear God, please punish me, don't punish him. Thinking if only I make a clean breast of it C. D. can be saved.

'Get a grip on yourself, Miss.' The attendant was cold, businesslike, indifferent. Why? Weren't they supposed to be angels of mercy or something? 'It only makes matters worse carrying on like this. If he's had a stroke you shouldn't have moved him. You don't want to move anyone with a stroke. Didn't you know that?' I stared at him blankly. No of course I didn't. Why should I? Wait. My father's first stroke in the Locker Room at the Club. Pauly had written to me about it; they'd moved him upstairs and that had been bad for him. So I did know. I put my head in my hands, sickening scared, hearing my voice over and over again insisting move him, move him, MOVE HIM, frightened beyond fear, staring finally at the rock bottom of the truth. Some reflex in me had kept right on trying to kill C. D. long after the joke had gone too far.

I had killed them all in one way or another. My father. Pauly.

With hatred. With neglect. My mother to begin with – just by being born. And now C. D. I would have to have myself committed. But I knew I wouldn't. I would have to go on living and hiding it from myself and trying to keep it hidden from everyone.

C. D. stirred.

'Easy now, Miss, we don't want to tire the patient out,' reproached the attendant mechanically.

I had fallen on my knees beside my victim, my hands cupping his, rubbing my cheek against it, kissing it, saying 'Listen to me, darling, listen but don't move. You've had a stroke, you mustn't be moved. We're moving you to the hospital so you'll be all right. And I'll go away. I promise I'll never see you again so you'll be all right.'

'Stay with me,' he whispered.

My heart was bursting inside me. 'I've killed you,' I said slowly. 'I couldn't help it. It was for the money.'

'I know—'

'No you don't. Now listen to me, listen carefully. I mean for my money. I'm your heir – your heiress I mean – don't talk, don't try, it's bad for you. I've got to explain. I tried to kill you. I never thought I really would when it got right down to actually doing it and most of the time it didn't feel like that at all, darling, my darling, listen to me – most of the time it felt like the only way I could keep you was to keep your money so you couldn't get away. That was what Pauly did to me, don't you see?' I paused. I'd spoken her name to him for the first time and my heart was racing so I couldn't go on. I waited for a reaction. None came. I wasn't making any sense. I tried again. 'She married my father and stole my money and then she married you and then she stole my money again and I couldn't help it but I couldn't let it happen again, could I?' I was trying to explain things too difficult to explain. It wasn't any use going on like that. I had to clear it up instantly. 'Listen to what

234

I'm telling you. Pauly Saegessor was my stepmother, do you hear? Pauly . . .'

'And you're Betsy Lou Saegessor,' he murmured weakly.

'Well now you know.' I subsided.

'Oh, I knew.' So faint I could scarcely hear.

'You knew?'

'Almost from the beginning. Because of Pauly. I could hear it.' He shifted slightly on to one side. 'Faint echoes of your voice,' he said to my astonishment.

'My voice! Me and that cheap little tart? My voice like that colourless little nobody's? You out of your mind? That affected priss, that little private secretary—'

'She tried to copy it from you,' he said. 'Didn't you know that? She admired you so, poor thing. In spite of what we did to her she admired us both very much.' I stared at him, feeling at last all the distress and failure that had made up Pauly's life, knowing here was something else I would never get over.

I got up off my knees and sat down and said, 'I am ashamed of everything I have ever done.'

'I know, my dear. And so am I.'

We were passing by the Ritz. 'You couldn't have gotten it just by my voice,' I began again.

'No I didn't,' he was eyeing me drily. 'But that was my first clue. There were lots of others. There was plain common sense. Why should a young girl like you make such a dead set for me? Money? Perhaps. But you were passing yourself off as very rich in the beginning if you remember. And something else – you knew too much about me already. Proud as I am I will not flatter myself with an international reputation. Also, it was completely out of character. You are not in the slightest curious about other people, you know. In fact it's one of your most striking characteristics to take people at their face value. Now why, I asked myself, should anyone as old and ugly – don't interrupt – as old and ugly as myself attract you so much? In short, what were you, at the peak of your power and glory, doing over here wasting your time on me?'

'I loved you. I adored being with you.'

He looked away. His spirit seemed to sag. He seemed to have a pain. He had lost interest.

'The way I made sure,' he said finally, 'was by asking for you under both your names on the BEA Paris flight.'

'That was your nasty, suspicious, evil mind,' I said.

'That was my nasty, suspicious, evil mind,' he agreed.

Immediately I was contrite. It was not the way a death scene should go.

'But if you knew who I was all along—' I started in again.

'And more. I even suspected you of trying to kill me as well. And I decided to let you. I decided to go along with the idea.'

Shock upon shock. 'But why, C. D., my precious Seedy, why?'

'The nights were drawing in,' he sighed, 'another sad winter coming on. Those womb places, it was all new to me. I liked the new womb places you took me to, their darkness and smallness as much as the youth and the excitement and the clutter. I reached for the truth in those places and it seemed I could see a little in the dark sitting in those places and thinking, at last I can see a little in the dark. And then, stronger – but I can see it in the dark! At last I can see it in the dark.' His voice died away.

'What? See what?'

'My end,' he said gently, suffering no longer. 'In a dark night-club with sad music and enough to drink. Watching my girl, so beautiful, so graceful, so contemporary – dancing – knowing she'll come back with me at the end of the evening. One gets tired of the coldness of life, of the darkness of winter, of the jagged edges of everything. That's an old man's tale, tired and baffled. What was it I once wanted? I forget. It's an awful thing to reach the age of fifty-six and still not know who you are.' He lifted himself up and began coughing, turning red. After a while he subsided. 'And there you were trying to do me in,' he went on almost cheerfully, 'and I just went along with it. You don't know how it touched me seeing you want that money, need the money that I had once needed and never would again. It is divine justice,' he said more gravely, 'fair payment for Pauly's poor death. My life for poor Pauly's. Odd, the guilt only began with having you around; feeling your hungry desperate claim. I didn't want to live. I wanted you to destroy me.'

We had arrived at the hospital and sat waiting. The ambulance was being prepared for the doctor who would come in and look over C. D. Finally he arrived. He had carroty red hair, greenish skin and was six foot five inches tall. In the bright ambulance light he looked like the undertaker. He poked and prodded at C. D. He made him cough and breathe and stick out his tongue. Then he rose and put his stethoscope away. I was crying.

'Move him out of here,' he said matter-of-factly to the driver and the attendant.

'No!' I cried, leaping forward to prevent them. 'No, you can't move him, he's had a stroke.'

'I've had a stroke,' echoed C. D. faintly. 'I'm going to die, am I not?'

'We'll see about that,' said the doctor and looked at him frowning. 'You're pretty run down, you know. What've you been doing?'

'No, me. Let me tell it, C. D. You rest.' Here it was: my chance for public confession, quick before I changed my mind. Spill it out, spew it on the pavement, blow it to the winds. The night by night blow by blow smoke by smoke drink by drink account. It's called racing the rat round the town till he drops. Oh-oh. Careful now. That doctor's looking at you very queerly. Watch it. Stick to the facts. No editorializing. Play it sly. Sure, we want to save C. D.

Got to save him from me for ever, no question. But save your own skin too, gal, save your skin. Remember, when it's all over, the authorities can make it hot for you. Preserve yourself. Protect yourself. Come in gently to the Zazou. Sit down quietly and then – God! The sudden shock. The horror. The unexpectedness. Play the heroine. Organize the escape. Save a life. There. What more could they expect? His own mother couldn't have done it better. Why is that damn doctor still looking at me so oddly?

'No you haven't had a stroke,' he said abruptly to C. D., cutting me off. 'Come on. We'll take you inside.'

'But what happened to me back there in that night-club?' asked C. D. 'I don't understand.'

'One of two things might have happened,' said the young red-headed doctor (just this side of impertinence). 'You might have fainted – but from this young lady's description of your recent activities' (just the other side of fed-up-ness) 'I'd be more inclined to believe you simply passed out.'

C. D. and I confronted each other appalled. 'You're sure?' asked one of us – whoever had found his voice.

'I'm sure.'

So he wasn't going to die after all.

Now what?

C. D. asked that we be left alone for a moment and the doctor stepped out of the ambulance.

My devilish syndrome was starting up again. 'Only I didn't destroy you after all,' I began babbling. 'I couldn't. And you didn't have a stroke, you only passed out.' I began to laugh bitterly and brightly, shock reaction of course, I was stark raving mad, out of my head. 'I can't be very anything, can I?' I said. 'Very mad, or very sad, or even very bad. Can't even kill an old man waiting to die.' And I began to laugh hysterically, right straight out of my mind. We two poor crazy nuts – what gothic nightmares had we not dreamed up?

And he giggled too, the ghost of that famous giggle. 'Never mind,' he said. 'At least you made me very ill.'

Then the doctor came back and they put me out into the night like a cat.

CHAPTER TWENTY-ONE

For three days I rang the hospital all the time, leaving messages and waiting for C. D. to call me back, never daring to go over there – an aura of such hopelessness hanging over my fear and cowardice – sensing rebuff, not only from C. D. but the doctors, the staff, the whole hospital conspiring to keep me from him. Everyone against me. Me too, in my way, of course. But such had been my life that year that without C. D. there was nothing.

They were polite on the telephone, even reassuring. He was fine, they told me. He was resting though. That was all. Resting resting, that was the key word. And firm too. No, he positively couldn't be disturbed, wasn't seeing any visitors. If you'll leave your name he'll get in touch with you when he can.

And so I waited. And that's all I did: waited. I almost disintegrated waiting, keeping myself in a shabby threadbare cocoon, aloof and waiting for him. Every day I put on the same clothes, and ate the same food. I watched the polish fade and streak and chip off my fingernails and toenails. I didn't wash my hair. Sometimes not my stockings. Sometimes I didn't even put them on. Some days I didn't go out at all.

One day, giving way to an impulse, I put in a call to Honey Flood in New York.

'Why, Betsy Lou,' her mother exclaimed. 'Why, Betsy Lou, where on earth are you? We've been looking for you high and low and nobody knew. It's as if you just disappeared off the face of the earth.'

'I'm in England.'

'Yes of course, that's what the operator said. I can't believe it. Honey's not here now, she's at work—'

'How is she?' That was what I had to know.

'Oh she's fine, Betsy Lou. She's just fine. That little bad patch, you know, when we had to take her out of college – well, that's all a thing of the past now, thank God. And, Betsy Lou – can you hear me? Betsy Lou, it's all due to you. We owe it all to you, we're so grateful.'

'Me?' I said startled. 'Why me?'

'Why she rang you at your office at the magazine one day – you know she wouldn't speak or go out with anyone for a whole year, I was so worried, nothing seemed to help – and oh really, I shouldn't—'

'Go on.'

'This must be costing the earth.'

'No please – what happened? Tell me.'

'Well, one day she said I'd like to see Betsy Lou again. Just like that. And that was the beginning, honestly and truly. We found out your telephone number at the magazine and she phoned and they said you'd suddenly upped and left, they didn't know where, and how the place was in an uproar without you, and do you know, she put down that phone and said 'Mummy, I've made up my mind what I want to do. I want to get a job.' And that very afternoon she went over to your magazine and they took her on as one of those coffee and errand girls at first and, Betsy Lou – this will thrill you I know – guess what her job is now. Just guess.'

'What?'

'And oh, she loves it so! And they're so pleased with her.

They thought after you left they'd never find anyone as good. It's given her such confidence. It's made all the difference. Betsy Lou? You there?'

Not altogether. But I sent Honey my best love and my best wishes and promised to write all my news and hung up. And I thought about Mother Nature some more.

The telephone that rang one day at last had the voice of C. D. I answered it languorously, savouring all the good things in the world: hope, happiness, renaissance, and, most of all, the possibility of a second chance. He wanted me to come right over.

I combed my hair and put on my shoes and went.

He opened the door for me, a complete stranger in a new brocade dressing-gown. Kempt and cosy and combed and spruce. And rested. And rosy. I forced myself to stand still in the doorway for I felt jittery and fidgety and wished I had taken more time over my toilet.

I said hello to him and nothing more.

He stepped aside to let me pass and then, with the far-off, pleasant but none the less intense curiosity he might have shown about the tribal customs of the aborigines, he asked me why I had a streak of red in my hair.

I didn't know what he was talking about. I even toyed with the idea that 'streak-of-red' might have some symbolic meaning that eluded me but he gripped me hard by the arm and planted me firmly in front of the hallway mirror.

What a sight I was! I hadn't looked at myself in a mirror, really seeing myself, for over a week (and he, all plump and smiling; fresh-linened, perky pocket-handkerchief'd, eau-decologned, thymey and healthy in the background for contrast). However, he was right. There was a red streak that ran curiously down my hair from the parting. I rubbed it gingerly. I had some idea that it might be blood but it didn't hurt. I rubbed my fingers together and sighed with relief. 'It's my lipstick,' I said.

'You don't put lipstick on your hair, you put it on your lips. How did you get it in your hair?'

'The top of the lipstick has been loose for some time and unless I pinch it hard when I put it back on, it keeps falling off. I must have forgotten to.'

'I didn't ask you that. I asked you how it got into your hair. Are you going to answer me?' He was very upset, shouting, and he was upsetting me too.

'The lipstick must have gotten on to my comb,' I explained, opening my bag and showing him. 'That's all. And then I combed my hair with it.' I was striving for that nice, right blend of logic and nonchalance. But my throwaway wouldn't work. He'd made me nervous and that thing, that desperate thing, that ever present possibility of my flip, kept coming through. I could see by the handbag twisting in my hands and it was worse than a pity. Damn that giveaway streak in my hair. It said danger to him. It said watch it, danger. The danger is still here, still playing around her, sliding up and down that crazy red streak in her hair.

I followed him into the drawing-room and we sat down. I was doubled up like a knife on the edge of the chair, fatefully waiting.

'What will you do now?' he asked. But first a large block of silence to cement our new relation. An ocean to establish our new distance. 'What will you do now?'

And still I sat, still doubled up, but very quietly so I could let it sink in, so I could get it, feel it in my bones. React. Recover. Stop making a fool of myself. I, who had once been held in the highest, in the utmost exaltation, not two weeks ago, fallen from favour, now come humbly to beg, humbly awaiting bread crumbs.

'Don't know,' I replied, cool as I could. 'Hit the road I guess. Looks like I've had Angleterre.' Then quickly, so as not to notice he hadn't said Don't go, stay, 'You're looking well.' Or did I say sexy? I hoped not but oh, how I yearned for him, that's all I could think about, his hands on me and his mouth on mine. Damn that red streak. What could I do while it was there? I kept touching my hair and my hands were getting covered with lipstick.

'I *feel* well,' he said, radiating. 'I've had a good rest. That's what I wanted to talk to you about. The other night in the ambulance—'

I forced myself back into the chair, curled into a tight ball.

'I told you I wanted to die. I really thought I could die with you helping me—'

'C. D.,' I was pleading suddenly. 'I am beyond strategy. I am speaking to you for the very first time in my life without strategy. The only thing I know is that I love you and need you and want to serve you to make it up to you.'

'—but,' he went on unheeding, he was up now, walking around the room so jaunty-stepped, so high-spirited, so fine-feeling'd in his skin, 'I couldn't. Looks as if I'm indestructible.' He chuckled. 'Weak, foolish, bad as I've been all my life, nevertheless I did not want to be destroyed and – what's more – ' crowing, '—I couldn't be. I am John Bull,' he added gleefully. 'Indestructible!' He looked it too. He looked Jolly John Bull for better or worse indestructible. 'And I shall be grateful to you for the rest of my life for pointing it out to me,' he finished gently.

I sighed and shook my weary head. I saw that my youth, my ordinarily strongest ally, was against me. For I was unused to failure, thrown by it, helpless to rise above it. He, the old man, so old and so vigorous; and me, young but so tired.

'Ah, C. D., can't I rest here awhile?' To twine my arms around him, hug his great girth and feel him there, the whole him, the sum total of my desires. 'I'll be good, I promise. Ah now, don't. Stop it.' (He, giggling again.) 'I'm being serious. I'm fighting for my life. What's to become of me? Look at me. Look at the way I look.'

'I have a plan,' he said, dominating the room from the fireplace, large, tubby and serene, one arm resting gracefully on the mantel. 'Here it is. You go back to America. You're better off over there, eh? America and England, hmm? Youth and Old Age, yes? You go ahead; I stay put. You forge on; I hold back. And,' he added ruminatively, 'I'll hold out too.' Very neat.

'Oh f— the analogy!' I cried out in my pain. 'I don't want to go back, I've seen them all, it's all the same. The prestige seekers. The Off-beat In-Groups. The Station Waggoners. People being fine old families and phony old fools. And this beach is private and that man's a local, and all the vast sparsely furnished apartments over-looking the East River. Why go back? I've seen them all.'

'Ah, but you haven't seen them on their knees.' Laughing and shaking and brimming over like Jolly Old St. Nick.

'What do you mean?'

'Simply that that is the position they will assume viewing you from the height of your X dollars.'

Then he drew up a chair vigorously – it was the first time I'd ever seen him even draw up a chair – and pulling it close to mine, and plumping himself upon it, he continued with anima-tion: 'Now here is my plan: We Nations split the loot. Agreed? Fifty-fifty. Can't say fairer than that, can I? Ah well' – giggle – 'I'd be afraid not to. Bad risk having you running around loose and poor, never knowing who the next victim might be. I'd have no peace of mind.' And he threw me one of his looks setting off those snakes of laughter, those little trilly snakes of laughter he was always able to, wriggling round inside me, so tingly they were like baby orgasms.

Yes, yes, you have me there, you sly old fox. Keep me laughing, boy, keep the picture frame around us picaresque, absurd. It's your strongest weapon now against my Tragic Queen of Sorrow: little nails of laughter piercing through my suffering.

However, the content of his last words had not escaped me. Half the loot. I let it sink in for a while. So it had come to that. Blackmail. The old pirate was paying me off.

'Aren't you ashamed to be sitting here like this bargaining for your life?' I asked with my first show of spirit.

'Certainly not.' He was still benign.

'Well I don't want the money,' I said grandly. 'What would I do with it?'

'You're going to take it and you're going to find out what to do with it,' he blasted at me, suddenly losing his temper. 'What's the matter with you, girl, you take a year out of your life, lie, cheat, assume false identity, attempt murder, go through elaborate silliness hourly to get the money and then you say you don't know what to do with it.'

'I only wanted it because it was mine.'

We both sat stock still, rocked back on our heels in our astonishment for we knew I had spoken the truth from the innocence of my heart and its ramifications stunned us. I had only wanted the money because it was mine. I'd never had any idea of what I would do with it, had never given it a thought; a truth as irritating to him as it was bewildering to me.

'Because it was mine, because it was mine,' he began, mocking me simperingly. 'Now you're going to find out what "mine" means. Now you're going to find out what money means. Only use it. Use it as Pauly did if you like, to buy a cad and a rotter for her second husband, or as I did – greedily on myself in the beginning, in the, what shall I call it? – my early Meissen china-cup days – and then as bait for you, my dear, to get myself destroyed. Or give it away as saints do, or gamble it away like fools. But use it. See its power to corrupt or save. But use it. Learn from our stupidities. Profit by our example. Have you got your fare home?' he asked, switching abruptly.

I nodded, licked.

'Good. Though if you hadn't I should have supplied you with it.'

'Thank you,' I sighed, at last remembering my manners.

'Not at all. Simply another use for my money. Protection money so I don't have to spend the rest of my life worrying about you sticking pins in my image.'

'How did you find out about that?' I asked startled.

He gave me a really terrible look. 'What?' he roared. 'This is the last straw,' he thundered. 'Out, out, OUT!' He had risen large and looming, filling the room with his fury, pointing a chubby finger theatrically towards the drawing-room doors. And I jumped up cringing, little Eva turned out into the storm.

But he recovered himself with a swish of his brocade dressing-gown. 'I must get dressed now,' C. D. was saying, suavely, looking at his watch. 'Sorry, my dear, I have people coming in. For drinks.' He kept advancing upon me as he spoke, sort of chesting me out of the room. 'Cheer up and think about the X dollars. You're too stunned now, I expect. That lawyer in New York will be issued instructions.'

'For drinks?' I murmured sadly, backing away towards the door, thinking of happier, cooler times.

'For drinks,' he replied implacable. C. D. had given me time. And the time was up.

I tried once more. 'I'll write you of course when I receive my – I mean your—'

'Please do.'

'And you'll answer me?'

'Oh, my dear child.'

'All right all right all right,' I said hurriedly, 'But someday . . .'

But I no longer existed for him. The wall was up surrounding him, the impenetrable wall of suavity behind which he hid without trace while he kept chesting me out into the hallway towards the front door. I turned, suddenly surprising him unaware with a final kiss on his lips, and was rewarded by a fleeting glimpse of my old mischief-making, mischief-loving soulmate Seedy. One glimpse was all I was allowed. When I left the house and looked back I saw him in the doorway: Bland. Brand-new. As if none of it had ever happened.

That year passed away like a day. Often it seems it never happened. Maybe none of it ever really did. Maybe it was all a dope-riddled dream. But here I am at 3.00 a.m. in the morning standing in the middle of my living-room in New York with xxxxxxxxxxxx dollars. And what am I going to do with it?